The Man from Sweetwater

A Western Tale

A Novel by Hank Scott

Co-Author: Susan Elizabeth DeLeon

Note:

My father, writing under the pseudonym Hank Scott, was the author of this book. In 1959, he suffered a stroke and was unable to work for a year. During his recuperation he sat at an old card table and wrote *The Man from Sweetwater*, with the hope that one day it would be published. He left this task to me, his loving daughter. This book is dedicated to his memory. For his grandchildren: John, Anthony, Aimee, Katherine, and Elizabeth and great-grandchildren: David, Sarah, Dominic, Adam, Ada, and Jack

INTRODUCTION by David Prescott

This story is about healing and recovery. It is a tale of grappling with unexpected events and radically changed circumstances. It is both the story of the protagonist, Dan Morgan, and the author, Hank Scott.

The author, my father, was an intense, focused, ambitious, and self-driven man. He was fiercely independent. He worked hard at whatever he did. More than once, he told me if it's worth doing, it's worth doing right!"

Providing for his family was central to his sense of self. As a young man living in the city of Philadelphia, he saw first-hand the impact of the Great Depression on his large family and the financial hardships of many families trying to make ends meet in the face of massive unemployment and the absence of a social safety net. I am certain that these observations must have motivated him to work hard to create a comfortable middle-class life for himself, his wife, and his children.

By and large, he was successful. We lived in a small but comfortable three-bedroom house he built in Fairfield, Connecticut, in 1949, just as the town was beginning to grow as a suburban community.

His life (and his family's) changed abruptly when, while driving to work one morning in 1959, he suffered an unexpected and severe stroke. My father had never been to a doctor and did not know he had excessively high blood pressure. He appeared to be in robust health; he was a relatively young fifty-three-year-old at the time.

In the late 1950s, rehab was uncommon after hospitalization for such medical episodes. Working with his oldest sister, who had been a physical and occupational therapist for the U.S. Army, my father was able to recover most of his physical capacities affected by the stroke, though he maintained an occasional small hitch in his walk and did not pronounce words clearly when he was physically tired. These disabilities were annoying for him but relatively minor.

Recovering physical capacity is one thing; mental capacity is another. I am certain that my father questioned whether his mental capacity would be adequate post-illness for him to continue to earn a living and support his family, which then consisted of my mother, my sister, and me. I was a high school junior focused on getting high grades, good SAT scores, and entrance into a good college. My sister was a freshman in high school.

My father was a man of few words. He did not disclose very much of what he was thinking. He told my sister that he worried about his ability to maintain his focus and remember words. He tested his vocabulary regularly using the *Reader's Digest* "Increase Your Word Power" column in each of the ten magazine issues published annually at that time. I can only imagine and surmise that he must have asked himself questions and doubted himself constantly: Can I articulate a complete sentence? Will I garble words or search for the right one and not find it? Are my thoughts and expressions clear and coherent? What more can I do to test or improve my mental capacity?

My father was a fan of Western novels and particularly

Western movies, which were so popular in the 1950s. He had traveled a bit in the West during his early life as an unmarried man and was taken by romantic notions of life in the Western U.S. in the late nineteenth and early twentieth centuries. His fandom was reinforced by novelists such as Zane Grey and by Technicolor movies such as *Gunfight at the O.K. Corral* and *Shane*. So as part of the healing and rehab process, my father decided to write a book. Maybe the decision was months or years in the making, or maybe it was spontaneous. He never said.

My father was not an author. He did not have an editor. He did not send drafts to friends or colleagues to read and comment on. He did not solicit or accept suggestions. He set up a card table in the living room, sharpened half a dozen pencils, and started putting words down on yellow foolscap pads. My sister was kind enough to type the handwritten manuscript as it progressed. I suspect the book was never completely finished until my sister harmonized the several competing drafts recently. My father had sent some versions to several publishers without success.

The story of Dan Morgan is one of recovery from the inexperience and mistakes of youth and dealing with the unexpected. The event that disrupted Dan's life starts with his innocent presence at a poker table. As a result, Dan's life is unalterably changed, and he must overcome fear and unexpected circumstances to clear his name.

The author's story is a parallel. The author's life changed dramatically as the result of a debilitating medical incident. Like Dan, he had to come to terms with an unforeseen event and its consequences. Unlike Dan, an exuberant and inexperienced youth, the author, a mature man in the prime of his life, dealt with recovering from the effects of a serious, life-altering illness.

The story of my father's recovery in the writing of this novel is the story behind the story written on its pages.

David Prescott
Santa Fe, NM

Notwithstanding the rigors and the hardship of his calling, he lived his life in the sun and like the mountains about him, endured.

—Hank Scott

Prologue

The sorrel stopped responding to the pull of the reins as the young rider eased himself forward in the saddle to reach for his pack of Bull Durham. Carefully and deliberately, he fashioned a cigarette with the dexterity of deliberate practice, touching a match to it as he hooked his leg over the saddle horn and drew deep and long on its mellow fragrance. A wisp of blue curled from his nostrils as he watched, curiosity more the element than surprise, a rolling dust cloud gathering momentum behind him.

As he looked down the road, he saw the stagecoach careening dangerously around the bend. "Old Charlie's still raisin' hell," he muttered, reining his mare out of harm's way, not a whit too soon—the lead boys snorting and wild-eyed sweeping by him in a cloud of yellow dust that hung like a curtain to obscure the rapidly vanishing coach. He could hear the thin, penetrating, high-pitched voice of the driver and pictured him jamming down the foot brake hard for the downgrade roll to the stage line depot on the edge of town.

Grinning, he recalled that old Charlie, with his handlebar mustache and frayed Mexican sombrero, was somewhat of a fixture—almost a tradition—on the Sweetwater-Abilene run. He remembered, too, how the Ladies' Society complained each and every time he turned the air blue with his hell raising "Wahoo!" as the stage came charging into town. Regardless of their opposition, old Charlie continued to bring in the stage—year in and year out—with his outlandish verbosity.

Dan watched as old Charlie pulled up his team to discharge the passengers. One by one, he helped each person step down as a strong gust of wind came spinning toward them. When Charlie was satisfied everyone was safely removed, he proceeded to turn the horses into the corral while Smitty, who rode shotgun, threw down the luggage. On his way back from the corral, Charlie stopped to shout something to his teammate, almost tripping over the last of the bundles left on the ground. Smitty, hiding a mischievous smirk, hurried down to help his buddy gather up the scattered bags. Loaded down with luggage, both of them jabbering like two old magpies, they disappeared inside the station. Minutes later, they reappeared arm in arm, promptly heading for the one and only saloon in town.

Dan remembered his father's stories about old Charlie and his good friend Smitty. Sidekicks for what amounted to a lifetime, they were inseparable. Drunk or sober, on duty and off, they were never far apart. Psychological liars both of them, they continually amused and abused their listeners with unbelievable stories of bloodthirsty Indian atrocities, hair-raising escapes, and high adventure.

Here, almost invariably, they could be found after every run, wetting down their thirst with good whiskey and swapping old stories in jocular good humor. If it was common knowledge that Shotgun Smitty couldn't hit the side of a proverbial barn door, short of ten feet, the fact never did seem to bother Charlie. Whether or not it was a case of failing eyesight or just old age getting to his friend, any attempt to fire the old gent always met a barrage of guilt on his part.

The young rider stood in the stirrups and stretched. He

remembered that it had been just about a year ago that he had come to town at his sister's request when she had run out of baking supplies. But today, he was in no particular hurry and for the first time in many months, he was on his own and looking forward to a great day.

Dan Morgan stood a trifle over six feet in his stockings. Lean and hard—though somewhat gangling—he weighed around 170 pounds of solid bone and muscle. A shock of unruly black hair fell over an alert pair of deep-brown eyes that accentuated the bluish cast running along a strong jawline that was left unmarked by a close shave that morning.

He was no different than any other young man in Sweetwater—a typical cowboy, except for his complete lack of firearms, if one were to make a point of it.

A faded red kerchief with black polka dots was knotted loosely at his throat. His only claim to any degree of elegance—if such could be presumed present—was a broad leather belt with an ornate (but dented) silver buckle that emphasized a slender waistline. One might include the colorful denim shirt neatly tucked into a pair of worn but clean blue jeans. A dusty black Stetson pulled slightly over his eyes cuffed and pummeled into shape, sat on his head at an angle. Characteristic of men born to work in the sun, crinkly patterns of tiny wrinkles and valleys furrowed his temples when he smiled.

It was good, indeed, to get away from the ranch, if only for one day and he was looking forward to taking advantage of a good poker game and perhaps attend the town square dance that had been on his mind all week. He hoped that Sarah would be there. He longed to hold her close once again, as he had a week ago when she'd accidentally tripped and fallen into his arms during one of their regular walks on the trail. He remembered how tranquil he'd felt when her body had rested upon his for what was seemed too short a duration.

The dust had settled by now. Dan kneed the mare back onto the road. His gaze wandered back across the valley below. Color was everywhere. It touched the hills and the mountains and the slopes to catch the day in shimmering brightness. Buffalo Gap—located in Sweetwater, his father's ranch, the Boxed M—was nestled between the mountain peaks, the only access point for the giant prairie wagons going from the east to the west, slightly off the beaten path.

A rough border town, Abilene was a jumping-off point away from Indian territory. It had become a mecca for the wanderer and families seeking a new adventure and a place to settle and raise their children. Deserters from the army, gamblers, outlaws, and renegades also found it to their liking.

Rumor had it that the railroad surveyors were working as far west as one hundred miles east of Buffalo Gap. A church was under construction at the edge of town, and folks were thinking of bringing an instructor from Kansas City to teach their children the three Rs.

The American Mexican War, over now for many years, and the subsequent Guadalupe Hidalgo Treaty, signed by a defeated Mexican republic, did not happen without its' onset of challenges. It served to establish questionable boundaries for both the immigrant moving west and the native Mexican population as a condition of settlement. Treaties were made and rapidly broken. The Apache no longer constituted a major threat.

They surrendered to the onslaught of the white man with great resentment as families continued to migrate west and build farms in areas that had been designated as Indian lands. But as the army withdrew their forces, the Apache struck with savage fury at the few white folks who still ventured too close.

Due to a growing population, the law had come to Abilene. Justice was a matter of harsh on-the-spot judgment. The town fathers would rather hang the outlaws than feed them. Eventually, the nearby ranchers and the business townspeople conceded to appointing a sheriff, even if his practices were not always to their liking.

The long winter was over. Spring, with its transient greenness fought against the restless hot breath of summer and colorful flowers staged a painted look of elegance everywhere. The wild geese, wedged high against the blue sky, flew into the open prairie and crossed over the distant horizon. A roadrunner with its rounded wings, curved bill, and long floppy tail, leapt into the air, then crashed into the dense brush along the prairie as he rode.

It was into these surroundings that young Dan Morgan rode on this special day to celebrate his twentieth birthday.

The warmth of the sun on his face, the immensity of the vast sky above, and the feel of a good horse sent a thrill of anticipation through him. Straight and tall in the saddle, he cantered down the main street with nary a worry in the world. Turning the mare in front of the Silver Dollar Saloon, he tied up the sorrel and ducking under the hitch rail, headed for the porch steps, taking two at a time.

Chapter 1
A Twist of Fate

Dan walked into the saloon and spotted a game of poker just beginning. He confidently walked up to the three men sitting at a ratty old wooden table and grabbed the fourth chair.

"Hi, I'm Dan," he said, his hand extended and ready to shake. "Do you mind if I join you?"

"Zeke here, and this is Ed and Will. What's your interest here, Mister? Aren't you that rancher John Morgan's son? Are you old enough to handle this, kid?" Dan countered Zeke with a smug look.

Ed Crawley, a cheeky-looking character, who was seated to his left enumerated, "Let's see what you got then. Our game is five-card stud—so get ready to bet." Dan immediately recognized Ed. Most everyone in town knew he was the elusive brother of the town's most notorious sheriff with a reputation as a skilled gambler.

Although aware of the clandestine reaction to his introduction, Dan was satisfied. As far as he was concerned, these men posed little or no threat to his poker-playing ability. Once seated, the game began without a hitch. About twenty minutes had passed when Dan began to further observe his fellow players. He turned his attention to Zeke, the only person to shake his hand sitting to his right. He appeared immaculate in a white shirt, grey-striped vest, black tie, and frock coat with a velvet collar; the man had the distinction of a professional gambler. Slim, and darkly good-looking, he played silently, handling his cards with consummate skill and artistry. Confident and seeming imperturbable, he sat well away from the table with his back to the wall, an unlit cigarette clenched between even white teeth. Begrudgingly, but not without admiration, Dan could sense the man's magnetic personality.

Opposite Dan was Will. He had deep-set eyes that were brown, nearly black, and a crop of greying hair that sat proportionately around his face. A narrow close-trimmed mustache on his upper lip completed the perfect look. If the man had any nerves whatsoever, it reflected only in his long slender fingers that seemed to be moving constantly.

Soon there was a crowd watching, with men sitting at the bar catching an early start to their drinking day. Excitement ran through Dan as he began winning. But it didn't take long before his luck changed and Ed started to gain the upper hand despite Dan's near-perfect cards. It seemed that whenever Dan took the pot, Ed would throw out accusations. "What the hell's going on here? Are you cheating us, kid? Must be a peach of a hand," he would say loud enough for everyone to hear.

Before long his badgering become contentious.

As the game continued, Dan started getting angry at Ed's insulting comments and confronted him. "Why all the questions, Ed? Are you accusing me of cheating? If anyone is pulling out cards, it ain't me."

Ed was now fuming. He belligerently got up from his chair, pulled out his gun, and aimed it directly at Dan's chest and yelled out, "Nobody can call me a cheat!" Dan knew he had no choice but to respond. He stood up to face him. But before he had a chance to counter, a sudden and unanticipated challenge came from the direction of the bar. A stranger who had been watching the entire incident unfold intervened.

"Don't try it!" The man's voice cut across the room like a knife as he looked directly at Ed, who glared at him in disbelief. This was the first time Ed had noticed the man. He was suddenly nettled by the gruff insistence in the stranger's comment.

Everyone knew that Ed Crawley, town gambler and bunko artist, was no coward. He was a shrewd judge of character, a quality that had enabled him to take advantage of countless men in his checkered past. But now having been jarred out of his usual confident composure by this surprising intrusion, he felt trapped and knew he could expect little help from his so-called friends hanging around the table.

Ed's face flushed at the direct impact of the stranger's demand. "Don't butt into something that's none of your business!" Ed looked straight into the man's eyes as he spoke. "Why don't you just mind your own business, Mister?" he continued, his voice rasped with irritability.

There was a sudden clatter and scraping of chairs as men jostled one another to get out of the possible line of fire.

Ignoring Ed's comment, the stranger gazed inauspiciously at him and stated firmly, "You'll notice the kid's not wearing a gun."

Ed hesitated. He knew what the man said was true, but the situation was getting out of hand. It was ridiculous that a mere incident with a boy from one of the local ranches should put him in the humiliating position of losing face among his friends...and just because some itinerant trail hand had happened along with an overdone sense of justice. Ed was not backing down. But as time passed, his uncertainty as to his next move was becoming evident to everyone in the saloon, especially to the stranger whose hard blue eyes never left the gambler's face. Ed tried to size up his antagonist. Had the card shark been observant, he would have noticed the stranger was no run-of-the-mill traveler. His right hand was bronzed and weather-beaten. His long, tapering fingers fell within easy reach of a heavy gun belted low and thronged down for action. A black Stetson topped his muscular six-foot frame. He wore what appeared to be custom-made peaked boots of fine leather. The man's eyes were disconcerting—cold, hard, and penetrating. From his head to his feet, he had the indelible stamp of a man who had lived a life on the open trail, not one to play fast and loose. One would have pegged him to be in his early thirties, although there was a timeless quality about the black bearded face that made definition difficult.

The room had become uncomfortably quiet as Ed looked around. Seeing the hard, unsmiling faces about him did little to boost his confidence. And now at the point of no return, he began to regret that he had not disregarded the stranger's remarks.

Again, the stranger spoke, "You'll notice the kid can't defend himself."

Gambler Ed hesitated. He grumbled under his breath. If he didn't act soon, he knew this encounter would end badly.

To retreat from his position was not an option. Nervously, Ed ran his tongue over his dry lips, contemplating his next move. He knew he had pressed his luck too far this time, providing scant hope that he could bluff his way out. The choice was his; lose or draw.

The stranger seemed aware he had shattered the gambler's nerves. He stood with composure, poised, and waiting. Unhurriedly, he placed his whiskey on the bar and stepped away... He hadn't meant to intrude in the matter, but he had always had a profound contempt for unprincipled men who cheated at cards, especially this man, a professional gambler, whose skill should have been sufficient to enable him to win without deception. Only a sharp eye could have detected the ever-so-slight movement of palming a card. The fact that this young lad had chosen not to back down had inspired the stranger's sense of fair play to the degree that he felt he had to intervene.

The gambler studied the stranger, shifting his weight a trifle as he edged closer to Dan. The air was suddenly hot and oppressive.

Outside, the town lay peaceful and quiet in the glaring haze of the noonday sun, blissfully unaware of the drama being enacted in its midst, while inside, the silence, broken only by the rhythmic ticking of the big clock behind the bar, hung heavy and awkward. Time held its breath.

"Pick up the pot, kid. It's yours." The stranger's voice carried an air of authority. His tone was sharp and abrupt.

The lad, somewhat nonplussed by the stranger's intervention, nodded, and reluctantly scooped the pot toward himself, sweeping it into his hat.

Then it happened.

Ed Crawley, seizing upon this distraction as his opportunity, suddenly dodged behind the lad, grabbed him around the throat, and using him as a human shield reached for his shoulder gun.

Those who saw Ed said he was fast, but those who watched the stranger said his move was a thing of beauty. His forty-four came out of leather with a rush of speed. The thunder of the heavy gun rocked the room with a deafening explosion. It was snap-shooting at its best. The shot passed over the lad's left shoulder and then magically, a neat hole appeared in the forehead of the gambler. He gasped as the bullet struck home and he slumped against the boy. He was dead before he hit the floor.

So sudden was the action, everyone stood rooted to one spot.

Quickly tossing off his drink, the stranger was halfway through the swinging doors before the crowd shook itself out of its trance. Then men came alive quickly. A babel of excited voices rose sharply as they crowded about the gambler's body.

"That was a close 'un alright, boy!" an old-timer spoke in the lad's ear. Dan was anchored to the floor as though mesmerized. The old-timer continued, "Better git afore Sheriff Crawley gits here. That's his brother who just got kilt an' he ain't gonna take it layin' down."

The place was booming with commotion. People ran out of the saloon to flee the chaos.

Dan looked up, startled, his face white, scared. Emotions kicked in and he was galvanized into action by the old-timer's words. Moments later, he was furiously booting his sorrel down the main street, sweeping by the depot in a cloud of dust, almost running down a group of people gathered near an empty stagecoach. His mare broke stride to avoid them, and a man walking yanked two young ladies near him out of harm's way.

Agitated and shaken, his mind in a turmoil, he wiped the sweat off his brow with the sleeve of his shirt. Indecision tugged at him as he cast anxious eyes back toward the depot.

Dan swung his weight to one side as he caught the startled look of a young woman whose face was framed with long yellow hair as she peeked from under her gingham bonnet. For a fleeting second their eyes caught and held. "*Oh no!*" he thought. It was Sarah. Her questioning gaze left him with an awkward feeling as he raced along the back trail out of town. His fault or not, he knew he was in trouble.

The sorrel was snorting as they rode. He knew he was pushing the mare to her limit. Once on the ridge where the trail forked over the mountain leading to Sweetwater Valley, the lad pulled up to breathe his animal and take stock of the situation.

Confusion and bewilderment plagued him and restricted his will to act. He had handled it badly, he thought, yet he knew the incident was beyond his control. It was now a part of his history and he was reasonably sure that it would be useless to attempt any explanation to the sheriff who would never acknowledge his own brother was a cheat—and even if he did, he would never accept the circumstances of the incident.

Dan's eyes burned with the memory of looking death in the face. He shivered momentarily as he turned his attention to the trail. He had to keep moving.

He noticed where the dirt was soft, having been freshly flung from the iron shoes of a fast-moving horse, telling him his benefactor had taken the fork in the road in a mighty big hurry. "My friend wasn't wasting any time," he muttered aloud. "That guy was sure superb with a gun."

As Dan suddenly snapped back to reality, he noticed an insect buzzing about his head and the impatient movement of the sorrel. Again he turned and looked back. But there was no sign of pursuit. He lifted the reins and directed the mustang toward the slope. The sun indicated that the afternoon would be well on its way by the time he reached the bottomlands. He nudged the mare to step up her gait. As he rode, he chewed on conjecture. Where to? The more he thought of it, the greater his conviction grew that the most logical place for the sheriff to look for him would be his father's ranch. Knowing full well that bad news travels fast, it was a foregone conclusion that his father would be one of the first to hear about what had happened, especially since Sarah undoubtedly would get the story from the townspeople and report back. He could only surmise the immediate reactions and repercussions his family would have; however, he was certain that any judgment on his father's part would be held in abeyance until he heard his side of the story.

Coming out on the Valley Road, Dan instinctively turned west. He had no particular reason for his choice. Uppermost in his mind was the need to put as much distance between him and the sheriff in what remained of the day. He hated to run. But what could he do? The easiest solution to the immediate problem was staring him in the face—just keep going.

He had no gun, little food, no bedroll...only the clothes on his back and money in his hat from the game. He felt a wave of panic as he rode away from the people he loved and respected most in the world. What would his mother have said were she alive? His only memory left of her was a picture that stood on top of the old, scarred bureau in the hall. His older sister, Elizabeth, now twenty-five, was like a parent to him, and she would be beside herself with worry if he did not come home. Several years his senior, she'd never lacked for suitors. Tall and willowy, singularly attractive with honey-colored hair, he pictured her in the kitchen up to her elbows in flour, making bread and rolls. More than one errant cowboy had been interested in dating Elizabeth but had been fended off and adroitly sent on his way. Most of them never did get their proposals underway or really knew that they had been outmaneuvered. Dan surmised she was sweet on Clay Elkins, the ranch hand whose ardent attention to her seemed to be mutual, yet for some unknown reason Clay had failed to take the relationship to the next step. He kept himself busy with his own interests and activities and it seemed to Dan he was surprisingly reluctant to declare his feelings when it came to Elizabeth.

There remained, though, the basic fact that in addition to being a marvelous cook, Elizabeth cared for Dan and his father unselfishly and with affection and understanding. This included giving them both a stern talking-to whenever the occasion warranted—and he recalled that such instances had been quite frequent over the years, especially as he had gotten older.

Then there was the close association of his father's old-time friend and ex-ranger Jeb Smith, whose ranch abutted the Boxed M. A fine man in every sense and a capable rancher, he bred and raised horses for the army. Dan had always been a welcomed guest at Jeb's dinner table. As a routine, Dan had spent considerable time in Jeb's south pasture learning to handle a gun, something his father was unaware. He would have been surprised to have seen his son cutting the black out of the ace of spades at twenty paces with a smooth fast draw, a fact that never failed to bring a glint of admiration to Jeb's tired old eyes.

As time passed, Dan seemed to find excuses to visit more often, especially when Jeb's granddaughter and his ward, Sarah, came home from school to spend vacations with her grandfather. It didn't take long for a strong friendship to develop between Dan and Sarah, although Dan had hoped it could be more.

The mare snorted and shied at a startled jackrabbit under her feet. Dan rode steadily along, daydreaming until he came to the bend in the road where the main trail swung left, meandering south across the flatlands. A weather-beaten marker, bearing evidence of having served as a target on more than one occasion, was nailed to a dead cottonwood and pointed to Big Spring.

Dan pulled up. He calculated he had come about twenty miles along the main road. If he were to follow it to the town of Big Spring, there could be trouble. If he left the trail at this point, he could take a shortcut to the old game road through tall canyon country and probably be safe. Wild, rugged, and seldom traveled—except by deer and wild horse hunters—it offered shelter and represented the most direct route to the Texas border and the territory of New Mexico.

Apprehension gnawed at him. Was the passage still open,

or would it be blocked by the rock falls that came crashing down from the towering walls after every severe winter? He decided to find out.

At first, he found the ride cool and inviting. It was a pleasant relief from the hot, piercing rays of the sun, now high in the sky. The sorrel led the way along the soft earth floor. Oak, willow, and gum leaves caught and held the darting shafts of sunshine penetrating the dense foliage. Flowers blossomed in the rock crevices, prospering in bright array. But gradually, the terrain changed. As the trail penetrated deeper and deeper into the canyon, traveling became rough. The trees and the underbrush thinned, taking on a stunted, straggly appearance. Here and there the canyon dipped, dropping into a wash, dangerous and unpredictable, boulder-strewn, and almost impassable. Several times the trail ended and reappeared as a small corridor cleaved through jagged black rock ledge that had grown layer on layer. Shadows hugged the hollows and the narrows. Plant life tenaciously gripped the sand-swept bedrocks.

Several times Dan spotted horse tracks in the gravel, and once he stopped to examine them. Acutely aware that he wasn't alone in the canyon, he kept a sharp vigil for the unexpected. He surmised that the horse tracks he found were from someone who was riding furiously to get away quickly from something or someone.

"Whoever is riding ahead of me sure knows this trail, that's for certain," muttered the lad out loud several times, dismounting to study the deeper tracks before the trail started to vanish completely. Now he was in the maw of the canyon. Walls rose on both sides and closed in on him. Rock falls forced him to lead his animal through dangerous narrows. Half a mile further he could see the distant skyline through the far end of the canyon and the V slash in the mountains giving egress to the west.

"If I can only make it through the gap," Dan spoke to his horse, "I can make it out of Crawley's jurisdiction."

Rapidly the trail climbed. The canyon twisted and turned in serpentine fashion, barely wide enough for horse and rider to squeeze through. The mare bulged in and out through jumbled underbrush. Gradually the floor sloped to a new low level. Dan slid out of the saddle by the river to duck his head in the clear, cold water as his horse drank deeply, making great sucking sounds. With a full canteen, refreshed, and feeling more like himself, he got back on his horse and splashed through the still water, sometimes at stirrup depth, the mare shaking her head, distrustful of the footing beneath. Once clear of the low spots, the trail improved, and the clanking of iron shoes rang in eerie echoes as the mare began to gain higher ground. The severity of the walls held for the next mile or so and abruptly tapered off, to finally disappear into the rolling hills. Then, suddenly, he was out in the clear on the widening valley floor and riding for the notch in the mountains ahead.

Relief swept over him. He was finally away from it all. Slowly the strain of travel eased. Night would soon close the gateway of pursuit and lock him in the security of the foothills. He had hit the path toward the old canyon trail and was on his way to New Mexico.

Dan began to realize that everything that had meaning to him would be gone at least for now; something that he would not have predicted earlier, when he'd sat down to take part in a poker game that had turned deadly. Suddenly he was questioning what had induced him to run for the mountain passes rather than seek out the sanctity of his own home. Two things were bittersweet and mitigating in circumstance: he was being pursued, labeled as a criminal, and he was very much conflicted and alone.

It was his attempt to temporize that brought him to a conclusion. Acknowledging his vulnerability and his inability to survive without arms or food, he had but one choice: Go back. He would bed down for the night and with the coming of the daylight, head for home and take his chances with the law.

Chapter 2
The Posse

Jud Crawley was sitting in his office, overcome by the heat. The sweat ran down his face as he swatted madly at a pesky fly that was making his life miserable. He scratched his chin to satisfy the itch of a two-day stubble. His sweat-soiled bandana partially balled into his shirt pocket was, even at this early hour of the day, too damp to be of much use. Grumbling about insect life and the unbearably hot weather, he swung his feet down from the scarred roll top desk, grunting as he opened the lower drawer and reached for a cigar.

Sheriff Crawley was a rough-and-tumble, barrel-chested individual who had given in to obesity. An easy life had piled the pounds on him these last few years. Not overly tall, he stood on long, spindly legs that gave a crab-like shuffle to his walk. Not graced with good looks, even in his younger days, he had fleshy jowls, a flushed complexion, and close-set eyes. A large hairy mole mushroomed alongside his bulbous nose that had been flattened from too many fights. Now pushing fifty and balding, a fringe of gray hair straggled untrimmed down over his ears.

Incongruous with his general appearance was the unusual caliber of his voice. It had a deep resonant quality—basso profundo—providing a welcome contrast to an otherwise curmudgeon personality. It was the characteristic of which he was most proud.

He had come to Abilene when the town was a mere small point on the trail west. His brother Ed had preceded him and a year later sent word for him to come join him. That same year he had been appointed the sheriff's deputy. He had learned the ropes the hard way, and after the mysterious death of his predecessor, he had taken over the office as a matter of course.

Living in Abilene had taught him how to take care of himself. The townspeople were raw and rugged and mainly concerned with their own problems. It surprised no one that he was elected sheriff in a unanimous town vote despite some questions about his brother Ed, a known troublemaker having had a hand in his election. Since then, he had had the luxury of running the job to his own liking, bending the law whichever way necessary to satisfy himself and those who'd put him in office. If there remained any questions about Jud using his authority to keep Ed out of jail, most people had found it healthier to forget what they knew.

Lately the town had been quiet. Occasionally, a drunk got too rambunctious, but, on the whole, Jud had almost no complaints about his work, which mainly consisted of sleeping and drawing his pay. Few men could say the same. Indeed, the last five years had been very much to his liking, and he hoped it would remain so.

It was at this most pleasant point in his daydreaming that the office door burst open, and a wide-eyed youth stood before him. Agitated and disheveled, his eyes were popping with excitement. The boy shouted at the sheriff, "Yer brother's been kilt!"

The sheriff, in the act of lighting a cigar, almost fell out of his chair. He looked up in disbelief. "What?!" he yelled at the terrified lad.

"The Silver Dollar!" The boy now ducked quickly out of the office. A second later, he reappeared in the doorway. "Jest a few minutes ago," he added, as though anticipating the question. "Better come!"

Sheriff Jud lunged to his feet with a speed that belied his bulk and grabbing his six-gun, hurled through the doorway, nearly sending the youth sprawling into the street. He roared, "Out of my way—my God, Ed!"

He bolted to the Silver Dollar Saloon and breathing heavily from the exertion, burst through the batwing doors.

"Here's the sheriff now!" someone yelled. "Move back an' give him room." Jud Crawley elbowed his way through the crowd until he got to his brother. He dropped to his knees beside his brother's still body. His mind flashed back to their childhood spent living with an abusive father; his brother bearing the brunt of his father's wrath. Their mother had died when they were young boys, leaving their father to run the ranch while raising two rambunctious sons. His father hadn't handled it well. Drinking had become a daily ritual. When he was drunk, one never knew what to expect. One time, he and Ed had been playing together when his father had come home from the bar and decided to lock the two boys in the shed because they had not cleaned up the stalls to his liking. It was at that point they had decided to take an oath in a special bond of brotherhood. They would always be there for one another, no matter what. As the older sibling, Jud had always been responsible for his kid brother's well-being. He was the one person Ed could count on.

He felt dizzy and sick, but Jud knew he had to gain control

as he remembered his position in the community. Anger then took over as he bellowed, "Who done it?"

Before anyone could answer, Doc Smith came hurling through the swinging doors with his black satchel. "Here's the doc!" the barkeeper's voice squeaked off-key. "Let him through, gents." The doctor lost no time in taking command of the situation. After a cursory examination of the body, he straightened up and snapped his black bag shut. "He's dead, that's for sure," he announced. "Never knew what hit him. So sorry, Sheriff. Let me know if there is anything I can do for you. Will someone get his body over to my office?" With that he headed for the door, jostling a few onlookers who stood in his way.

The sheriff, still on his knees, attempted to get up but found his legs were buckling and he needed to hang on to a chair. He looked up at no one in particular; just directed his gaze around the room. As he struggled for strength, he repeated, anger rising in his voice, "Who done it?"

The barkeeper spoke: "A stranger—we dunno who—came in after that Morgan kid. Them two guys there..." The speaker pointed at two men and continued, "The kid an' yer brother Ed was playin' a game of poker when young Morgan accused Ed of cheating. The kid wasn't wearin' no gun or nothin', so a stranger cut his self in by sidin' the kid. Then he put a bullet through Ed when yer brother tried to stop the kid from takin' the money. The stranger shot him cold." There seemed to be consensus with this account among all present except for an old-timer, who retreated to the back of the crowd and said nothing.

No one mentioned the fact that Ed had reached for his gun first or that he had tried to use the lad as a shield. Slowly regaining his composure, the sheriff questioned, "Which way did they go?"

"South," about a half-dozen witnesses said at varied intervals.

"I always knowed that spoiled Morgan kid would git into a jam sooner or later. I'm gonna ride out to his ol' man's ranch an' git thet kid for murder." The sheriff looked hard at the faces of the men about him as he spoke. "I'll deputize anyone who'll ride with me."

Jud stopped at his office to pick up a rifle and throw some things into a saddlebag, then joined a posse of volunteers waiting for him in front of the saloon. Threading his way through the milling onlookers, he signaled his men about him. Less than an hour after the killing, the posse thundered out of town, heading for the valley road and the Boxed M ranch. Two of the posse who had witnessed the ordeal and had been close friends with the sheriff's brother rode up in the lead with Jud. The remaining two respectable members of the group, who were from neighboring ranches, kept well behind. They had joined the sheriff's posse only because they had been asked to and individually felt it their civic duty. One of the men up front spoke to the sheriff. "Yer brother Ed didn't have no chance— that Morgan kid blocked Ed from defendin' his self." The other nodded in assent, then said. "Them two was in cahoots iffen yu ask me," supporting his friend's testimony. "What yu gonna do when we catch 'em?"

"Jest between us 'n," Jud's voice dropped so he would not

be overheard by the others, "I'm gonna kill 'em both." And with that remark, he lifted his animal into a gallop. When he reached the turn-off, the sheriff pulled up and waited for the rest of the posse to catch up. "Look," he pointed to the fresh hoof prints. "They both stopped here for a spell—ground's all torn up. That proves they was in cahoots. Trail ain't more than half hour old." He squinted into the sun for a second, then spurred the bay into a run. The others followed suit as they rode along the trail in single file. Coming to the juncture where the trail met the valley road, the sheriff wheeled his mount toward the Boxed M spread.

The men rode the remaining ten miles in relative silence.

Sheriff Crawley held his forward position as he eased into the rhythm of his mustang's loping gait. His face was grim and harsh with determination. Some two hours later, they rode up to the Morgan homestead. The Sheriff stepped down and handed the reins up to one of the men. The remaining members of the posse stayed mounted while the lawman approached the house and knocked on the door. He was about to knock a second time when one of the posse exclaimed, "Here's John now."

John Morgan was re-shingling the north side of the house and having heard the commotion, appeared around the corner of the building. "Howdy, Jud," he greeted the Sheriff, nodding to the mounted men. "What brings you and the boys out to the Boxed M?"

"We're looking for that young son o' yours, John...he's wanted for aidin' an' abettin' a killer," answered the sheriff. "We aim to take him in!" The words were abrupt and devoid of any friendliness.

John Morgan stared, speechless, his face changing color, his jaw working. Seldom had anyone or anything caught the rancher by surprise. Somewhat phlegmatic by nature and slow to anger, he placed the few shingles he carried on the porch step. With mechanical deliberation, he arranged them in a neat pile, carefully placing the hatchet on top. Caught off guard, he fought for time.

John Morgan was not a big man. Well under six feet in height and a little on the fleshy side, he carried his weight well. On the wrong side of sixty, he nevertheless presented like a man in the prime of life. A square jawline and full head of iron-gray hair were his distinguishing features. A well-trimmed mustache added a military touch to his bearing. His open and direct manner enabled him to stand up to most challenges. He had struggled with a whole range of unfortunate experiences through his earlier years, from Indian fighting to hanging rustlers, but none of these things had shaken him as the sheriff's words now had.

"I don't believe it—you must be mistaken about Dan," he recovered his voice. "What happened?"

"Ed Crawley was killed in a gunfight, and Dan had a hand in the killin'..." stated one of the men.

"That can't be true, Jud," answered John, coming to his son's defense. "Dan would never hurt anyone. He wouldn't get into trouble. Dan gave his word never to wear a gun to town. In fact, he doesn't own a gun anymore. He uses mine, and my gun is inside hanging on the hall rack."

Jud Crawley barked, "Search the place! You two men take the barn and you," he designated the remaining two, "look down by the corral. If Mr. Morgan has nothing to hide..." He didn't bother to finish the sentence but added, "I'll take a look inside myself."

He was hardly done speaking when three riders, led by the ranch foreman, Clay Elkins, came up to investigate. "What's up, John?"

"Jud Crawley and the boys are looking for Dan. Jud says Dan was mixed up in a killing in town. Claims his brother Ed was killed in a gunfight," John replied.

"You heard right," snorted the sheriff. Do I get tu go in or not?"

Clay swung down from the saddle with the typical ease of a Westerner. He bent slightly to tie down his holster. He wore a black Stetson and kept his head low. The sheriff began to back away as he waited for Clay's next move.

Clay Elkins had worked alongside John Morgan for five years. He'd found a sense of family at the Morgan Ranch. John's daughter Elizabeth was central to his life. He had struggled to find the right time to declare his love to Elizabeth. He and Elizabeth had found each other one day at the end of the pasture. The sky had been beautifully clear. She had been riding the grounds and had settled on a blanket to enjoy some solitude when he'd approached her. Sitting on the blanket together, they had both gotten caught up in the moment embracing one another with their lips touching passionately. He had not wanted to ever let go of her. But the moment was over too quickly and he'd known he was needed back at the ranch. He always made sure any job required of him was completed—he wanted to remain in good favor with John, and he was content for the time being just knowing there was hope for a future with Elizabeth.

"Say the word, John," Clay said as he straightened up, "and I'll run him and his whole gang off the place."

"Crawley," Clay's words hit the sheriff with intensity. "You open that door without Mr. Morgan's permission, and I'll nail your hide to that barn door. If you came here looking for trouble, you shore as hell came to the right place."

The sheriff stopped short. His face flushed with anger. He didn't know Elkins, having seen him only briefly on several visits to town, but had always been intrigued by the man.

Jud noticed that whenever Clay came to town, he was alone, unless he was accompanying Miss Elizabeth. He never frequented the saloon or mingled with the townspeople. Once, he had spotted him through his office window examining the "Wanted" posters tacked to his bulletin board. After Elkins had moved on, a quick check of the board had revealed nothing of interest, and a review of his files had shown no one meeting the foreman's description. Another time, he had watched him enter the Wells Fargo office, learning later that he had only asked when the new post office would be built and had left after picking up his mail.

In truth, the sheriff could find no reason to be disturbed by Elkins' presence in town. Good-looking, with blue eyes and well-defined features and a full head of black hair prematurely silvered at the temples, Jud guessed he was in his mid-thirties. Long, thin nostrils accentuated the hawkishness of a somewhat curved nose. Even, white teeth showed slightly when he spoke, and there was a sternness about his mouth and a significant set to his jaw. Slim and muscular, he walked catlike on the balls of his feet. This tall Texan had a distinctive quality about him that commanded others to listen when he spoke.

The quiet voice of John Morgan broke the tension. "Let him look all he wants, Clay. Dan hasn't come home yet. Help yourself, Jud," he added. "You're welcome to look inside..."

Somewhat intimidated by Clay's threat, Jud hesitated. "I reckon I don't need to look in the house," he said, turning from the door. His walk was a trifle stiff as he passed the spot where Clay stood eyeing him with a cold stare.

"Find anything?" Jud asked the men who were returning from the barn. Both shook their heads.

"Nothin' in the barn," answered one of the men as he mounted his pony. The other shook his head in confirmation. "Call the other two," ordered the sheriff, "He ain't here that's fer sartain sure." The other two deputies came running and sensing the hostility in the air, swung into their saddles to await further orders. It was evident from their actions that these last two appointed deputies were not comfortable with their assistant position, especially since they were both longstanding friends and neighbors of the Morgan's.

Jud mounted and leaned forward in the saddle in one last demonstration of authority. "We aim tu git Dan one way er the other, John, dead or alive. He can have it either way when we ketch up with him." He yanked his horse about and sank his spurs with a glaring disregard for the welfare of his animal. Two of his deputies caught up hastily with him as he headed for the main road. The two other deputies hesitated long enough to reach out to the rancher.

"Sorry, John," said one of them, who Morgan regarded as

a friend. "Can't believe it myself. Didn't really see it, come to think of it—all hearsay. Me and Bart rode in just in time to see Dan run for it—was movin' in one hell of a hurry, too. Crawley was dead when we got inside the saloon. Never saw Jud this way afore. He's mad clean through. I'll help Dan iffen I can."

"That goes for me, too, John," said the other man, pulling his bronco around. Both men rode off to join the sheriff waiting for them down the lane.

Jud Crawley was no fool, and he wasn't one to buck the odds if there was any other way to investigate. He was wrong this time. Dan simply wasn't there, and little or nothing could be gained by belaboring the fact, especially in view of the resentment he had encountered from Clay Elkins. He had been so sure the lad would head for home to the protection of his father's ranch. An old hand at the game of hide and seek, he had wasted too much time already and intended to make use of what was left of the day. He knew there were two probable courses of escape that Dan could have considered. First, there was the easy access to the Mexican border that precluded the likelihood of pursuit beyond its boundary. Second was getting to the border of New Mexico through the sanctuary of the rugged mountain recesses. This last one seemed the most natural hedge for anyone running from the law without the likelihood of meeting up with a band of roaming Apache, an incentive since a lawman in most cases would not risk his scalp against such odds.

It was very late in the day when the sheriff and his men reached the turn-off. The small posse had pushed their horses hard and by dusk had reached the path slanting south. Here the sheriff signaled a halt. "It makes sense they may have gone on to Big Spring—country's wide open. If they cut south to Mexico, they'd have to go through Fort Concho an' then they'd be taking a chance runnin' into some cavalry an' those boys in blue will shor as hell ask questions. Nope!" He added, "Let's take a look at the old canyon trail. Seems like it's the best bet considerin' New Mexico Territory would be the more likely choice. Old trail still open most of the way—I reckon."

Here the sheriff pulled up to study the ground for tracks. The posse milled about as he dismounted to get a better look. It had been a rough day so far. The ride had been hot and dusty, and the sheriff's frame of mind did nothing to alleviate their exhaustion. Leather creaked as the sheriff returned to the saddle, ready to address the posse.

"Men," his voice was testy and surly. "I think I know whar them varmints are holed up. It'll take some riding, and we won't git home 'til late tonight or afore tomorra' morning. It's still early an' if I aim tu rout them killers out, it might jest take some doin'. Those who want to see justice done will ride with me. I got vittles enough in my saddlebags fer anybody that want to come. Gotta warn yu though, there might be shootin'!" The sheriff's two friends nodded assent, but the two ranchers both shook their heads. "Gettin' kinda late, Jud," said one, speaking for both of them. "An' we got chores back at the ranch that won't wait."

The sheriff looked at them with disdain. But he nodded his acknowledgment and wheeled his bay about as he continued along the trail without them.

"Good riddance," remarked one of the ranchers as they

left. "Them's my sentiments, too," echoed his companion coming up behind him. "An' fer one I hope he don't git within ten miles of Dan."

"Looks like yu hit it, Jud," said one of the deputies, riding into the brush. "Look here," he said, pointing to the trampled bush and the cut-up turf. "Shore shows signs o' hosses."

The sheriff spurred his horse into the thicket. "What're we waitin' fer?" he exclaimed, looking at the hoofprints in the soft earth. "Maybe we got 'em after all. They's a good chance they'll camp som'ers along the trail, cause they ain't no way out o' thet cannon cepten maybe a deer run jest this side of it, if they gits thet far, an' they won't see it in the dark. Let's go!" he commanded, then added, "Moonlight tonight, boys. Keep a sharp eye peeled fer ambush, an' be quiet." The sheriff turned in the saddle, his eyes on the outline of a pale moon hidden behind an evanescent cluster of clouds.

"Gettin' cold," said the man named Miller, turning to his partner who had fallen slightly behind and for whom he waited to catch up. "Yu can say that again," answered his companion as he approached.

It had been a long day and a grueling one. His deputies straggled behind, but it did not deter the sheriff from the heat of pursuit. The whole matter had become a personal grudge, and he was willing to sacrifice anything or anyone to achieve his revenge. Someone had to pay for his brother's death.

Night was on them when the trio skirted around the last of the rock falls in single file, the barriers barely discernable.

When they were finally through, Jud yelped, "Shut up an' follow me—an' stay close. It can git purty bad here at this part of the canyon." He led his deputies through the final squeeze into the widening valley trail. His arm went up as he motioned for silence. His companions crowded their mounts to a halt behind him. Malevolence stained the lawman's face as he noticed smoke from a campfire ahead. He signaled the two men to wait as he swung down from his bay to get a better look. "Can't see nobody at this distance," Jud continued. "I'll sashay around back o' the camp and git the lay o' the land. Iffen yu hear a shot, come arunnin."

The two deputies remained mounted as Jud pulled his Winchester from the scabbard.

As he made way through the thicket, he chortled to himself. "They's most like beddin' down fer the night in the clearin' yonder." Once he had a better idea of where they might be, he treaded his way back to report to his deputies.

"Can't see much. Might take some doin' tu work my way aroun' the camp. They's a crick back yonder. Could be they's down by the water. Only spotted one saddle, though. Didn't see no hosses, neither. Won't be long now," grunted the sheriff as he levered a cartridge into a chamber of his rifle, "an don't ferget to come shootin to kill whin I flush them coyotes out with this here thirty-thirty."

"Muzzle yer traps til I get back," he ordered. "An keep them hosses still." Without waiting for a response, he turned and vanished into the shadows.

The two men dismounted to talk in whispers. They both agreed that the cold fury in the sheriff's voice confirmed this was his hour of vengeance. "Let's git on with it," growled Deputy Miller, shivering. "I'm saddle sore now an' getting more weary by the minute."

"I don't rightly set much stock in this here way of doin' things," said the other man, Josh, as he squatted down to wait. "It's more like shootin' fish in a pickle barrel then anythin' else. Wish it was over, though, so's we could go home. It'll be sun-up afore we git back an' I could use some shuteye right now. I'm jest too blame tired tu move."

Miller hunkered down alongside his friend and replied, "Yup. Kinda goes aginst the grain tu see 'em cut down in cold blood without a chance."

"Yu thinkin' of thet foreman back at the Morgan spread?" He might be watching us right now. Maybe he is hiding in the brush." Josh waited for a reply with his eyes on his partner's face.

Miller stirred uncomfortably, easing his position slightly. His answer was slow in coming as he pinched off his cigarette and carefully tucked the stub into his vest pocket. "To put it thataway, and nows yu say it, I ain't hankerin' to keep lookin' over my shoulder all the time. An' yu can shor as hell bet thet iffen Jud put a slug intu that young'er, he ain't gonna be fur behind all o' us." He rose to his feet. "Bout time tu mount up." Josh joined him, grinding his smoke under his foot. Tossing up the reins he vaulted into the saddle. A disdainful expression crossed his face. "Jud oughta be 'round t' other side by now. Been gone a tolerable time." Josh laughed aloud, as though pleased with himself. "He'd be plumb surprised if they was awaitin' fer him."

Miller nodded as he pulled himself wearily into the sad-dle with visible effort. Both men sat wrapped in silence, their horses jostling each other at close quarters.

A shot exploded in the night, and both men shot forward as though propelled out of a catapult.

When Jud had left his two deputies, he was certain that the conundrum had been solved. He had finally cornered his prey. The chase was about to be over. Getting revenge was but a matter of time. Victory was at last imminent. He moved stealthily, pausing just to reorient his position. Suddenly he saw him. Silhouetted against the light of the campfire, the sheriff could make out the figure of a man moving between him and the camp.

"Thet white towel over his shoulder ain't gonna hurt one bit. Makes a right good target." Jud's inner drive to kill became larger than life. He pictured his brother Ed lying dead and bloody on the bar room floor. Carefully, Jud brought the Winchester to his shoulder, squinting along the barrel. The white cloth accentuating his target, the sheriff nestled the gunstock firmly against his cheek to line up his sights. He could hardly miss at thirty feet. Every detail of the man's figure stood framed in the light of the campfire. Jud squeezed off the shot. The man staggered and went down. Jud levered another cartridge into the chamber and waited.

The stranger was injured, and Jud knew it. He lay for a moment in obvious pain. He dragged himself to his knees, coming upright barely in time to meet the charge of the two deputies cutting across the glade. Their guns glittered in the moonlight as they bore down on their victim. It proved to be the last act of their lives. Both had made a fatal mistake, rushing in for the kill, only to be confronted by the stranger in the shadows, rifle in hand, weaving on his feet while trying to stay upright. Simultaneously both tried to gain control of their twisting, sliding horses, but it was too late. Two shots rang out, hitting the targets with unerring accuracy. Bent down under the burning lead, Miller was swept from the saddle and fell backward, under his rearing mount. A split second later, Josh collapsed and jack-knifed to the ground. The stranger then disappeared into the shadows.

Jud Crawley, standing in relative safety, witnessed the stunning abruptness of the entire incident. He had seen death come swiftly and horribly from the stranger's gun. Fear gripped him. He had thought his shot killed the man—now two of his deputies were either dead or wounded, and he knew that he had only succeeded in arousing a killer. Jud turned, and in utter desperation, he plunged madly through the brush to get away from this savage gunman. Half-crazed with fear that he was now the hunted instead of the hunter, haste succeeded caution as he fought his way through the undergrowth. He was relieved to reach the open trail where he had left his bronco.

The horse shied skittishly as Jud grabbed for the bridle piece. The bit cut deep as he hit the saddle and yanked the horse about. Seconds later he was in a headlong flight, his horse pounding away into the night.

Chapter 3
Three Graves

The day was well-nigh spent and Dan was bone tired. A cold wind had sprung up, and the shadows were lengthening as the sun began to set. It hung over the horizon like a big red ball, then began to sink over the western hills. The world came alive, with all the colors of the rainbow leaving it aflame with crimson and gold. All of nature arose, fixed in her own regal beauty. Then, the majestic vista faded into the deepening dusk. Suddenly it was night.

Better make camp up in the rocks, Dan thought, pulling his mare to a halt. *Never would make sense to be caught in the open like a sitting duck.* Suiting his actions to his words, he moved the sorrel to higher ground.

A slowly rising quarter moon cast an eerie light on the giant boulders that loomed like gray ghosts along the way. Underbrush and overgrowth tore at his clothing, and several times, he had to hold the branches from whipping across the mare's face. Once off the main trail, he dismounted. There seemed little choice but to camp for the night on a shelf rock at the base of a parapet, offering some relief from the wind and the trail below. It took but a moment to strip the mare of her saddle. Dan inched into a rock crevice with the horse blanket about his shoulders for warmth as he sat back and began to mull over the events of the day and his gullibility. He continued to defend his right to have called the gambler at his deceitfulness, but sheepishly had to admit his foolhardiness, especially since he wasn't armed. He was disturbed and annoyed that what had started as a pleasurable day in town had suddenly become his misfortune. He tried not to dwell on the event, but sitting there alone, so many miles from home, nostalgia swept over him. Stetson cocked forward covering his eyes, he chewed on supposition. It was hard to fathom that a man was dead. Certainly, he was innocent of any crime other than his right to expect fair play. Perhaps the old-timer was wrong. Maybe the sheriff hadn't blamed him after all. Maybe he wasn't even wanted. There were any number of witnesses that could testify on his behalf. Either way, he would know more when he was finally able to go home.

He had just ground out his cigarette butt and pulled the blanket closer, snuggling deeper into his nook, when the sorrel whinnied. Instantly he was on his feet. Sleep was suddenly forgotten as the movement of an animal caught his attention. Almost immediately, he heard the drumming beat of running horses. Riders were coming along the lower trail at a fast clip. Quickly he muzzled the mare to listen intently. His best estimate was that there could be at least three horsemen—maybe more. They must have been pushing their broncos hard. The beat swelled as they passed a point below, and then the noise gradually faded away and was soon gone.

A thought struck him. He had made no attempt to cover his trail—had been too self-absorbed and in too much of a hurry. If these men riding were the law, they would rout him out of his cover sooner or later. The odds could be against him either way. And suppose the stranger who had helped him was ahead of him in the canyon and had stopped to make camp for the night? If he was in danger, Dan couldn't in good conscience ignore the matter. After all, the stranger had stood up for him when he'd needed help—probably even saved his life.

He shivered in the night air. Innate caution fought a wild urge to run—to get away from this place before the riders reached the canyon's end. Hurriedly he tossed up his rig, leading the mare down the rubble-strewn mountainside, rock and shale clattering past them as the mare turned and twisted to avoid the pitfalls of questionable footing. Dan stepped into the saddle for a moment, sitting still, a sixth sense pulling him into breathless immobility. The movement of the light and shadow in the night was playing hide and seek with his nerves. He could hear the gurgling sound of a fast-moving stream. Then—suddenly—a shot shattered the night, then two more. His horse reared in fright. Holding a tight rein, Dan literally threw the spooked mare off the trail into the concealment of a nearby wash, tension growing as he hugged the gully bank. Soon the sounds of someone crashing through the undergrowth became very loud. Someone cursed, and a saddle creaked. Dan stood in his stirrups for a better look as a rider loomed into sight, breaking stride as he swept onto the trail. He then flashed by the lad in a bewildering flurry of speed. Gradually the hoof beats died away, and the hush of night returned.

Considering the poor lighting there had been no chance to get a good look at the horseman. He'd been in one hell of a hurry, and it seemed only a matter of logic, since the man had headed for the canyon pass, that he was one of the nightriders that had come through behind him. Leaving the sorrel tied in the seclusion of the brush, Dan ventured to investigate the shots. A cautious approach brought him a few short steps beyond an outcropping of rock to the edge of the glade. Less than fifty feet away, the darkened shadow of timber created a tiny amphitheater that was bordered on the north side by a hilly rise of exposed rock ledge. Above and beyond, but discernible, the sandy soil of an embankment reared up to serve as a protective slope to the lee of the wind.

Approaching cautiously, Dan noticed a campfire burning briskly in a cradle of rocks. A coffee pot was boiling over furiously, sending up geysers of steam as the lid popped under pressure. Nearby, a rifle was propped against a saddle, and left of the clearing stood two horses. He continued to circle the camp when he stumbled upon the bodies of two men awkwardly sprawled on the cold ground. Turning them over, he recognized them from the Silver Dollar Saloon. Their badges pinned to their vests pegged them as part of a posse. Both men were dead. Where was the sheriff? Was he the rider that had passed him back on the trail? The enigma grew as he started back to camp. He had gone only a few steps when his spine prickled with fear. A groan came from the thicket. Instinctively, he dove into the shadows. He lay still—nerves taut—hardly daring to breathe. Cautiously, he crept into deeper coverage. His eyes searched the darkness. The obscurity of the night shadows appeared unreal and ghostly, the pale moonlight concealing its secret. Again he heard a man crying out in agony, the anguish of his pain making a prolonged torment apparent.

Holding to the brush, he became close to the shadow of a man sitting upright on the ground with his back to a tree. A paroxysm of coughing shook the man, and sensing danger, he made a feeble effort to reach for his rifle but lacked the strength

46

to move it more than a few inches. His chest heaved and a deep sigh escaped him as he slumped over on his face. Warily, Dan turned him over as the moonlight flickered through the trees to catch the face of the stranger who had come to his defense back in town. Sensing urgency, Dan half carried, half dragged the wounded man back to the campsite to make him as comfortable as possible. Cutting away the man's shirt revealed a bullet wound to the back. He was bleeding profusely. Dan ineffectively tried to stop the bleeding with the shirts of the other dead men. He dressed the wound as best he could, but the blood continued to flow. Helplessly, he sat watching the man's life fade away.

"If only I could do something." Dan's utterance echoed his thoughts, yet he knew, from the course the bullet had taken, it must have torn a big hole in the stranger's lung. He tucked the man's blanket about him and used his saddle for a pillow. Finally, he set about to rekindle the fire and making beans and coffee taken from the stranger's supplies. The activity helped Dan feel useful, while the good taste of hot strong coffee warmed him. The man's breathing now had become labored and heavy and, in the dim light of the fire, the pallor of death showed on his face. Dan removed the man's boots—recalling this to be protocol for one who was at life's end. Unable to do more, he settled himself with legs crossed, his arms around his knees, gazing into the glowing embers of the campfire. A star flared across the night sky on its way to oblivion. He began to piece together the reality of the moment, slowly crystalizing the facts with clarity. The sheriff and his posse had deliberately set out to kill them both. The blanketed proof of that rested with the injured gunfighter and two dead deputies left unattended. Not only did it offer an excellent opportunity for the sheriff to save face, but the charge against Dan had just turned into three killings.

Tired, distraught, and homesick, the memory of better times swept through him. He had only to close his eyes and he could smell the fresh oven-baked bread from the kitchen and the tantalizing aroma of crisp cornmeal muffins for breakfast. He realized that he had never attached any importance to such things before.

A sigh escaped him. It had been a long day—a very long day—and he was learning that even youth had its limitations. The summer night was heavy with the rich smells of the good earth, and the fire sank slowly into glowing ashes. Heavy-lidded, his eyes closed in weariness, and slowly his head sank to his chest as fatigue caught up with him. In the night a bird called to its mate, the last thing Dan heard before he fell into a deep sleep.

A false dawn was seeking out the night shadows when he awoke. Around him the wildlife made music as he stretched the stiffness from his muscles. Tossing his blanket aside, he rose and bent over his patient. A cursory examination revealed the man to still be alive—but barely. Dan had never watched a man die before, but now he had witnessed two, very close together. He marveled that this man had the strength to have lasted through the night. It was difficult to tell if he was unconscious or asleep, but the man finally stirred slightly as his breaths became spaced farther apart. Dan felt the man's forehead. It was cold and dry. He reached for the stranger's canteen and let a few drops of water trickle between his lips. A slight cough shook the man, and the faintest show of foam tinged with blood bubbled through his lips. He looked up, and Dan found himself gazing into a pair of clear blue eyes. A look of recognition crossed his face. It was as though he was trying to make a feeble effort to speak. Dan leaned over, and putting his ear to the man's lips, he thought he heard the words "take care of Lady." With a rattle in his throat, the man's body wilted. Dan felt for a pulse. There was none.

Straightening, he looked down at what until a day ago had been a strong virulent man in the prime of life. Who was he? Where had he come from? Where was he going? Questions crowded through the lad's mind in helter-skelter order. Daylight had broken, and everywhere he looked was bright with the golden promise of another day. Dan shivered in the cold morning air, and a moment later he was rekindling the fire. Shortly, with a brisk flame going, he picked up the coffee pot and headed for the creek. Halfway down the path, he spotted the colt in the grass.

"Must be the stranger's," he ventured mechanically, detouring around the bodies of the two dead deputies. Shifting the empty coffee pot under his arm, he noticed a gun belt hanging off the saddle. He hefted the gun. Surprise brightened his face. A forty-four caliber with a big walnut stock—satin smooth with years of use—fit his hand like a glove. It lay like a thing alive, and its weight and balance felt like a part of him. The hammer thumbed back to full cock under the gentlest pressure. Further investigation revealed the initials JR inscribed on the butt, but he gave it no thought, shoving the gun into his waistband and continued on his way. Soon the aroma of fresh coffee spurred him to keep moving.

The coffee scalded his throat as he swallowed it in huge gulps. After finishing his meal thanks to the stranger's supplies, he promptly set about searching for a suitable burial ground. A few minutes of browsing the glade revealed an empty spot on the slope, just north of the camp, ending his search.

Selecting the stranger's frying pan to serve as a shovel, he dug feverishly, and his body was wet with sweat by the time he had scooped a grave out of the sandy soil. Then, on each side of the stranger's grave, he dug another—one for each of the deputies. It took him the greater part of the day to work the graves down to a satisfactory depth, and his hands were torn and bleeding by the time he had wrapped the dead man in his blanket and deposited him in the center of the grave. Many hours later, all three men lay in their graves, ready for burial.

Dan had decided to place the stranger's personal effects with him, a fitting way to bury a man—at least a kinder way. He was about to drop the stranger's boots into the grave when he hesitated. An audacious idea, myopic and incredulous at first, gradually took on a basic realism. Was this, perhaps, an opportunity—a golden one—or was it too presumptuous, too offensively bold, to consider taking a pair of boots better than his? Would its inference divert pursuit or buy a little time— maybe a whole lifetime?

He looked off across the sylvan scene where the three horses were grazing as he raised his brow in thought. Slowly, he picked up the boots and turned them over in his hands. He noticed they were made of strong black leather, well stitched, and relatively new. Dried clay crumbled into dust as he broke the earth from the jagged edges of the high-fashion Mexican spurs. He squatted down to yank off his own worn pair and tried them on for size. To his pleasant surprise, while not snug, they fit quite well.

"Not bad," he muttered half aloud, as he stood up and walked a few steps. "Seems a shame to waste them in that hole. I am sure he wouldn't mind if I swapped with him."

A moment later he was busily backfilling the grave, his own boots deposited at the foot of the enshrouded body. The grave was topped with a mound of solid earth, sand and gravel, and heavy stones were securely placed to keep the wild animals away.

The chore completed, he returned to camp, where he stripped the saddles from the horses—including his own sorrel—and with a slap, turned them loose in the high grass. Toting the saddles up the glade he stashed a rig at the head of each grave, his own at the center, as he stepped back to wipe his brow and survey his handiwork. Convinced there was nothing more he could do, he picked up the personal effects he had decided to save and headed for camp. Some distance away he came on the dented utensil that he had tossed aside and kicked it into the brush before going to the water's edge, where he cleaned the coffee pot and filled the stranger's canteen with fresh water. A few minutes later, the dirt and sweat washed from his hands and face, he returned to camp, doused the fire, and finished packing the stranger's saddlebags with efficiency. Adjusting the stranger's well-filled cartridge belt around his waist, he holstered the forty-four, and with a final look around, he shouldered the stranger's saddle and headed for the thicket and the big black horse.

The mare's ears cocked forward inquiringly. She whinnied softly at his approach. With a tuneless whistle, he began to appreciate the specifics of Lady's strength and beauty and how fortunate he was to find at least some solace in this whole unfortunate experience. Dan's eyes began to glimmer with excitement as he gazed at Lady—she was majestic in stature and as black as the night. Sleek and well groomed, the mare's muscles rippled and flowed beneath her black hide with every movement. She had white stockings on all four legs, and a coat like polished metal. *One in a million,* he thought. She was everything a man dreamed about in a horse.

Dan smoothed the blanket in place and tossed up the saddle, bringing the cinches tight. Then he saw the initials JR burned into the saddle leather on the lower right skirt. He had heard his father talk about Jace Randall, the outlaw, but could not bring himself to truly believe he had just buried him. He pondered the thought only momentarily before proceeding to search the stranger's saddlebags for other clues but only found a few silver dollars, some Mexican coins, and a crumpled paper, which he ignored.

Dan gripped the reins and stepped into the saddle. A last look around convinced him it was time to move on. He passed within a few feet of his own sorrel, grazing contently with the other two mustangs. Hesitation brought him to a halt. A memory swept through him, as he guiltily recalled the pride with which his father, many years ago, had cut the pony out of the herd. He remembered the thrill of ownership and the impor-

tance of the moment when his father had adjusted the stirrup lengths of his first saddle. Now it all seemed so long ago.
He looked at the plenteous supply of the glade's green grass
and heard the murmur of the brook. Surely, he thought, the
animals would be found before the season changed and the
snow came. Or perhaps they would eventually join one of the
wild horse bands that roamed this far west of the central Texas plains. There remained the strong likelihood that someone
would do a search for the missing deputies and find the animals. Someone would discover the bodies in time.

He lifted the reins and moved out of the glade to the gap
ahead giving exit to the valley.

"Take care of Lady," he repeated the dying words of the
stranger aloud. "You can bet your bottom dollar I'll do just
that." The mare picked up her heels, heading west. Several
miles later they were through the mountain pass, crossing a
creek at low depth. The mare's hoofs made squishing sounds as
the bottom mud yielded to her stride. When the horse's jolting
lunge cleared the bank, Dan found himself reluctant to let go.

"Best be safe than sorry," he stated. And with those words
he swung the mare off the trail to make his way alongside the
inlet. The sun poured down with enervating force. Several
times Dan stopped to splash his face with the cool water. Traveling along the waterway, now shallow and wide, was a garnish
of undergrowth and trees. There was cottonweed—willowy,
colorful, and lacy green—reaching for the water; and oak,
twisted, sturdy, and tough, flourishing in profusion. The hum
of insects, the creaking of saddle leather, and the uncertainty
of the moment lent a weariness that Dan found disturbingly

difficult to combat. He catnapped as he rode. Time passed. The morning was well gone, and the sun became hot and merciless.

As Dan left the area, guesswork switched into reality. For several hours, they climbed as treacherous hills and rocks made their ride arduous. More than once, he was forced to reorient himself to avoid boxed canyons. Eventually, he found himself on a wide tableland holding a westerly course. Red shale and sandstone baked in the sun's shimmering glare. Tendrils of heat rose from the hard earth—the wasteland was beginning to take on shape and definition. Although the terrain was rugged and uninviting, the mare seemed to find the footing to her liking. Soon the last vintage of underbrush vanished almost completely, and the stark vastness of the badlands seemed to swallow them up. The hard shale cracked and crumbled into puffs of dust as Lady's iron shoes rang sharply against the rock. Scrambling, and at times fighting for balance, she skillfully negotiated the trail as she moved ahead.

The hours passed. Finally, cresting a slope, Dan stopped to look ahead. He could make out the distant V slash in the mountains to the southwest. The desert lay behind him. A limitless expanse of lowlands stretched away to the north and west. Directly below them the river flowed sparkling and glistening in the late afternoon sun like a broad stream of virgin silver. It meandered, in serpentine fashion, to disappear beneath him, under the overhang at the bottom of the slope, only to reappear further south.

A fresh fragrant breeze touched his face. A sigh escaped him. A feeling of relief ran through him. Dan dismounted to stretch and mop his brow, grateful for the breath of cool air.

He stood there, looking back. It had taken him hours to come this far, and he was feeling the effects of a long and rough ride. His decision to continue moving began to make sense now. He looped the reins over a bush and climbed to the top of a nearby hump of rock ledge for a better view of the backcountry. He was on top of the world. Shading his eyes against the sun's glare, he squinted into the distance. Somewhere to the west lay the border town of Hobbs in the territory of New Mexico and freedom. He began speaking to Lady, "Maybe some time away is not such a bad idea."

Satisfied, he scrambled down from his perch and climbed into the saddle, nudging Lady into cautious descent. He let the mare pick and choose her way to reach the river's edge. Making good time, they traveled well.

Several times, he saw signs of wild game at the watering hole, and once he spotted a pair of antelope vanishing over the plain.

Twice they approached a river crossing, but the current was too strong, and he had to turn back. Finally, he gave up the idea and continued along the water's length until they came to the bend in the river. The mare snorted and shook her head, the bridle jangling noisily. Dan pulled up short. The earth was churned from hundreds of milling hooves. He whistled softly.

"Wild horses," he murmured as he eyed the foaming white water. "Here's where we cross, old girl," and with a flick of the reins, they went into the water.

Lady stepped out vigorously, breasting the deepening current with a snort. The water was up to her haunches now and was getting deeper. The mare fought for footing against the force of water, her eyes rolling, and her head held high. Suddenly, the jolting ceased, and the mare was swimming clear of the bottom. Her powerful shoulders and legs working in superb coordination, she moved ahead with tremendous surges, and the bottom ground soon sounded under her feet. A final lunge—ears back, muscles taut—shook her clear of the entrapping mud at the river bottom. Catlike, she scrambled to safety, breathing hard, but none the worse for the wear.

Dan slid to the ground and unsaddled the mare to turn her loose and watch her proceed to roll in the tall grass. Blowing noisily, she came to her feet. A minute or two later, she was docile, grazing in the deep grasses, raising her head only to catch the sounds of the day. Satisfied that the mare would not stray, Dan undressed, wringing out the excess water and hanging his clothes on a bush to dry. Then with a running plunge, he dove into the cold water, only to come up struggling to catch his breath from the unexpected chill that engulfed his body.

After a brisk swim, he climbed up the bank and flung himself full length on the grass to let the warmth of the hot sun permeate his naked frame. This moment of reprieve from running brought some peace of mind, even if it was short-lived.

A man...a horse...a gun. A typical process of thought for a young man, if only his life had not turned upside down. The murmur of the river and the hum of the insects lulled his senses to slumber. How long he slept he did not know, except that he awakened with a start. He sat up, looking around. Nothing had changed. The mare was still cropping grass. His gun and his clothes were all in the same place. Gradually, he relaxed, lying on his back, watching patches of white clouds, high against the blue sky, billow and spread and band together.

When hunger pangs began to overtake him, Dan struggled into his damp clothes and wet boots. Twenty minutes later, he had finished a sparse helping of food, hastily made over a small fire. The utensils washed and packed, Dan prepared to ride. He rounded up the mare, threw the saddle up, and kneed the cinches tight. Then an urge—perhaps it was only a brief burst of energy—led him to feel for the holster on his hip. He turned and stood poised, ready to draw. The gun came out of its casement smoothly and easily—almost, it seemed, without effort. Returning the gun to its leather, Dan looked around for a suitable target. His hand swept down, then up, to a loud boom, startling Lady. A loose piece of bark had disappeared from the tree—nothing but the raw pine testified to the accuracy of the shot.

Dan hefted the gun, watching the wisp of blue smoke spiral from the muzzle. He holstered his firearm and stepped up on the big black. "Lamesa must be somewhere close," he mused aloud. He knew that he needed to stock up on supplies before too long. His best estimation of distance was that they were some twenty miles from the town. Traveling was good, and the mare swung alone in an easy canter that carried Dan along with the wind in his face and a lightheartedness that took him by surprise. It was then that Dan, on the spur of the moment, decided to give the mare her head and let her run. Touching the spurs to her flanks, he let her go. Immediately sensing the free rein, Lady moved energetically for the next couple of miles. Big and powerful, the mare stretched out and settled low, covering the ground in tremendous strides. It was evening when horse and rider finally clattered across the old wooden bridge into Lamesa and turned into the livery stable near the edge of town.

A dozing stable hand almost fell off his wooden crate as Dan's voice startled him.

"What a horse," he said as he gave the mare an affectionate pat. The big black flicked her ears at the sound of Dan's voice and impatiently chafed at the bit. "Take good care of my horse!" A silver dollar spun through the air and was caught by the grinning stable boy, now thoroughly awake.

"Yes, sir!" exclaimed the lad. "Yes, sir!" he repeated. "Nothin' but the best here."

The boy turned up the lantern and tested the coin between his teeth. "Iffen you lookin' fer a place tu bed down fer the night, stranger, there is a hotel right up the street a piece," he indicated the direction with a jerk of the thumb. "Nice horse you got here, Mister," he added, running a knowing hand over the black.

"Special care," reiterated Dan, untying his bedroll and slicker and ignoring the attempt at conversation. "See that she gets the best."

Dan waited until the boy had stripped the saddle from the mare before tucking his gear under his arm and heading in the direction the boy had pointed, toward the hotel. His spurs jingled as he walked along the wooden boards. Within the hour, he was in his room. He fell fast asleep, oblivious to the sounds of the night emanating from the saloon across the street.

It was late morning, and the sun was streaming through the window, when Dan awoke. He lay for some time watching a breeze ruffle and billow a pair of tattered curtains. He yawned and stretched to full length as though relishing the luxury of a bed, then one final stretch and he was on his feet. A quick glance through the window showed the town to be deserted—not unusual for the hour—except for several early-bird cowboys perched on the porch railing in front of the saloon across the street. Jumbled voices drifting up reminded him that the day had begun.

Twenty minutes later, washed and dressed, his bill paid, and his bedroll over his shoulder, he crossed at the far end of the street to get his horse. A moist morning breeze with just a hint of rain swirled puffs of dust around his boots. He paused to look up and down the street. An eerie silence hung over the town. An uneasy feeling stirred in him as he walked to the stable. He immediately noticed that there was not much to the settlement. Adobe shacks squatted between the weather-beaten fronts on one side of the road. A square saw-toothed style livery with its adjoining blacksmith's shop was connected to the local barbershop, made obvious by what once served as a barber pole. Next to the general store was the saloon.

Dan turned on his heel to enter the stable. "Anybody here?" he called, walking into the dark interior.

"Right here, boss," came the answer from the depth of the rear stall. "Be with you in a minute." Almost at once, an old man emerged, leading the mare out of the stall. "This is yu hoss right, Mister?" Dan replied with a nod.

"Only hoss in here, so figured as much. Real hoss, too," the old man said as he ran his hands over her glossy coat. "They don't come like that around heah. Be an extry two bits fer rub an' curry. Right with you?"

"Right," echoed Dan, handing over the money. "Where can a man eat around here?" The old man waited until Dan had saddled the mare. "Yonder," he pointed toward the saloon and the general store.

Dan thanked the old man and led Lady down the street to the beanery, where he looped the reins over the hitch rail and went inside. He was ravishingly hungry. Breakfast went down easily, flushed by huge cups of strong coffee.

Meanwhile, across the street, things had started to brew.

The town barber (and village gossip) was shaving a local customer when he happened to glance out the window of his shop and see the black hitched in front of the restaurant.

"Look at that big black hoss over in front of the beanery," he exclaimed excitedly. His eyes were aglow. "Did yu ever see a hoss like that afore?" The customer, towel in hand, slipped out of the chair to squint through the dirty glass window. He pulled back the ragged curtains to stare.

"I seed that hoss afore, all right," he said, slowly getting back into the chair—a perplexed expression on his face. "But I shore can't recollect jest whar. She shor is a beauty, ain't she?"

A few minutes later he left the barbershop to walk across the street and stare at the mare in deep contemplation. "I shore seed it afore this," he repeated, running his hand over his smoothly shaven chin. "But fer the life of me..." His voice trailed off. "I got it!" he cried. He headed for the saloon, taking the porch steps two at a time. Pushing his way through the swinging doors, his excited, strident voice broke the quiet.

"Jace Randall's in town. I jest seed his hoss out front." In no time at all, their drinks forgotten in the excitement of the news that the famous outlaw was in town, the men began to vacate the saloon, though most remained at a safe distance on the porch. A few braver individuals approached the mare to stare at her in questioning disbelief.

"That's his hoss fer sartain," stated the smooth-shaven on-looker as he pointed. "Ain't no doubt about it. Them white stockin's makes it so—seed him up Pendleton way a year back."

The barber, watching the excitement from the seclusion of his shop, shed his apron, and hurried across the street to join his friends. Word ran like wildfire that Jace Randall was in town. It seemed, as though people came out of nowhere to gather in groups of twos and threes, watching and waiting.

Dan, meanwhile, having finished his breakfast, paid his bill and helping himself to a toothpick, stepped out into the sunlight. He halted when he observed the many townspeople on both sides of the street.

Something must be up, he reasoned as he turned into the general store adjacent to the restaurant, almost colliding with the storekeeper who was headed for the front door. The man, visibly shaken and upset, mumbled an apology, and retreated behind the counter.

"What can I do for you?" he managed, his voice somewhat high and squeaky.

"Some supplies and a box of ammunition," ordered Dan.

"Right away, sir," the man scurried about, hastily filling the order.

"What's all the excitement in town?" asked Dan, picking up his cartridges. "Seems like something special," he added, turning to select a pair of socks from the nearby counter. "I'll take this too." A wool shirt completed his purchases.

"Will that be all?" inquired the perspiring storekeeper.

Dan nodded, while the storekeeper added up the bill and packed the goods into a neat package for traveling. Once the transaction was completed, Dan headed for the door. He halted at the threshold and spoke to the storekeeper over his shoulder.

"You still haven't told me what the excitement's about." There was no answer. Dan looked around in surprise as a rear door slammed. The store was empty. "Mighty queer goings-on," he surmised, shaking his head, and stepped outside, only to hesitate, an odd feeling in the pit of his stomach. Several men were gathered around his horse, but as he approached, they backed off to a respectable distance.

Surprised as he was at finding his horse the center of attention, he was even more amazed to find his every movement watched by the crowd. He began to have the feeling that he was the one all the excitement was about. Curiosity ran through him as he stuffed his purchases in his saddlebag, sensing that something was wrong. He had just untied Lady's reins from the hitch rail when a man elbowed his way through the crowd to come to a menacing halt about ten feet away.

"Thet yer hoss?" The words were thick with whiskey. Dan nodded.

"So yer the great Jace Randall, eh? I heered about you! Me an' the boys would like to see -just how good you are with that hog leg." The man stood swaying unsteadily, his feet spread wide apart.

"You've made a mistake. I'm not Jace Randall. I'm—" Dan

hesitated.

"Yeah!" the man pursued the point, "If yer not Randall, what air yu doing with his hoss? An I'd know that mare anywhere. Yu wouldn't be a little aferred now, would you?"

One of the men in the crowd placed a restraining hand on the man's arm.

"Yer drunk, Slade, you ain't good enough to buck Jace Randall when yer sober, let alone drunk."

"Lemme alone! I'll show yu whose good enough!" the man retorted and shook himself loose.

Dan went tense, his stomach balling into a tight fist as the challenge took substance. The name of the man buried back in the glade rang its warning as he pulled the slip knot free. His surprise died quickly. How stupid of him to have doubted it. Jace Randall was one of the fastest guns the West would ever know, and now, he, Dan Morgan, was being mistaken for this legend of a man. After all, who hadn't heard of the lone outlaw who fanned the flames of campfires where men gathered to talk of guns and challenges?

"I don't want to fight." Dan's voice carried to all within earshot and especially to his antagonist. "I'm riding out, and I don't want any trouble." Deliberately, he turned his back and prepared to mount. He was about to step up when he heard the clickety-click of a drawn hammer. He whirled around, his gun flashing down and up, the mare reacting as the forty-four roared. Gun in hand, the man who had threatened him stood with a look of stupefaction on his face, lifting both arms instinctively, as though to stem the searing pain in his chest. He stood erect briefly, then pitched forward on his face. His gun exploded as death triggered his reflexes.

Dan knew he had killed a man for the first time, and a feeling of weakness ran through his body. Holstering his gun, he stepped into the saddle and pulled the black around to move slowly through the crowd, the townspeople giving way to let him pass, no one making any attempt to stop him. Halting the mare alongside the dead man, he said something, utterly surprising himself.

"The fool," he said, contempt in his voice. "The damn fool." Then he bent low in the saddle and lifted the black into a gallop. Not knowing the mood of the townspeople, his mind started racing. Once having gained the open plain, he knew the black could hold its own against pursuit—even to the New Mexico border if necessary.

No sooner had he begun to think he had won clear of a bad situation, a stinging pain seared through him like a hot iron. A chance bullet had found its mark high in his left shoulder. Cold dread gripped him as he felt the warm blood run down his back, and he watched with consternation as a red stain spotted the front of his shirt. Surprise gave way to action as he hunched low against the mare's neck and sank his spurs into her sides as the big black's gait smoothed out and the desert wasteland began to swallow them up.

The sheriff, back at his office, having heard the shots, arrived on the scene a few minutes after Dan had left.

"Jace Randall was in town," one of the men milling about the scene informed him as he was inspecting the dead man. The sheriff looked up, startled, an incredulous look on his face. "Jace Randall," he repeated the name, trying to grasp the fact that Randall had been here in his town, and he hadn't been aware of it.

The storekeeper pushed his way through the crowd. "It was Randall, all right," he confirmed. "But Slade forced him into it. In fact, he was going to shoot Randall in the back. Randall was just too fast for him. Slade's gun was in his hand when Randall started to draw—got him dead center, too, before Slade could pull the trigger. Good riddance to poor rubbish, I say. Slade always went looking for trouble, and, by golly, this time he found it." With that he turned on his heel and walked back into his store.

"That so?" The sheriff threw the question out to everyone listening.

"That's so," said the barkeeper. Some others nodded their heads. "Some of you fellows lend a hand here and take him to my office," ordered the sheriff, indicating the dead man. Following the men carrying the body, the sheriff spit out a stream of tobacco juice, turning a surprised grasshopper upside down. "Now where in the hell did I put that shovel?" he muttered, mostly to himself, as he stopped to discard his chew at the jailhouse door.

Chapter 4
Fate Stacks a Crooked Deck

John Morgan stood in silence as he watched the posse ride out. Confused by the belligerence and truculent attitude of the sheriff, his world had been turned upside down in just a few minutes. It seemed implausible to him that this thing could have happened...and yet it had. In a trance, he walked up on the porch and dropped heavily into a rocker.

Clay Elkins followed him and perched himself on the banister, steadying himself with one foot on the floor.

"Don't worry too much, John," he exclaimed. "Dan can take care of himself." His tone belied his words and sounded hollow and lacking in conviction.

Unmoving and staring into space, John Morgan made no comment.

"How about me ridin' to town an' doing a little snooping? Maybe I can get a line on Dan an' find him first. If you say the word, I will take that sheriff an' that posse of his apart piece by piece 'til the truth comes out. He is no damn good anyhow!"

"We'll both go." The rancher cut his words as he came to his feet. "Have my horse saddled. I'll be right out." He flung his hat over his shoulder as he disappeared into the house.

The rancher went directly to his first-floor bedroom and slipped his gun belt from the peg on the wall. It had been a long time since John Morgan had worn a gun, but he strapped it on with a familiar motion. Pulling the gun from the holster, he thumbed back the hammer and with a deft flip, spun the cylinder. Satisfied the weapon was loaded, he eased the hammer down on the empty chamber and slipped the gun back into the case. Before he left the room, he let his eyes travel over the familiar objects in it until his gaze ultimately came to rest on a silver-framed tintype. Walking over to the bureau, he stood for a moment, looking down at the beautiful face in the photograph.

"Dear Mary," he said with a tremor in his voice. "Give me the strength to meet this day."

Mary and he had shared their life in the West. He had proposed to her one evening after knowing her for only four months. He'd known she was the one he wanted to share his life with the first time he had laid eyes on her. She'd had a gentle nature and instantly made him feel as though he could accomplish almost anything. When she'd died at only twenty-six, he had been devastated. He had vowed to take good care of their two children and live a life she would have wanted for all of them. After talking aloud to her picture, something he had done throughout the years since her passing, he got up and strode briskly through the front door, where Clay was waiting with the horses.

His foreman was already mounted, and as John swung up to get on his horse, he noticed Clay had his Winchester tucked in his boot, and he was sure, from the bulk of his saddlebag, that he had packed more than enough supplies.

"Keep your eyes open," Clay ordered his two ranch hands. "Maybe Dan will show himself. If he does, tell him to lay low. We will be back tomorrow." Then he added, "Tell Elizabeth not to wait supper. Don't tell her about Dan. I will do that when I get back."

"Ready, Clay?" Clay nodded and touched his spurs to his horse. Without further comment, they rode out side by side, turning onto the valley road toward Abilene. Preoccupied, they jogged along, exchanging only monosyllables. Clay at long last opened the conversation. "Something about this whole thing don't make a hell of a lot of sense. Why would Dan get involved in a gunfight without a gun? Dan always had too much sense to do a thing like that."

John hurried his bronco to a faster gait. "Been wondering about that myself," stated the rancher.

It was a good, long trip from the ranch to Abilene. Both men stepped up the pace, speaking little as the miles rolled by.

As they rode, John Morgan became more engrossed in the privacy of his own thoughts, falling slightly to the rear as reality began to take over. He was finding it more of a challenge to displace the inference of things evil and foreboding, but he had to know the truth.

Looking back through the years there were numerous times he questioned his choice to remain in the west. Had he done the right thing by joining the successes and sharing with others in their moment in history? The West had become more attractive as the land officially became part of the United States. However, few had been ready for the perils of life on the trail, which included limited food and water and overwhelming fatigue. There was hardly a family along the trail west who had not paid the toll. The unmarked graves along the way were unquestionable proof of that. Vivid—as though it were yesterday—was the unforgettable journey by wagon train and that last summer's sweltering hell of broken country, where hardship and heartbreak were almost a daily ingredient and tragedy the common denominator. He remembered how difficult the journey had been as they'd been faced with the threat of an early winter, with the cold blasts funneling through the passes nipping at their frozen limbs. They'd barely made it in time to weather the first light snowfall of the year. They had been bogged down in a sea of mud that had turned the prairie into a morass of sludge. The decision to winter down had been a matter of pulling the wagons into protective formation in the foothills. Here, to provide cover from the rising winds, they had set up camp.

A community cabin had been the first order of the day, and the men set to the chore with a will. Working with haste and against time, they had built a good-size cabin that grew at unbelievable speed. Shortly thereafter, a shelter for the animals had been added to provide safety for both man and beast alike. A split log floor interlaced, flat side up had made for a rough but serviceable dry floor. A loft had served as ideal sleeping quarters for the women and children, who had bundled for warmth during the cold long nights...and as a private area for couples when privacy was imperative. A massive fieldstone fireplace had almost constituted the entire wall of the far end of the cabin—lending a crackling and blazing warmth to the eternal chatter that usually happened while family and friends routinely gathered about the open hearth. Magically, from the mysterious women's world of bits and pieces, curtains had appeared at the shuttered windows and the odds and ends of touches of home had softened the bleak austerity of the walls. More than one shaggy buffalo rug had tickled the bare toes of the children as they were readied for bed. Four families had been housed in cramped quarters—three of the original seven families having elected to leave the wagon train some miles south of Abilene. The tantalizing aroma of mulligan stew simmering in the big black kettle had served to constrain the testy and irascible frustrations of daily survival.

Winter had struck with a vengeance. John remembered the night a nor'easter had howled down in all its fury to seal them off from the rest of the world in a blinding glare of white and frozen silence.

It was in the wee hours of the following morning, just before dawn, that the first squeal of a newborn child had broken the quiet. Dan Morgan—the first true Texan of the Morgan clan—had arrived. The price had been high. Mary Morgan, her energies taxed beyond her human limit, smiled on her son, turned her face to the wall, and died. John; his young daughter, Elizabeth; and newborn son had buried her that terrible day on a windy snow-swept knoll among the willows overlooking the quiet valley. A simple white wooden cross marked her grave.

Gradually, winter had passed and with it had come the hustle and bustle of preparations for leaving. It was then that John Morgan had decided to stay. Through the ensuing years, bound by the poignant memory of Mary who slept on the hill, John Morgan had made his decision to build his ranch. At times against almost insurmountable odds, he'd held on. Soon the hardships became less of a struggle and the years passed by quickly. Gradually the ranch had grown and prospered. The old cabin, now adjacent to a new bunkhouse, was home to more than one wandering cowpoke. Corrals had been added and enlarged. Nestling in the shadows of the easternmost end of the valley, the low sweeping lines of a comfortable hacienda had spoken with functional affluence. The Boxed M had made it. John and his two children, Elizabeth and young Dan, had somehow survived.

Clay finally pulled up and patiently waited for John to catch up alongside as he turned onto the trail leading to town. The remaining miles slid by and before long they had cleared the rise on the edge of town. Together they rode up the main street, the clip-clop sounds of horses' hoofs muffled by the splaying dust that spurted beneath their iron shoes.

"Looks kinda deserted," remarked Clay as they rode up to the hitch rail outside the Silver Dollar.

John Morgan nodded and swung down. Clay quickly followed suit, and together, both men ducked under the rail and went inside.

John held the swinging doors for Clay to pass. The place was empty—unusual for that hour—except for the barkeeper busily filling the coal oil lamps lined up like tenpins on the bar.

"Howdy, John," he greeted the rancher, nodding a recognition to Clay. He dropped his chores to wait on the men. "Thought we'd see you soon after the ruckus. The sheriff been out your way yet? Left right after noon with some of the boys. Fact I just saw two of the posse ride in a minute ago. What'll u have?" he asked as he wiped his hands on a soiled apron.

"Clem," said John Morgan, "You've known me for a long time, and you know I don't mince words. If you saw what happened with Dan, tell me the truth. If you lie—I'll break every bone in your body. Now! Let's have it."

"Honest, John, I didn't see too much of it—it all happened so fast. Your Dan was settin' here peaceably playin' poker with Ed Crawley when a stranger came in. I never saw him before. He was standin' right where you are now when your Dan called Ed a cheat. Ed got mad an' threatened tu run Dan out of town, but this stranger who looked like a gunfighter took Dan's part...him not wearin' a gun or nothing. Then when Ed went fer his gun, it looked like Dan interfered with his draw. Anyhow, the next thing I knowed, Ed was dead, and the stranger lit out an' Dan followed...an that's the truth, so help me God."

It was a long speech for the barkeeper, and beads of sweat were standing on his brow when he finished.

"What's the matter, Clem?" questioned Clay, who until now had been listening to every word and watching the barkeeper closely. "You sound plenty nervous. Afraid Jud Crawley 'll hear you?"

"It's the solemn truth," Clem hastily defended himself. "Yu can ask anybody. Dan didn't even wait to git all his money. Spilt most, he was in such an all-fired hurry tu git outen here. I never did see a man so fast with a six-gun as that stranger," he added, picking up a towel to wipe the spotlessly clean bar with an almost mechanical motion.

"Just how did Dan interfere with Ed's draw?" questioned Clay, his cold, hard eyes fastened on Clem's perspiring face.

Clem swallowed hastily as though he had a lump in his throat.

"It appeared tu me from here that Dan grabbed Ed when he was makin' his draw—that's the way it looked from here, anyway." The barkeeper repeated himself, and his eyes fell in embarrassment and confusion.

"Shore as hell sounds fishy to me," said Clay succinctly. "A kid without a gun gettin' mixed up in a gunfight—'specially between Ed Crawley and a total stranger—don't make any sense atoll."

Clay leaned his six-foot length over the bar, clamped his hand on Clem's shirt front in an iron grip, and yanked Clem's two hundred pounds against the bar as though he were a sack of potatoes.

"Yu lyin' whelp! I ought to beat your brains in—with a story like that. I have just a notion."

John's voice cut in. "He's not worth it, Clay, let him go." With a shove, Clay flung the trembling barkeeper backward, sending him crashing against the bottles on the back shelf, then followed the rancher out into the sunshine.

The shaken barkeeper regained his equilibrium with considerable effort and righted the overturned bottles. "Sometimes," he muttered, "I don't think Jud Crawley is worth the trouble I get...fer jest the few favors he does fer me." Then pulling his shirt and apron upright, he returned to the lamp wicks, appearing disgruntled with his lot in life.

John Morgan and Clay paused just outside the door. The heat of the day was beginning to wane, and the sun was well along as they walked to their horses.

"I'm gonna ask that buzzard which way Dan went," stated Clay, turning as though to reenter the saloon. "I'm jest dyin' to take a poke at thet skunk..." John's motion arrested his move, and Clay turned to follow his gaze down the street toward the livery stable where a man was signaling to them.

With that, John pulled the slip net and led his mount toward the stable. Clay reluctantly followed, apparently displeased at the turn of events denying him the pleasure of debating things on a more personal basis with Clem.

Both men approached the barn and were beckoned inside by an old man. John thought he recognized the old timer, but in the dim lighting of the stable, he wasn't too sure.

"You wanted to see me?" The old man nodded, furtively probing the inner darkness about him as though making sure they were alone.

"Yer Mr. Morgan, ain't yu...I'm Shuey. I knowed yer boy. He used tu come in an' we'd set a spell an' talk when he came tu town an' we get tu be right good friends..."

"What did you want to see me about?" John spoke as he approached the man.

"Jest so," answered Shuey, stuffing a wad of chewing tobacco into a toothless hole in his mouth. "Thought maybe so you ought's knowed what happened today. That's whyfer yu come to town, now ain't it?"

"That's right, Mr. Shuey, Did you see it?"

"Yer dern tootin' Mr. Morgan—an' thet was a humdinger iffen I ever seed one..." Shuey gave his thigh a resounding slap. "I never in my borned days..."

Morgan's voice cut him short. "Go on."

Timothy Shuey was a small man who'd loved horses all his life. He had a way with them beyond all understanding. Some townsfolk believed that he was a little touched because he claimed he could talk to a horse, and it would understand him. Nobody ever paid any attention to the little man's meaningless ramblings and babblings. Timothy liked to talk, and now that he had a captive audience, he was reveling in it. Patiently and without interruption, John Morgan and his foreman listened with an attentive ear as Timothy told them the whole story. As both men listened, they knew from the intensity in the old man's voice that they were finally hearing the truth. By the time he had finished his narrative, Clay was wild with suppressed anger, and it was all he could do to restrain himself from going back to the saloon and beating the truth out of the barkeeper.

Sometime later, the two thanked the old man and climbed into the saddle to head for home. "Shuey, my home is always open to you," stated John as he rode away.

Timothy Shuey watched them go, his faded blue eyes watering. "He invited me tu his ranch," he said, talking to himself. The change of voice caused a mare in a nearby stall to raise its head. "Ain't nobody ask me tu visit for a long time." And he disappeared into the shadows of the stable, mouthing his thoughts over and over again as though he liked the sound. "That Mr. Morgan...he's a nice man...a nice man."

"Well! I think we've got the story fairly straight now. Sure makes things look a lot different and some better." It was a simple statement entirely without rancor. A definite relief lifted John's voice. "You reckon Dan'll be home when we get there?" he waited patiently for a reply.

"Nope!"

"You don't think Jud..."

"No! Not what you're thinkin'," Clay hastened to allay the rancher's inference. "Depends on how much the posse crowds him. Figure if Crawley gets too close, Dan'll keep running. Remember, the lad knows this heah country like the back of his hand an' knows a dozen places where they can hide out."

A wave of fear took over John. "You think he and that gunman will stick together until this thing blows over and Jud gets to know the truth? Dan's unarmed and can't weather it long on his own. Sooner or later he has to come back." The rancher struggled for the right words, purposely not letting himself think the worst, in an effort to dispel unfeigned concern.

They turned south and started to dip down into the valley before Clay picked up the thread of conversation once again. His words were weighted and carefully chosen.

"Can't say for shore aboot that. Figure he knows the risk of teaming up with an owlhoot. Figure he'll make it on his own. Got a mind of his own, too. Most likely he'll hightail it for home soon as the coast is clear. Maybe a look at what's on the other side of the mountain will shoo him along quicker than we think."

John nodded. While somewhat a libertarian, both in thought and action, he knew Clay was right. Conjecture and fact had little in common...if anything at all. Without further ado, he changed the subject.

"Jud will surely be in town before long to bury his brother. Now that we have a witness, we could set him straight on the facts. At least we can reason with him."

"You'd have to kill him before he'd take your word for it, an' for shore he wouldn't take much stock in Timothy's story. Probably kill the old man, too. Nope! I don't reckon it'd do a mite of good."

"Maybe you're right." He picked up the reins as he continued, "Let's go home. It's getting dark, and we've a distance to go. We'll cut Dan's trail tomorrow if he doesn't show tonight."

Clay nodded. Both men bent to the trail.

After a restless night's sleep, dawn finally appeared to the Boxed M household, and the bunkhouse was aglow with lights as the rooster's raucous crowing ushered in the day.

John Morgan awakened early—unusually so—partly because he'd slept restlessly and partly because he wanted to get an early start. He was riddled with worry about Dan. When he came downstairs, he rushed to eat his breakfast—hot buckwheat cakes and sausage, along with cups of steaming black coffee.

There was noisy activity in the bunkhouse. Doors opened and slammed shut, and snatches of talk drifted in from the kitchen, with men moving about, getting ready for the day's chores.

John had just finished his third cup of coffee when a knock sounded at the door.

Looming in the doorway was Clay. "Ready, John? Got the horses outside and ready to go." "Got enough grub for overnight?" questioned the rancher, rising from the table.

"Shore do." Clay nodded as he spoke.

"Be with you in a minute," responded John, walking to the clothes rack, from where he took down his gun belt and buckled it around his waist. Slapping his battered Stetson on his head, he followed Clay outside.

Clay Elkins was born and bred in the Western Plains. He had come out of nowhere late one night about five years before and had stopped at the Boxed M to ask directions to the nearest town. It had been a wild, stormy fall evening, and both horse and rider had spent long hours on the trail. John Morgan had answered the knock on the door himself. After giving directions on how to get to Abilene, he was about to dismiss the incident, when, in the light of a flaring pinecone from the fireplace, he had caught a good look at the man's face. The rancher, struck by the man's clean-cut features and straightforward manner, and playing a hunch unhesitatingly, had thrown open the door with an invitation to enter. The man had stepped back to shuck his wet poncho and take off his hat. After striking the outside of the doorjamb to shake off the surplus water, he'd stepped across the threshold.

John Morgan could not help but notice that the lean, lanky stranger towered over him as he'd followed him into the spacious living room.

"Thanks," he'd said, walking toward the big fireplace to extend his hands over the fire, rubbing them together to generate warmth into his cold fingers.

The rancher had recalled the incident as though it were yesterday.

"My name's Morgan—John Morgan," said the owner of the Boxed M, moving forward to extend his hand. "You are welcome to spend the night here—plenty of room to accommodate a guest."

He then turned to his housekeeper, Maria, a lovely Mexican woman who had served him for many years, cleaning, and cooking for the family. "Maria, please have the front room on the south side made up for our guest," he directed.

"Si, Señor," she answered as she finished up the washing

from the evening meal.

"Clay Elkins," the tall man met the rancher's hand with a firm grasp. "Don't like to impose, but thanks. That valley wind is a mite cold—chills a man clear through."

"Mind if I look after my hoss?" he added, taking his hat from the rack where he had just hung it.

John Morgan nodded, satisfied he had read this man right. "I'll have some hot coffee ready for you when you get back. Stable's right down a piece to the left. Help yourself to whatever you need. You'll find feed and some dry blankets for your horse hanging over one of the stalls."

Clay nodded, slipping into his wet poncho as he stepped out into the storm.

That evening the two men talked long into the night.

"This," said Clay, as his somber eyes watched the flames on the hearth flicker and hearing the snap and crackle of the chestnut logs, "is the nearest thing to home I have seen in twenty years."

The next morning at breakfast, the rancher offered Clay a job—no questions asked—and so it was that Clay Elkins had come to the Boxed M.

That fall and the ensuing winter convinced John Morgan that he had hired himself a real man who knew the cattle business as well as he did, and it wasn't long before a deep and mutual respect for each other's ability had blossomed into an abiding friendship. Clay had become an asset to the ranch.

Clay had met Elizabeth during breakfast that first morning and was immediately taken by her warm manner. He found her striking in her gingham dress, with her hair placed just perfectly on the back of her head. Many times, he thought he caught her looking over at him but dismissed the idea quickly. Dan was just a teenager who was learning about the cattle business. He spent most of the time with the hands on the ranch. John wanted him to learn everything there was about ranching, as one day he and Elizabeth would be given full responsibility.

Over the last several years, Clay had grown to love the ranch and considered it home. He had watched young Dan grow up and had seen something of himself in the boy. To Clay, Dan was as much his son as he was John's. He had developed a strong bond with John and was happy to be riding by his side, although kept most of his feelings to himself.

"Ready," he said, following Clay out to the porch. The ranch hands were rounding up their ponies in the usual hubbub of excitement. The rancher and his foreman were well on their way before their absence was noticed. The miles passed rapidly under them without a word exchanged. They reached the junction leading west away from the town of Sweetwater. Only the muffled sounds of horses' hoofs, accompanied by the pleasant creaking of saddle leather, disturbed the early morning quiet. John Morgan dropped back slightly to let Clay take the lead. His eyes followed Clay, who continued to set a stiff pace.

"Tell you this much," said Clay, breaking the silence, as he waited for the rancher to come alongside. "If that sheriff harms a hair of Dan's head, I'm going to kill him—that's for sure, an' nobody's gonna stop me."

Mile after mile slid by rapidly beneath the horses' feet, and a strong rein held them to a canter as the road wound its irregular pattern westward along the valley floor. It was several hours later when they reached the fork leading toward Big Spring.

Clay spoke first, as he carefully kept his eyes on the trail. "Looks like somebody cut off here and headed for the old canyon pass. The trail's been used some," he stated as he pointed straight ahead. "Appears that five...six horses went this way." Morgan nodded as he guided his mustang into the brush. "Let's go," he said, uttering his first words since leaving the ranch.

Clay nudged his horse onto the canyon trail after John, his horse's hoofs clattering on the loose gravel as he left the main road. Both men rode carefully, following the narrowing trail between the gradually rising escarpments on either side. Not a single disturbed stone failed to catch Clay's eye as they went deeper and deeper into the canyon's maw.

"Watch out for slides!" Clay called ahead to John, whose horse was skillfully picking her way around piles of rocky rubble and shale, the result of winter's erosion on the overhanging cliffs. After several hours of arduous riding, they were through the narrows at the far end of the canyon, where the walls had deteriorated into boulder-strewn embankments. A wider trail permitted them to ride more easily, although John had again dropped behind. He had been deeply steeped in thought about what he might or might not find at the end of their journey.

It was during one of these instances that Clay pulled back his horse and, motioning to John to catch up, pointed to the ground ahead and spoke.

"Only four horses on the trail now. Coulda sworn there

was five back apiece. Looks like they are being pushed hard, too." Clay's soft Southern drawl accentuated his words as he moved out again. Several miles further, the lead mare's ears cocked forward, and she emitted a soft whinny. Clay pulled up and slipped a restraining hand over the mustang's muzzle as he slid out of the saddle. John came up to join him. Motioning to stay still, Clay tossed up his reins and, gesturing him to remain put, cautiously stole forward along the trail.

John Morgan, watching Clay go forward afoot, felt his shattered nerves shake his body. He was trying to remain calm, telling himself it would be okay, and he would find his boy soon. He was considerably relieved when he saw Clay some distance ahead, waving him forward. Kneeing his bronco, he rode up, returning Clay's reins to him as he took in the scene. They had approached a beautiful glade. Trees—willow, oak, pine, and cottonwood— stood like sentinels, verdant and lovely, almost completely encircling a grove. Only the north side, showing an elevation of rock ledge and gravel, broke the symmetry of the landscape.

John was startled out of his reverie by Clay's practical and matter-of-fact voice.

"Horses, yonder." Leading his mare, he approached the center of the green.

"That is Dan's sorrel!" called Clay, coming up short. "And there are two others." He started forward, changed his mind, and waited for John to catch up.

John Morgan's heart leaped as he heard Clay's shout and spotted Dan's horse grazing off to his left. He whistled and the sorrel raised its head. Her ears flicked forward at the familiar sound, then she resumed grazing.

"Wonder where Dan is," queried the rancher, dismounting, his chest heaving. "He should be hereabout, somewhere close. He wouldn't go off and leave his horse. Look here, Clay, that looks like something up there on the hillside." Cupping his hands around his mouth, he shouted at the top of his lungs. "Dan!" No answer. Again, he shouted. "Dan! Where are you?" The hills returned only the echo.

"Must be someone around," shouted Clay, from halfway up the slope. Then he came on to the three crudely fashioned graves, each with a saddle at the head. Hardly able to control his voice when he recognized Dan's saddle at the head of the middle grave, he called John, who was about to fire his gun in the air.

"John," Clay's voice floated down to the rancher in an eerie pitch. "Come up here."

John eased the hammer down and made his way quickly up the slope to where Clay stood. He followed Clay's gaze, and his face went white as horror drained the blood from his body. It was as though his heart had plummeted to the bottom of his stomach. Sick with cold fear, he stood too paralyzed to speak or move. With a cry torn from deep inside his soul, recognizing his son's saddle, he brokenly spoke out. "Dan, Dan...please, don't let this be happening, God, not my boy!"

Gently Clay took him by the arm and led him to the campsite, where he made the rancher sit down to get control of his emotions.

"Stay here, John," he said, "I'm going to have a look at those graves." John nodded numbly, without looking up.

Clay Elkins knew that John Morgan, grief-stricken as he was, could not go through the ordeal of opening those graves, but he had to know if Dan was buried in one of them. Clay removed the larger stones. Using a camp utensil as a shovel, he then scooped the sand and gravel from the first grave. It did not take long to uncover the blanket-wrapped body. Carefully, Clay turned back the corner of the blanket. He was looking down on the face of the deputy called Miller. Clay covered the face and refilled the grave, packing the earth as best he could and replacing the larger stones securely on the mound before he moved to the second grave. With determined vigor, he opened the grave on the far side to stare in surprise as he recognized the second man as another of the sheriff's deputies, whom he did not know by name but recognized as one of the Posse who had come to the Boxed M ranch that day in search of Dan.

"Hope the next one is the sheriff himself," he mumbled as he refilled the second grave and set the stones in place. In his heart he knew who was there. Finding Dan's horse and the three saddles neatly arranged at the head of each grave told the story only too well—but at least he would be able to tell John Morgan the truth. The soft ground and gravel gave way rapidly to the bent and battered utensil, and before long, Clay found himself holding one of Dan's boots in his hand. He swept the dirt away with his hand and uncovered the other boot.

A sound startled him, and turning quickly, he found the rancher at his shoulder, looking down at the shrouded figure just visible under the loose gravel. Wordlessly, the rancher reached out his hand, and Clay passed him both boots. He knew there was nothing that he could do or say that would assuage the pain that would be there for the rest of John's life.

"Shall I go on?" asked Clay. "He's here," indicating the blanketed body not yet fully exhumed.

"No!" The answer came slowly and abruptly as John let his eyes wander over the peaceful valley aflame in the golden radiance of the late afternoon sunshine. "No!" he reiterated, more to himself then to Clay. "Let him rest here in peace. I can't bear to look. Just cover him up as gently as you can...maybe someday..." Then he handed his son's boots to Clay and made his way blindly down the slope.

Clay watched him go with mixed emotions, waiting until John had regained his footing before he replaced the boots at the foot of the grave. Quietly, he set about refilling the excavation, topping it with heavy stones to make it secure. He finished the unpleasant task and paused only long enough to hurl the makeshift shovel as though it were an evil thing. Then he rejoined the rancher, who was holding the reins of his horse. Clay swung up.

"Shall we go?" Clay asked, a strange softness in his voice. John mounted without a word. His world had collapsed. Something in him had died up there on the slope.

"I'll pick up his sorrel," Clay ventured. John shook his head negatively but said nothing. Clay understood, aware there was plenty of grass and shelter to provide a means of subsistence for the animals and that they would in all probability return to their wild state and join one of the roving wild horse bands. Satisfied on that count and sensing the rancher's wish to leave everything as he had found it, Clay directed his mare across the glade, passing the campsite enroute to the canyon trail. Here he halted and looked back. John Morgan, still in the glade, sat on his horse, motionless, head bowed. Clay kneed his mount out onto the trail to ride on at a slow pace. He sensed John Morgan's need to spend these last few moments with the son he loved more than life itself and whose warmth he would never again know.

The foreman glanced at the sun sinking in the west. The day was done, and in the soft stillness of early evening, a cool breeze was lifting. Soon, hoofbeats sounded over the muffled clip-clop of his own bronco, and he knew John Morgan was soon to join him. Once abreast, both men dug in their spurs, retracing the partially familiar trail through the canyon toward home. Neither spoke. Night was closing in fast, and both men realized they would ride all night. For them, sleep was out of the question.

Dawn was breaking when the two men turned into the ranch road and dismounted at the house.

"I'll take care of your horse," said Clay, swinging down and taking the reins from John. Without further conversation, he led both ponies off to the stable to be watered and fed.

John Morgan stood on the porch, watching the long figure of his friend lead the horses into the shadowy depth of the stable. Then, with a heavy heart, he went inside the house to break the news to Elizabeth.

A few minutes later, the horses groomed and fed, Clay wearily climbed to the hayloft. Pulling off his boots, he stretched his long frame in the fresh-smelling hay and fell fast asleep, troubled intermittently by bad dreams and forebodings.

Chapter 5
Mustang Draw

Dan rode hard, pushing the mare to get as many miles between him and Lamesa as possible. Tendrils of pain were shooting down his left arm. Numbness had crept into his shoulder. He knew it was imperative that he stop and examine the wound. Consequently, he turned into a grove of cottonwood, reasonably sure the element of surprise back in town had slackened things enough to give him time to escape to safety. There was a knot in his stomach, and the feeling of nausea overwhelmed him at the sight of warm, sticky blood darkening his shirt. He grimaced with pain in his effort to create a makeshift bandage with his bandana. Fortunately, the bleeding was not profuse, so he had some hope. However, despite his efforts to disregard the severity of the wound, it continued to seep blood.

From his place of concealment, he looked around. There was still no sign of his discovery, and being well hidden in the thicket, his emotions gradually calmed.

Somewhere ahead was the town of Seminole, an intermediate settlement near the New Mexico border. Knowing full well his need for medical attention, he wrestled with the idea of going into town. To ride into Seminole could spark recognition, and it would be delusional to think he could keep his wound a secret. His blood-soaked shirt was too conspicuous to escape embarrassing inquiry. He also knew the swift frontier justice of the unscrupulous men who sought public office in such towns. Thus, while the town of Seminole could offer medical attention, it also carried an unwelcome risk.

Satisfied he had tended as best he could to his wound, he left the thicket to follow the stage road west. Although the jolting action of his horse heightened the pain, gradually the trickle of blood stopped. While the coagulated flow had encrusted his shirt with a stiffness that continued to give him some discomfort, it helped hold the bandages in place. Encouraged by the short respite, he had made up his mind. He would ride south to circumvent the town. In doing so, it would almost certainly make it harder to find him.

While not sure that his sense of reasoning was other than delusional, he felt comparatively safe for the moment as he reviewed the day's events. He had been somewhat surprised with his own behavior in Lamesa. It had all happened so fast that he hadn't had time to think. He certainly would have gone to almost any length to avoid being embroiled in a gunfight and the death of a man. He was quite surprised by his voluntary instinct for survival that had triggered his automatic response to draw and shoot. His sudden reaction to defend his own life was etched indelibly on his mind. Suddenly, his gun had been in his hand, aided by the natural impulse to defend his life.

If the truth were known, the man he had killed could hardly have been more surprised at having been shot than Dan had been at shooting him. He wondered if he would ever forget the look of stupefaction on the man's face as his body shuddered under the smashing impact of lead.

Thinking of it now stirred up a feeling of revulsion in him, and it took a conscious effort to dismiss the whole affair from his mind. A stabbing pain caused him to bite his lips. The arm had grown stiff and sore during the last hour. Gingerly, he felt around the wound. The bandage was still in place, and the bleeding had not started again.

He pulled the mare about. The immobile prairieland met him, and the white road stretched ribbonlike over the table-lands, still and deserted. Southward, the desolation of broken canyon country shimmered and danced in the haze of the hot sun. In the distance, far to the west, the horizon emerged, leading into a bluish-black endlessness.

Momentarily, indecision returned to plague him; it seemed the more he thought about his situation, the less capable he became of his decisiveness. One inescapable fact, however, remained incandescent and was fast growing in significance. He had to get off the beaten trail—and fast. He had little doubt there would be a cry for his capture; a posse was overdue.

Amid such a quandary, his problem was solved suddenly and expeditiously by an easy egress at a likely offshoot of the stage road. It was just what he was looking for—a chance to cut directly through the badlands, thence continuing toward New Mexico. Either way, he figured the percentages were in his favor no matter which way he elected to go—and he would be safe from the long arm of Texas law. Perhaps he would find someone to tend to his wound. With his first choice, he rode light-heartedly into the sun where, despite the throbbing ache in his left side, he headed the mare into the brush.

The day was young, and the miles slipped by with unbelievable swiftness. The sun climbed, and soon the wastelands swallowed them up. Gradually the meadow grass petered out, and brown shale and red sandstone greeted him. Growths of barrel cactus with the promise of life, holding moisture within its spiked body, grew sparsely along the way. Underbrush and tumbleweed danced on the landscape as far as the eye could see, and slowly the red sand and sheet rock encompassed horse and rider with a mystical quality of desert silence.

Before long the under footing rose to waylay them, and travel steadily roughened. Eventually the undergrowth thinned as it struggled in isolation, burrowing for substance in parched soil.

A dead cottonwood thrust its withered arms aloft, beseechingly, to the high sky, and the quiet hung like a curtain broken only by the cracking sounds of steel-shod hoofs ringing on shale.

Evening's chill settled quickly, catching them well into the lowlands. Camp was but a matter of timing. Unwilling to risk an attention-drawing fire for warmth or to prepare a meal, Dan resigned himself to the unappetizing taste of a cold supper. Here, in the cover of a rock formation, he managed, despite the anguish and torment of his injury, to look after his horse. His Stetson served to water the animal, leaving little more than a swallow in the canteen for himself.

Dusk began to close in as he sat trying to light a cigarette, hoping it would give him some gratification. The evening's soft glow in the gathering night was a portent of the end of the day.

Eventually the desert came to life under the transfiguration of a rising moon. A sidewinder slithered across the sand, leaving a series of concentric circles to mark its progress, and a frightened rodent scampered to safety under a nearby rock.

Dan spread his bedroll and stretched his lanky figure at

full length to lie on his back, looking up at the stars. Nestled against his saddle, he pulled the blanket around his shoulders as he listened intently to the sounds of the night. Tired and weary, the end of his cigarette found him heavy-lidded and drowsy. He winced with pain as he turned on his good side and closed his eyes. Soft were the voices of the summer night as the still, crisp chill of the desert air closed in around him. The stars twinkled down in perfunctory elegance, oblivious to the disturbing and shattered dreams that took ahold of him as he slept soundly. The night winds continued to provide some sense of peace.

Morning came with unexpected suddenness and Dan awoke, cramped and sore. A dull pain had spread through his chest and his left arm had begun to throb. Soon the chill of night was gone and within hours—he was again on the trail.

"Hell!" his desperate word was twisted from his parched throat. As he spoke, he could have sworn the temperature had increased with suffocating intensity. Whenever and wherever he turned, there was no relief from its blast-furnace effect. Thirst caught at him as the burning heat took its toll.

The endless terrain of rock and rubble from the broken mesa and stretches of red shale lay ahead. The sand-whipped sage brush under the withering desert heat made it difficult for him to push ahead.

Things were beginning to happen to him that were increasingly difficult to understand. Several times, a sense of familiarity left him with the impression of having passed the same way before. His stops became more frequent, and as the day wore, mounting thirst continued to plague him. Fatigue grew swiftly and with it...regret. Regret that he had not taken his chances in Seminole rather than in this withering, hellish inferno. Several times, when the pain of his wound became almost too great to bear, he considered retracing his steps and taking his chances with the law. But he could not estimate how far they had come since leaving Lamesa. And when he thought of the multiplicity of canyons and the labyrinth of washes through which he had already traveled, he realized the futility of trying to find his way back. Finally, considering his physical state, he knew he had to deal with his present predicament.

Deeper and deeper they plunged into the maw of searing hell and damnation, the unrelenting fingers of nature digging at him. Twice that day he and Lady found themselves in boxed canyons. A near accident on the way out of one canyon ended in a rockslide and almost cost them their lives. Terrible and stunning were the implications of the treacherous travel. Forced to slow the mare to a snail's pace, he eased the pressure on the animal. Dry watercourses crossed his path to confuse him and blot out all sense of direction. Working his way through the uncharted mazes of limitless wasteland, he learned a basic truth: He had come upon an implacable and cruel foe. In all his life he had not been faced with such a wild, unrestrained adversary. The arid and profitless desert asked for nothing and gave nothing. Without pity, it hammered and tore at his physical being like something alive. Only the desert inhabitants—the scorpion and the lizard—were equipped to fight or even exist on near-equal terms, and they too scurried hurriedly to some cool hidden crevice to survive.

A flitting shadow across the rocks appraised him of a lone

visitor. A buzzard had circled overhead, wheeling silently through the sky like the ominous presence of evil. Soon it was joined by another—and still another. Gimlet-eyed and ever watchful, the three buzzards rode the skyways with the untiring patience of ones that would not be denied. As his bleary, bloodshot eyes followed their flight, Dan was aware that soon there would be more of them. Frustration rose in him. After one or two attempts to drive them off with his Winchester, he gave up, but he could not ignore their presence—or the implication. He daydreamed of better times—not too long ago life had been so peaceful, so certain, so pleasant and happy. It had all been so secure. The ranch, the green mountains with their cold running streams, and his friends and family were his life. Where had those carefree days gone? Why? Surely there was some purpose to all of this. Was this going to be the end for him?

An elusiveness of will and a deepening fatigue came over him. He was totally and irrevocably lost in the badlands, with seemingly no possibility of a way out. Suddenly Lady stopped. No amount of urging would prevail on her, and Dan, rousing himself from his lethargy, looked about. The mare had halted by sheer instinct and stood on the edge of a plateau overlooking a tremendous valley. Dan slid from the saddle. A steep cliff fell away beneath them. Hundreds of feet down, the valley floor hastened away to a distant escarpment. They were on the rim of a great draw. Amazed by its immensity, he stood looking down. The path ran a zigzag course within walls of precipitous rock. Across the void, the far escarpment humpbacked its way to touch the distant skyline, like the jagged backbone of some prehistoric creature.

Momentarily, he was able to turn his attention away from his wound and pain as he stood on the very edge of inordinate splendor. He thought of the millions of years that had gone into its making, and the hand that had dug its fingers into the crust of the earth to gouge out this massive expanse across the land. This dramatic picture momentarily cast a spell on him as he looked across the miles.

Gradually, a sound came to his ears. The mare trembled and tossed her head against the tight reins. Dan led the animal closer to the lip of the canyon and scanned the valley. A dust cloud—he could scarcely estimate the distance—was rising from the throat of the draw. He stood in amazement as hundreds of wild horses spilled into view and cascaded down the draw. They poured out the upper end in ever-growing numbers and fanned out across the floor of the valley. Slowly, the sound welled up until it beat like jungle drums against the escarpment wall to roll back like thunder in an ever-increasing crescendo. Far in the lead, a magnificent white stallion ran with wild abandonment known only to the natural environment, the flock converging to pound after him. Finally, the dust rose, obscuring him from view.

Suddenly, Lady whistled—a shrill, piercing blast that bounced and reverberated from every nook and ledge around them. Her eyes flared and rolled at the call of the wild. Finally, she stood, neck extended, and nostrils dilated, inquiring of the familiar sounds. Far down the draw, still hidden from sight, the white stallion squealed his reply. Wheeling into full view, he swung a tight circle, searching, then followed by the herd, he vanished through the lower end of the pass.

Then Dan remembered. Jeb Smith had told him of the wild horse bands that ranged in the west. This then, was Mustang Draw—known to all wild horse hunters as the breadth of the Southwest. This was that remarkable place where only the strong and determined hunter could appreciate the importance of these splendid creatures. The draw consists of sloping terrains surfaced by quartz sands, gravels, clays, and sandy loams that support brush and grasses. How well named, he thought—Mustang Draw, a name that captivates its audience. Surely this was a place to excite the imagination and whet the appetite of all those who loved horses. Tales of images such as these had intrigued the young and old whenever told around the campfires of the West and had grown with every telling.

While he was mesmerized by the unfettered beauty and independence of the horses, he had to face reality. He had come to an insurmountable impasse that virtually imprisoned him in the trackless wastelands behind him. His mind reeled, stripping him of will, leaving him vulnerable to whatever lay ahead.

Throughout that day—and the next—across the vast reaches of scorched earth, horse and rider moved like tiny specks. Marshaling their strength with frequent rests, they pushed on.

He knew the sun was getting to him now. Several times, he had been fooled into believing he had come through this hell, but a mirage—one of many—had dashed his hopes, always leaving him the worse for the experience. Aware that his mind was beginning to wander, he heard imaginary utterings. On one such occasion, the sound he heard was the unintelligible ramblings of his own voice.

It was now a question of surviving the day. Sick and exhausted, he crawled into the shadow of a gigantic boulder where sleep took over the dim consciousness of his tortured body. The spent mare stood with her head low and motionless. Eventually the sun's rays lengthened on the mesa, and the first hint of a cooling breeze brought with it some relief. Steadily, the sun sank to touch the distant escarpment. Slowly and gently, twilight blended day into evening. Soon darkness came, and the inscrutable night looked down, cold and remote, as a tiny spark of life force continued to keep him going.

The sun was well up when Dan awoke. Excruciating pain persisted. As far as he could remember, this was the third—or fourth day in the wastelands.

Delirium—being somewhere between the conscious and the unconscious—superimposed itself on his ability to reason. All he could salvage of his situation was that he and his horse were still alive. He was vaguely aware that he was holding on to the reins of his horse with a grip so tight that his fingers ached.

Mechanically, he slipped down from the saddle. Painstakingly he labored to unhook the canteen and hold the flask to his lips. The gesture was as automatic as was the habit. He had done the same thing several times yesterday and the day before. The canteen was as empty as the desolation around him. At times out of his mind, he could no longer account for the hours of the day—or the direction in which he was headed. It made little difference where they went or how. They would never survive another day.

It was at the close of the day when the mighty fighting spirit bowed its head in defeat. He had given his best, and it was no longer good enough.

Darkness was abruptly on them again, and a full moon brightened the dark sky with a spectral effect.

Dan stumbled, staggering against Lady as she came to a halt. The horse was done...exhausted and unable to move. Dan dismounted and immediately fell. On his knees, in these last minutes, he knew what he must do. Doggedly, racked with pain and beaten, he hauled himself erect, hanging on to the stirrup for support. His last thoughts were for his horse. He was feeling now like a man in a drunken stupor, trying to bring the mare's head into focus. He had to do it—now. He felt the mare give against his weight as he came to his feet. Babbling—driven by the madness of a bedeviled man—he managed a backward step. Barely able to stay upright, he tried to force his hand to do his will. Desperately, he sought to free the heavy Colt from its holster. Suddenly the ground gave way beneath him. Down— down—down—he fell into what seemed like limitless space. Briefly, he was conscious of the soft touch of death on his face. Abysmal darkness—deep and impenetrable—engulfed him.

Chapter 6

A Timely Stitch

Zeke's voice was shrill and high pitched with his customary annoyance at his partner's gait.

"Hurry up, yu ole horned toad-frog. Can't yu see it agittin' dark?"

Shaking his head with an air of disgust, he started to unpack one of the burros.

"Mights' well do it meself, as usual," he added, loosening the pack containing their food supply. Next came the utensils for their evening meal. "Rightly don't know what he'd do 'thout me to keep 'im movin likely he'd jest sit down an' wait tu die," he chuckled to himself, easing the equipment to the ground where Amherst, his partner, was building a fire.

Amherst busily nursed a tiny flame to life with small tinder and did not respond to his partner. He was used to Zeke's rumbling to the point where it went in one ear and out the other. He knew, too, that the sarcastic remarks were Zeke's way of letting him know he had them pains in his bones again. No one within earshot was spared, but then there was never anyone other than Amherst around, unless you wanted to count the four of them—Zeke, Amherst, and the two mules, Henrietta and Jake. Amherst didn't mind Zeke's outbursts and rantings any more than Zeke minded Amherst's long silences.

"Jest too dead-boned lazy to talk," Zeke said when Amherst's only answer was to spit tobacco, a distance of five feet and hit a target nine out of ten times with unerring accuracy.

The two old-timers, now in their early sixties, had met

years ago while prospecting and had joined forces. A lasting bond of friendship had grown between the two men.

Zeke Billings, with his disgruntled mien, which served to disguise his true feelings, had a deep regard for everyone and everything that lived and grew. Orphaned by an Indian attack when he was only fourteen, he had made his own way in the world ever since.

Zeke had been tall and skinny as a young man—and painfully shy—and he had remained remarkably spry and agile for most of his years. Prospector in both action and appearance, the habit of talking to himself—or to no one in particular—had grown with the years of solitude on the trail. He was the more articulate of the two, and his words were whetted by a better-than-average sense of humor. Patience, bred in him from the years of his never-ending search for gold, had become second nature to him. Now, somewhat bent over and crowned with a bushy head of snow-white hair to match a bristly crop of chin whiskers—of which he was most proud—he and his partner had become a familiar sight to the gold camps of the West.

Zeke gave his suspender a hitch as he doffed his battered old sombrero and hunkered down to open a sack of beans. He poured its contents into a skillet and placed it over the briskly burning fire.

"Better git the coffee goin," he said, "whilst I tie up them mules."

Amherst Slocum grunted unintelligibly, half filling the pot from a canteen. A few minutes later, the tantalizing aroma of coffee and beans made him drool with anticipation. *This is the life,* he thought, as he spit a sizable chew from his mouth—

which he did only because Zeke kept after him to remove it before he ate.

"Make you sick tu death, yu old coot," he would say many times. "An' I ain't agoin' to even bury you effen you die o' thet chaw terbacca poison."

Amherst said nothing, only stared at his partner exasperatingly and spit defiantly until Zeke shut up in disgust. Amherst never could tell whether Zeke was serious about not burying him or just being his grouchy self. But he had to admit that since he'd been getting rid of his chew before he ate, his stomach hadn't been acting up on him.

The shorter of the two, Amherst's entire make up was almost the direct opposite of his partner's. Inarticulate as Zeke was articulate, Amherst's shy grin and self-effacing nature won him instant friends wherever he went. He was unpretentious and somewhat outlandish in appearance. It was not unusual to find a piece of rope substituting for his suspender or his shirt front held together with a horse blanket pin, not to mention a tear in his pants pulled together with a string of rawhide. Only in patience did the two men have a common denominator; that and their friendship for one another. Tobacco-chewing, lovable, and with a sheer delight in living, they had searched for gold all their lives and loved every minute of it.

To Amherst, Zeke was more than a partner; he was like a brother. Amherst could remember only a few people on the ranch where he was raised. He'd never known his father but did remember his maw telling him that his father had gone away and wasn't ever coming back—and how she'd cried when she'd told him. He'd been too young to ask questions about his father. Then his maw had died. At times, when his chores became too hard to bear, he would go over to the burial plot on the hill and sit by her grave and talk to her about his problems. It was during one of these visits that he'd decided to run away and find his dad. As the years sped by, his pursuit had become an empty dream.

Now in the closing years of his life, all he had in the world to care for him was Zeke. Although Zeke sometimes called him an old scrawny piece of sawed-off buzzard meat, Amherst knew he was a genuine friend.

Amherst never complained of the pain in his own rickety old bones. Lately, whenever he got chilled panning for gold in the cold-mountain streams, he would wait till Zeke turned his back so he wouldn't see him trying to rub the circulation back into his legs. More than once, lately, out of the corner of his eye, he had seen Zeke working his arms to ease the rheumatic twinges that plagued him, too, with increasing frequency.

Now here they were, enroute to the mountains of New Mexico. Zeke had been right about one thing. He had wisely selected Mustang Draw as the best possible route west. While unbearably hot during the mid-summer days, it did provide some relief with shade in the canyon depths during the late afternoon. They had followed its almost direct course as they cut through the badlands and managed to find sufficient refreshment in the water holes to keep them going. A lateral passageway, slashing its way from the great south plains of Texas to the lush green, grazing lands of the north, this quirk of nature provided a natural escape route and passageway for the wild horses and cowboys of the Southwest.

The two old prospectors had learned to respect the sounds that veritably shook the canyon whenever they raced through this hidden gateway to greener pastures. Several times during their journey, they had felt the earth tremble as they watched these surging, spirited herds thunder by and disappear into a haze of dust.

Most days that passed for the two men were pleasantly tranquil. Born to the trackless desert country, the two old prospectors kept close to rivers and streams. There seemed to be little need for haste. Their method of telling time was a clock divided into the four seasons of the year.

News of rich strikes in and west of the Alamogordo range had been the subject of many discussions everywhere prospectors gathered, as far south as Old Mexico. It was here they'd decided to try their luck. Several fortnights ago, they had put all their gold dust into a grub sack and equipped themselves with enough supplies to last them several months.

Amherst leaned forward and poured two cups of steaming coffee, handing one to his partner.

"Smells right good," said Zeke, sipping his first taste. "Makes yu feel nice an' warm inside. Gittin' kinda chilly, too."

Amherst nodded and helped himself to the beans. "Night here comes in a mite of hurry —gittin' along bout thet time o' th' yar," continued Zeke, placing his tin cup of scalding hot coffee on a flat stone and making himself comfortable against his saddle. He was just reaching for the plate of beans from Amherst when he heard it. At first, he was sure his old ears were playing tricks on him, but when one of the burros began showing signs of uneasiness, he knew something was amiss.

Finger to his lips, Zeke indicated silence and sat motionless, listening as a new sound of rolling stones and the muted rumble of moving earth died with a final clatter. Amherst, the plate of beans still in his hand, stood frozen, peering into the night shadows in the direction of the sound. Zeke rose quickly but quietly to his feet to stand beside Amherst. All was still. Both men listened. The mules quieted—whatever had disturbed them had evidently gone, at least for the moment.

"Thought I heard a hoss heave," ventured Zeke, "but it coulda been a cat. Gonna git me ole Betsy." He was back shortly at the fire, his carbine in his hands.

"Can't take no chances," he volunteered to Amherst, who had hunkered down to resume eating his beans. "An' don't just sit thar an' cram your mouth full o' beans like a heathen."

Amherst swallowed another mouthful before he answered. "Warn't no cat," he said, reaching for his coffee.

"Why not?" demanded Zeke, settling down to his meal with his rifle handy. He pointed his fork at Amherst, "Whadda yu know about cats?"

"I knowed they ain't much on making' no noise like that thar, Smarty!" Amherst put down his food and, reaching across the fire, picked up Zeke's rifle and rose to his feet. "Now whar yu goin'?" shouted Zeke. "Yu wanna git yerself kilt?" But Amherst had disappeared into the semi-darkness of the night.

"The danged fool," Zeke grumbled angrily under his breath as he hastily put down his tinplate and rose to follow Amherst. "He'll never learn effen he lives tu be a hunnert—which he won't."

Suddenly, a horse whinnied, and a shout from Amherst

spurred him into a run. Cursing at the rocks that stabbed at his ankles through his heavy boots, Zeke fought his way through a dense growth of underbrush through which Amherst had vanished.

Again, he heard Amherst's call, "Zeke! Help!"

"Tarnation," swore Zeke, banging a knee against an outcropping of rock. "Where air yu?" he called, hobbling in pain as he stopped to rub his aching leg.

"Har," the words jumped at him out of nowhere as Amherst acknowledged the call. Zeke swore again at his old eyes not being able to pierce the darkness, but he eventually made out the figure of Amherst kneeling beside a man half-covered by sand and gravel. Amherst was busily moving away the rubble. Zeke dropped to his knees to help.

The man stirred and groaned. "He's alive—jest about." Amherst straightened as he spoke. "Most likely he tumbled down from up thar." Zeke indicated the rim of the ravine, barely perceptible, silhouetted against the night sky. "Lucky he ain't dead. Some little slide to jostle him like so." Gradually Zeke's eyes became accustomed to the gathering night. He stood erect, looking up the embankment.

"A hoss er I'm a jackass," said Zeke, tapping Amherst on the shoulder and pointing up the incline.

Amherst got to his feet and looked in the direction his partner had pointed. "A hoss! Whar?" he asked, searching the crest.

"I jest seed a hoss up thar on the bank," yelled Zeke. "Looks as big as a mountain."

"Wal, go git 'im!" the sharpness in Amherst's tongue caught

Zeke's ear. "Don't jest stand thar. This man's been hurt."

Zeke looked sharply at his partner. "Let's git him tu camp first, then I'll git the hoss."

Zeke bent to help his partner. "Careful like, now!" he grunted as he propped the man up to get a better grip under his armpits. "Git a hold of them feet effen yu ain't got nuthin' better tu do. He ain't zactley no passel o' feathers."

Sighs of relief were audible when they reached camp and deposited their burden by the fire. Amherst shook out his blankets to make a bed for the man, while Zeke removed the stranger's boots. Finally, with their patient settled on the blankets, Zeke rose, letting his partner administer to the stranger's needs. He stood for a moment, watching Amherst make the injured man as comfortable as he could. Stepping to the fire, he picked up a burning branch and turned to hold it close to his face. The flickering light revealed the unshaven face of a young fellow.

"Shucks," he exclaimed. "He ain't more'n a lad—banged his head some, slidin' down that wash. Git thet bottle o' snake poison outa my pack—an' don't u dare take a nip—I know jest how much is thar, so don't try any o' yer tricks. I'm gonna git his hoss afore she strays." He stepped into the darkness and disappeared into the night.

"I oughta have more sense, coming out this time o' night," Zeke grumbled. "Nobody in his right mind should come out heah, least anyways not for an onery ole hoss. Now, whar in tarnation you suppose that critter is? Dang it!" He swore as he tripped his way into the brush, rubbing a bruised shin bone.

At the point where he judged having seen the horse above

him, Zeke started the ascent. Luckily a sound guided him within reach of the mare.

While the bank was not too severe, its steep upsurge was enough to make it considerably dangerous, and more than once, he found himself back at the foot of the embankment, followed by cascading sand and gravel that filled his boots. Displaced stones following him down didn't improve his disposition any. By the time he had plowed his way through, it was his embittered opinion that anyone hunting a strange horse at night was just plain loco. Grunting and groaning, he finally sat on the rim, spitting dust and sand, and blowing his nose loudly and long. "Damnit," he swore as he tugged at his boots to empty them of sand and gravel. "Ain't no way tu enjoy life nohow," he spoke aloud. His boots, now comfortably replaced, he resumed looking for the big horse. A sound brought him within a hand's reach of the mare. Fearful he would spook the creature, Zeke moved slowly, speaking in soft, cajoling tones. The old prospector stroked her muzzle. "Whoa girl," he said quietly as he reached for her reins. "Now tu git down from this gosh–forsaken place ain't gonna be no picnic, hoss—so don't git skittish on me er' us'n both'll git our necks broke." Coaxing and swearing under his breath and holding the animal along the rim to where he could chance descent, he held firmly onto the bridle, half sliding, half walking on their way down the embarkment.

Back at camp, Amherst had worked feverishly to restore his patient to consciousness. Signs of life were beginning to show. He coughed as he poured raw liquor down his throat.

"How's the lad?" Zeke asked his partner upon his return.

He had unsaddled, watered, and hobbled the big mare in a patch of sweet buffalo grass before he returned to camp, joining Amherst by the fire.

"How's the lad?" Zeke repeated the question, hunching down alongside his partner.

"Been shot!" stated Amherst succinctly.

"What do yu mean, shot?"

"Been shot, jest like I said," Amherst handed Zeke the bandana he had removed from the boy's neck. "Blood," he said. "Look!"

Concern showed in Zeke's voice as he leaned over the lad. "Yer right; he's been shot sures' yer a foot high. How bad is it?" he asked, a tenderness creeping into his voice that contradicted its usual gruffness. His rough fingers probed at the wound with gentleness. Carefully, he cut away the blood-soaked shirt. "Hold that light so's I can see what I am doing, and don't burn him with thet twig."

He wiped the wound clean with a bandana soaked in whiskey and peered closely at the small hole. "Iffen I don't miss my guess, that bullet went clear through that left shoulder slick as a whistle. Too high to hit the shoulder bone and jest a mite low enough to git unner the muscle. Bleedin's stopped, purty much. Git me some water so's I can finish washin' thet wound."

Without a word, Amherst handed his partner the canteen. Zeke washed and bound the wound, thankful that his patient was not yet fully conscious and had been spared much physical distress.

"Lemme have thet whiskey," he said, reaching for the preferred bottle. He raised the man's head and let a few drops trickle between his lips.

It was almost an hour later that Zeke straightened to stand, looking down at his patient, a perplexed expression on his face. Slowly he shook his head, corking the bottle firmly with the heel of his hand.

"What do you think?" Amherst directed the question to Zeke.

"Don't rightly know—yit! Thet fever he's totin' ain't helpin' none."

Amherst stirred up the fire, mulling his chew, hard put to cope with the sudden turn of events. "Yu figure him to live?" He paused his fire making, looking up.

Zeke faced his partner, reading his concern, and their eyes met in an inscrutable moment of silence. Then, without answering, he skirted the fire to disappear into the darkness. Zeke needed time to think, and when he got back, there would be time enough for questions.

Ever so slightly, the lad stirred as Amherst tucked a blanket about his shivering figure and nestled warm rocks against his body. Zeke walked into the firelight and deposited the man's bedroll and saddle bags by the fire. A moment later he was on his knees beside his partner, examining the wound. The bandage was holding with no sign of bleeding, and gradually the trembling ceased. Many hours later, the lad's brow seemed to be cooler, and his sweating had finally stopped.

"Maybe!" Zeke muttered, adjusting one of the hot stones. "Jest maybe he'll make it."

That night the old prospectors took turns keeping vigil over their charge, administering to Dan's needs. The flickering light of the campfire made a small round hole in the night.

Dawn broke in a canopy of brightness out of the east, painting the high sky in colors of orange and reddish-brown, sweeping across the vastness of the draw, the slanting rays of silver cresting the western escarpment, and the golden light of another day stained the countryside. Zeke came out of his doze to rub the sleep from his eyes and stretch the cramping from his muscles. Hurriedly, he made a cursory inspection of their patient, while Amherst built up the fire. Soon the morning coffee brought them together over breakfast.

It was Zeke who spoke. "Fever's broke." He filled his cup. "Gonna be nip an' tuck lessen we git sumpin' in his belly." He reached for a tinplate. "Can't see a hint of his face with all them whiskers." Amherst had almost finished his coffee as he heard Zeke add something,

"Found this heah paper in his saddlebags last night." He fished about in his pocket and withdrew a frayed and wrinkled piece of paper. "This here sez that his name air Randall, can't rightly make out. Figger he's an outlaw." His stubby forefinger pointed to the caption beneath the indistinct frontal sketch of the face. "An' wanted—some bad."

Amherst stared at the blurred features of the man in the poster, a perplexed expression on his face. He returned to his breakfast.

"Wal! Ain't yu got nuthin' tu say?" Zeke, snorting in disgust, rose stiffly to attend the wounded man. Amherst was drawing the last dregs of coffee from the pot still grappling for an answer when Zeke called him. Together, they found themselves peering into a pair of defenseless eyes that stared at them in questioning appraisal.

"Where am I?" The words were little more than a whisper.

"Take it easy, son." Zeke reached for the canteen.

He hunkered down to hold the bottle to the lad's lips. Slowly, the trickle of whiskey brought a show of color to the lad's cheeks, as he struggled to sit up.

"How'd I get here?" The words were coming easier now. He touched his wounded shoulder. "What's wrong with me?"

Zeke, sitting cross-legged, held up his hand. "Whoa! One thing at a time. We uns found yu back yonder in a wash. Yu been shot an' purty near died o' us. This heah's Amherst," he pointed in the direction of his partner. "An' yonder's our mules, Henrietta an' poky Jake. Henrietta's a boy, but Amhurst ain't never tole her. That big hoss yonder is yore." Zeke chuckled at his own joke. "Call me Zeke." More conscious of the sound of his benefactor's voice than the words, Dan groped frantically for an explanation of his accident, but he was still reeling from what had happened.

"Wal! Maybe ponderin' this ol' paper can help yu." Zeke fished into his pocket, holding up a note for him to see. "Found it hidden deep in yore saddlebags when we brung yu in. Are you in trouble, lad?"

For a moment Dan studied the likeness before him and the caption beneath. Faded and almost illegible.

"Jace Randall," he read the name aloud. This was a name now familiar to him, but he was too tired to discuss the facts at this point.

The prospectors had breakfast going when Dan again woke and softly stated, "It shore smells good."

"Now," Zeke squatted, "how about some vittles and coffee? Think yu can handle it?" Even though the lad ate meagerly, the meal seemed to warm him. It appeared that his shoulder pain had lessened, but his eyes, heavy with exhaustion, refused to stay open. He remained awake long enough, however, to be conscious of the blankets being tucked about him. He was alive—and for the moment, that was all that mattered.

Dan Morgan, now alias Jace Randall, awakened to the routine activity of early morning, realizing he had slept round the clock. He tried to work himself to a sitting position. He grimaced with pain as Zeke and Amherst watched him reaching for his boots. Sweat stood on his brow, and his face was white.

"Where is my hoss?" A surprise pain jabbed him as he turned to look about.

"Yonder," Zeke nodded as the black hobbled nearby. "Oh!" Dan said, as though dazed.

Breakfast over, and feeling a little better, Dan stood up and walked unsteadily to his horse. Testing his strength, despite the strain on his shoulder, he managed the saddle and kneed the cinches tight. He turned as Zeke approached.

"Young feller," said Zeke, "it looks like yer in a mite o' trouble back thar, and since thet shoulder needs watchin', and me and Amherst ain't had no company for a spell, maybe yu'd like tu join up with we'uns—that is, iffen yu'd like. We're aheaden for New Mexico and then the gold hills o' Californy. Claim they's big chunks of it layin' on the ground jest waitin' tu be picked up."

At this point Amhurst came up on them, chewing his cud phlegmatically. He stood idly by. "Amhurst," continued Zeke, "ain't talked so much since I knowed him since yu come, an' it does him right smart tu have somebody that do understands when he do say somepin." Zeke stopped, slightly out of breath.

Amhurst nodded and turned a lizard on its back with a bullseye shot of brown juice. "Shore like yu tu stay, son," Amherst nodded, his Adam's apple bobbing up and down as his words wrestled with his chew.

The throbbing pain in Dan's shoulder was a prompt reminder that he was lucky to receive the invitation "If I won't be any trouble to you, I'd be proud to go with you," he answered without hesitation, a lightness in his heart at the thought of finding two good friends who were willing to support him.

The matter settled, quickly, the prospectors broke camp. The rising sun found them mounted and heading up the draw. Amhurst had done a good job bandaging his shoulder, and Dan was thankful the bleeding hadn't started again, in spite of the jolting motion of his horse. Slowly the hours wore on, and the days went by without incident.

Under a cloudless sky and unrelenting sun, the trio crept along against the travesty of nature. The immensity of the draw fascinated Dan. It wound like a serpent through the Great Plains, widening at times.

Sheer escarpments that rose to dizzying heights bordered the draw, and more than once, he experienced the feeling of entrapment as he eyed endless precipices that precluded any choice other than to go forward. Momentarily, he sensed a relaxedness of circumstance, but the thought eventually passed.

There were times at night—and even during the day—when the wind lifted, and he heard, or imagined he heard, the flutelike sounds of an organ. He asked Zeke about it, who stated that he had heard of the "mourning winds" many years ago. Amherst listened and nodded as he turned to the wisdom of his old partner. "Yup! wind singing through them rocks, was his final comment as he kicked his mule forward.

Dan removed his hat and wiped the sweat from his brow. The three sat motionless in the hot breath of the wind that carried the scent of the sweet grasses ahead. Dan stood in the stirrups and looked back over the draw to the south. Hot, dusty, and uncharitable, the trail etched itself against a magnificent gorge that Dan could not find the words to describe.

In the weeks that followed, Dan's wound, under the sharp eye of Zeke, continued to heal. It seemed that in no time at all its' only reminder was a small star-shaped, pink-white scar that stood out against his tanned skin and provided a slight twinge when he lifted too heavy a weight. As the journey continued, Jace, so called by his compatriots, became more absorbed with life on the trail with his two new friends.

Bothered by his new circumstances for survival, he began to assent to the fact that he was known as Jace Randall. It was somewhat frustrating that his plans had been suddenly changed, but he knew that he was very grateful for the prospectors who'd found him lying at the bottom of that dry ravine. At night, when the camp was asleep, he found himself wide awake, staring at the millions of stars twinkling against the black sky wondering what crimes Jace Randall had committed that had outlawed him.

He would toss about restlessly, throwing the blankets off himself even though he was cold. Sometimes the first touches of dawn would be painting the morning sky when sleep finally took over.

Although his nights were restless, he relaxed throughout the day. He listened with amusement as Zeke, at times annoyed, called down fire and brimstone on the head of one Amherst Slocum. With an air of disdain, Amherst would chew phlegmatically through Zeke's outbursts. Gradually, he came to understand and respect the interchange of the two old prospectors.

Only once did they see any evidence of riders. It happened one day well along in the afternoon. The draw had widened into a rolling plain, and the escarpments on both sides had fallen away in the distance. A group of riders appeared, momentarily, on the horizon. They were riding west and were soon lost to sight. Later, just before camp that night, they cut the trail of the horsemen. Traveling on what appeared to be an old stage road, Zeke surmised the men had been heading for the Texas Border.

Zeke squinted into the distance, shielding his eyes from the sun. "Recollect a settlement som'ar south o'heah a spell—least was last time we come through heah."

Zeke fell silent and turned in his saddle to look back at Dan. Dan glanced at his face, but it was Amherst who first broke the silence. "Looks like the weather might be kickin' up a spell," he added.

"Zeke," Dan spoke. "I've been here some time now, and you both were able to get me through a rough spot. I haven't told you much about myself, but you saw the poster. You will have to trust me on this one. I've got some money, and my plan is go into town. Maybe I can get some news. Look, I appreciate what you've both done for me, but I really need to move on. What do you say?"

Amherst looked at Zeke, shutting off what his partner was about to say.

"Hit shore do make sense tu me," he said.

"Wal! Maybe so," answered Zeke, scratching his chin whiskers, which he always did when he was thinking.

"I'd say he's got a right to do as he wants," interjected Amherst.

Zeke nodded. Amhurst continued, "No need for him to be worrying about us ole wart hogs. We will be in game country soon an' we can take care of ourselves."

Amherst stood firm. "Go ahead, son. Settlement ain't moren' five, six, maybe ten mile south o' heah."

"Maybe you're right," agreed Zeke. "We will camp heah in that slump of cottonwood yonder; we'll catch up with you sooner or later."

Dan replied, "If I'm not back by morning, go on without me. By the way, you guys are great; you saved my life. I will never forget what you did for me." With a gesture of a finger to his hat brim, Dan broke the mare into a run. "Wish me luck," he called out and hit the spurs.

The two old-timers watched him as he headed into the sun, soon to be lost from sight over a prairie ground swell.

"Wal. Don't jest stand around' an' moon all day. Let's hold up here a bit and maybe set up camp—be around supper time afore he gits back an' he'll be hungry." Zeke spoke gruffly, concealing his true thoughts. Amherst glanced at Zeke. They both knew that they were seeing the last of Jace Randall—whether he knew it or not.

A sigh escaped Amherst as he turned to help his partner.

"Adios amigo," he said, under his breath.

"Drat it." Zeke was still muttering to himself when he bedded down the mules for the night. "Young pup comes ridin' inter yer life without so much as a warnin an', the next thing yu know yer motherin' him like a—and then bye, he's leaves an'. . ." His words trailed off into the night.

Chapter 7
Alias Jace Randall

The day Dan rode away from his two friends, it was dry and clear. Horizon to horizon, the high clouds scattered across the sky. They hung with almost imperceptible motion bulging and swelling into soft, mushroom-shaped clouds. The world felt good to the lad as the black swung through tall buffalo grass. Cutting across the trackless expanse, the mare fought the restraining rein. A light-heartedness ran through him. Free of inhibition, Dan jogged along, enjoying the invitation of the open trail.

The settlement lay, according to the old prospectors, west of Mustang Draw and considerably south of their present position. To the west directly were the vast uncharted plains—home of the great buffalo herds. Beyond these level lands and rolling terrain, the distant timberline of the lower tip of mountainous territory rose to block the passage west. But the real challenge somewhere beyond this broken chain of western mountains were the Indians. For here, in the high and inaccessible wilderness, lived the most perilous of the Indian tribes: the Mescalero Apache, who had been involved in a series of armed conflicts with the United States to protect their land.

Around the greasewood fires of hundreds of camps, the stories were told of bold men who'd overcome Apache warrior attacks as they sought out any kind of reward for their capture.

This was the fringe of country where the two old prospectors were heading, and Dan wondered, as he rode if they were aware of the dangers that lay ahead or if they were to steadfast to even put any stock in the stories they must surely have heard. It did occur to him that they deliberately chose to ignore the risk rather than change their plans. True, they had seen only scant evidence of Indians. But by and large, their days had remained tranquil and infinitely pleasant and perhaps to them any interruption of their endless bliss seemed remote and far away.

The mare broke into a sweeping stride across the natural roll and swell of the prairie as the miles fell away. Isolated patches of desert floor raced beneath them breaking the continuity of greensward, the tips of which rode the ebb of a soft breeze. Saguaro stretched high into the horizon and yucca marched in profusion deeply through the mescal and cholla.

The scenery around him and the indulgence of time and distance soon distracted him. It was somewhat of an awakening on cresting a knoll to see thin tendrils of smoke rising from the valley below.

"Could be we're here," Dan pulled up to breathe the mare, his eyes shutting against the sun. Off to his left, the terrain swept downward, bottoming into a broad basin. The silver gleam of water sparkled in the bright sunshine, isolating a giant cantilever of red rock strata shafting out of its offshore depths.

As was his custom, he reached for his tobacco. A match flared, and he grunted in satisfaction as the blue smoke streamed from his nostrils. He heard the distant clang of a smith's hammer through the thin air...the noisy screeching of iron on iron. Black soot erupted intermittently from a stack, emerging through a shanty roof as a display of sparks shot upward into the atmosphere.

A moment later, horse and young rider moved on down the slope to find themselves following a deeply rutted road that ran around the perimeter of a lake and through the edge of a settlement.

A sound caused him to turn, and he nudged the mare aside to let a wagon pass that was piled high with freshly killed buffalo hide. A hail to the driver elicited the information that he was in Monument, New Mexico—the liveliest trading Post this side of the border. He didn't elaborate or say much else for that matter.

Evidently in a hurry, the wagon drove off, but the driver did gesture with his bullwhip to a dirty, broken tombstone, half buried on the side of the trail and almost hidden by the weeds. Dan rode close to make out the word "Monument" in fading red paint smeared across the front of the stone. Underneath, an arrow, its head missing where the stone was broken off, pointed to the town.

Now he realized that he had missed his objective. Having come further south than he had intended, he had stumbled on the trading post in error. Second thoughts brought the conclusion that one place was as good as another to do his business, so he pulled the black about and rode slowly down the main street holding the mare to a walk while he looked the place over. Passing several adobe shacks, mostly in a ramshackle state of repair, he went by the blacksmith's shop to find himself in the center of town.

The place was cluttered with rusting wheels and smashed Conestoga wagons, some with canopies still hung, shredded, and rotting to shambles.

Broken-down bits and pieces of equipment lay scattered in front of the blacksmith's shop, inviting anyone willing to make repairs to take what they wanted.

Further down the road, random tents appeared to be scattered in the hot sun to indicate the edge of habitation.

Stepping down out of the saddle in front of what seemed to be one of the more prosperous buildings, Dan found himself facing a two-story structure attached to a group of other buildings. A sign nailed to a porch column read "McNair's Trading Post." In smaller letters, underneath, it said "Saloon and Lodging." A well-filled horse trough just this side of a hitch rail overflowed to muddy the ground, already sodden from continual refilling from a shallow well pump. Surprised at the rustle and bustle about him, he watched with high interest the buffalo hunters and plainsmen move about in pairs and in groups to gather in conversation, interspersed with Indian sign language. The topic of the day—Buffalo. Their clothing stank with the odor of fleshed hides and bloody entrails that carried to the street as they haggled prices with McNair.

Some of these quick-tempered frontier's men were wild with excitement as they stood in the middle of the street, settling their differences by cursing and shouting at spectators. A random sampling of men, looking more like the general run of the border renegade, from deserters to the tin-horn gambler, milled about aimlessly, homing in on personal conversations for whatever selfish interests they were out to pursue.

With a tug on the reins, Dan led Lady to the horse trough, where she drank deeply. After the horse had finished, he primed the pump, and a second later, the water gushed furiously. Sticking his mouth under the spout, he quenched his thirst with the cooling water that flowed over his face and down his neck. A moment later he removed his Stetson to douse his head in the trough's cool depth. It was here that he made his first acquaintance of the day.

So engrossed in what he was doing, he had not noticed the approach of a young woman. She stood opposite him on the other side of the trough, an empty pail in one hand, waiting for him to finish his ablutions. A final plunge took him completely underwater, and he came up shaking his head vigorously, spraying water around himself as though he was a wet dog.

"Well! You certainly have a nerve." The woman's voice startled him. "Why don't you watch what you are doing?"

Dan looked up to see a young lady brushing water from her dress and attempting to dry her face on her sleeves. Sputtering in feminine furry and anything but coherent, she glared at him.

"Oh!" he said apologetically, offering his bandana, "I am sorry—I did not see—"

"And you did not look, obviously!" she arrogantly snapped at him in spite of his apology.

Overwhelmed to the point of embarrassment by the sudden tongue-lashing, Dan nevertheless became instantly conscious of the woman's attractiveness. She had soft chestnut hair coiled atop her head and a tiny yellow ribbon to the side with a tortoise-shell comb holding her hair into ringlets of curls.

Instinctively, he believed her eyes would be a lighter hazel brown when no longer darkened with anger.

"Here!" he blurted, hastily reaching for the bucket. "Let me help you." He submerged the pail.

"Not from there stupid!" She yanked the half-filled bucket from his hand. Her temper flared as she splashed water all over his front.

He saw it coming but could not evade the deluge of cold water that drenched him to the skin. Driven back, he gasped, catching his breath.

"What did you do that for?" His jaw dropped, speechless at her sheer audacity.

"Now you know how it feels, Smarty!" And he watched her walk away in a flurry of petticoats, the pail in one hand and a fistful of wet skirt in the other. She disappeared quickly down an alley between two shacks.

He heard a door slam and standing there with the water running into his boots and feeling more like a fool every minute, he knew she was gone and that this was one encounter in which he had, most definitely, come off a poor second best.

His temper rising and feeling more uncomfortable than he could remember, he grabbed his horse reins and made for the porch, where he drained his boots, swearing that if he ever ran across that female again, he'd duck her in the horse trough, good and proper, clothes and all.

But his rage quickly cooled, and he paused, boot in hand. *"What was there about this girl that affected him so...and why now?"* he asked himself. The realization hit him hard. It was another woman and the memory of happier times. He stood up, smirking, but he quickly forgot it all when he realized his altercation with the lady had not gone unnoticed. The confrontation and his bucket dumping had provided substantial amusement to a gathering, grinning audience. People on each side of him watched intently as he replaced his boots and led the black to the hitch-rail. Ignoring his audience, he headed for the saloon, pulling his Colt enroute in an attempt, at least, to dry his gun belt. He had the forty-four still in his hand when he stepped onto the porch and looked up in time to avoid a collision with a redheaded man blocking the doorway. The man had obviously been watching him. He filled the entrance, arms across his chest, leaning against the doorjamb with an amused smile on his face. Slowly he stepped aside, clearing the way for Dan to pass, his face collapsing into an offensive grin that spread from ear to ear.

"Got yer ditties wet, didn't you, Mister?" There was a twinkle in his eyes when his face straightened. "Amy sure ain't one to fool with—that temper o' hers comes up sudden-like sometimes. Maybe it'll simmer you down some to know you're not the first man I seen in these parts to tangle with that wildcat and not get your shins kicked."

The speaker removed the cigarette dangling from the corner of his mouth and flicked the ashes from the end.

"Thet gun in your hand, you ain't aimin' to throw down on any of us are yu?" The smile faded from the man's face, and Dan quickly noticed the change in him.

"I'll use it if somebody don't get off my back." Dan holstered his weapon, throwing a meaningful glance at the crowd that had grown slightly but was beginning to scatter.

"Some iron yore packing, hombre. Yu shore gotta be tolerable to handling a forty-four like that." Before long, Dan noticed a man shouldering his way through the crowd. He was joined by two other men who caught up to him, placing themselves on either side and halting some distance in front of Dan. The man in the center interrupted the conversation. "I'd shore like to handle your gun for a spell—friendly like, I mean." The gesture of the man to his right moving his holster forward to a more advantageous position caused Dan to stiffen slightly. Still riding the ragged edge of indignation and smarting under the embarrassment from his encounter with the girl, Dan was fully alert to the threat of violence and was in no mood to banter words.

A rapid appraisal of the three men showed the center antagonist to be a big hulk of a man, deep-chested with broad shoulders and a twisted bull neck—both indicating great physical strength. Two broken teeth protruded to brutalize his face. He had a large scar that had found its way from the left temple to his heavy jowls, narrowly missing the corner of his eye yet easily discernible under the heavy growth of his beard. He was not overly tall and a pair of very large hands with short spatula fingers hung at his side. Built more like a mountain man than the average plainsman, he stood on powerful legs, his oversized feet laced in Indian moccasins. The other two men were smaller in stature and not quite as threatening in appearance, but would still bear close surveillance if things got out of hand.

The circle about him hushed as Dan, his emotions suddenly capped and controlled, stepped from the porch down into the street. Mincing no words, he gave them his answer. He tapped the man's shoulder with robust force and replied, "The only way a man looks at my gun is if I draw it. You aimin' to take a look?"

Dan squared his position and watched a crimson stain flush the man's face.

"Wal! Could be, at that, and I shore could use that black." The big man's hand hung limply near his gun and only the twitch of his fingers belied the impatience Dan knew to be mounting in him.

"Look here! Luke, yu ain't gitten that mare for yourself," said one of the ruffians. "I say we match for the right to kill 'im. That right with you, Red?"

In the moment of silence that followed, granting time for the redheaded man to get a fresh cigarette going, Dan knew his moment had come. Confidently, he moved into the shadow that was lengthening along the building front. He knew his gun was fast—and a shadow of a smile crept across his bearded face as he prepared to meet the threat. He crouched, hand spread-eagled over his gun.

Finally, after what seemed an interminable length of time, the redheaded man, his eyes on Dan, spoke up.

"Might be a good idea at that," he conceded, stepping to the edge of the porch. "Maybe all three of you should try it, an' the one left gits the mare."

"Whadda yu mean?" The one that's left gits the black. He ain't that good...!" barked the man nearest him. The inference in the redhead's remarks brought about a need for clarification.

"Wall," the redhead switched his attention to the three men, "before you throw down on this hombre, maybe you oughta know who yore facing! He's Jace Randall—one of the fastest guns this side o'hell. An' one of yu air gonna die—maybe two—more'n likely he'll take all three of yu."

The sense of uncertainty that cropped up among the trio wasn't helped by the low murmur that ran through the spectators, now grouped safely at the far side of the street.

Dan saw the consternation on the faces of Luke's cohorts and made a mental note of the sneer expression on their faces.

Luke, by a considerable margin the youngest of the three, scoffed at the implied threat, albeit with a note of doubt. "Aw! He ain't no Jace Randall." He looked at the redhead for confirmation of what he hoped to be a jest.

"The hell he ain't." Red stepped down from the porch. "Yu jest might take a look at them four white stockin's on his mare—they's only one hoss like that in the whole West, an' she belongs to him. Yu gotta admit he ain't turned a hair when you threatened him—did he? An' he's all set tu take the three of yu. If yu still think I'm wrong, there ain't nothin' tu stop yu from reachin' for that iron."

"Count me out," said the last man to join the others as he beat a hasty retreat to the sidelines. "I ain't no gunfighter an' I don't want no scrap with Mr. Randall."

Dan, watching the metamorphosis, stood quietly as the knowledge of his identity shifted the odds. Quickly, the bulwarks of support faded. Luke, his tongue licking his dry lips, appeared bewildered; his ego became deflated when his remaining partner spoke.

"Listen, Luke!" he said pulling the big man by his arm. "Don't be a damn fool!"

"I c'n take 'im, Pete—honest to gawd I c'n." Luke tore his arm free, his eyes a baleful stare.

"Luke! Hear me, I heard o' this man. He'll cut yer heart out afore yu could blink twice—an' Paw'd turn over in his grave iffen I let yu."

Luke was ready to pull the trigger, and the crowd sensed it. But the man on the porch intervened.

"Boys!" The redhead approached the two men. "Looks like yu ain't gonna die after all, so I'm inviting Mr. Randall in for a drink—an I'll split the backbone of the first man who tries to gun him in the back. That clear? Yu hear me! Luke?" He waited for Luke's nod before he turned to Dan.

"I'm Big Red Reagan," he said by the way of introduction. "Come in, Randall, and let me buy yu that drink." He disappeared inside with a backward glance at Luke, who reluctantly followed the crowd through the swinging doors to gain a favorite spot.

Dan followed on the heels of his host and lined up at the bar to join him. They touched glasses in the classic frontier salute and gave themselves over to the unforeseen pleasantries of the occasion.

In the interim, Dan had had a chance to size up his benefactor. While his first impression of the man had been one of respect for the control he exercised over the hoodlum element in town, he had mixed feelings about his precise motives. Dan's face remained passive as he mentally catalogued the man over meaningless chatter. Tall and slender and good-looking, Red was well-suited to the role of leader. His head was crowned by a shock of close-cropped curly red hair, and his pair of keen blue eyes missed little of what went on about him. He had a toothsome smile when he was pleased, and an aquiline nose of good proportion flattered his face. He wore no gun and was dressed in the casual garb of a range rider. A pair of eastern riding boots in good repair, high-heeled and well-kept, augmented well-filled corduroys. He spoke with the easy manners of the range and with friendliness, simultaneously infectious and dubious.

Dan thought he should concede some authority to appease this person. Along about the third round of drinks, he had concluded that this man could be either a fast friend or a deadly enemy.

"By the way, Randall, what brings you to our country—you a Texas man, I heah?" The question was offhand, obscure, and probing in a friendly fashion. Red was engrossed in refilling Dan's glass, and he kept his eyes averted as the question was posed.

Dan, quick in repartee, held up the plug of chewing tobacco he had managed to grab when they had first come in. He picked up his drink and ignoring the question, replied, "This, is for a good life on the trail."

Big Red searched Dan's face for a second and then replied, "I guess I'll have tu drink tu thet." Both men broke into pretentious laughter before the conversation got around to Luke. A loner, he was withdrawn and uncommunicative, ignoring Big Red's invitation to join them at the bar and drink with them. He sat at a table apart from the others, sullenly drowning his sorrows in a half-empty bottle of whiskey with his brother Pete. His obnoxious voice carried across the room.

The scar that had nearly cost him an eye, Dan learned from his benefactor, had come from a brush with a couple of

Apache. Luke's old man hadn't made it, but young Luke had managed to get away, but not before one of them had left his mark on him. Keenly aware of his disfigurement, he'd developed a withdrawn, unsociable personality that kept him apart from everyone except his brother, Pete.

Later, when Dan took his leave, he passed by the table of the two brothers, who eyed him coldly as he approached.

"Mr. Randall," Pete addressed him as he neared their table, reaching for his last swig from the nearly empty bottle. "No offense, but I'll shore be glad when yu leave town, cause my brother Luke here sez you shamed him in front of his friends when yu called him out that way. His eyes git kinda big when he looks at thet horse o yorin. So, I'd watch my back iffen I was you."

Dan looked Pete squarely in the eyes, hands flat on the table, ignoring Luke completely, and stated, "You tell your broth er that if he gets in my way again, I'll kill him!"

Luke half rose, but Pete pushed him back in his chair and with authority stated, "Sit still, you damn fool. Don't you see he's trying to bait you."

Once outside, Dan untied the mare and stepped into the saddle. Big Red, who had followed him out, stood by stroking the velvet nose of the big black. He looked up at Dan.

"By the way, Randall, I wouldn't want anything to happen to Luke or his brother Pete there. Luke's not too bright and he's—well, kinda difficult. Needs a lot o' growin' up—an' I kinda like them both around, if you know what I mean."

Dan replied, "You heard what I said. If he tries again, it better be worth it because he won't get another chance." Dan lifted the reins as the redheaded man moved back with an irritated expression on his face.

"Hasta luego!" he said, raising his hand in salute.

Big Red stood for a moment, watching Dan ride down the street, and eventually saw him dismount at the blacksmith's shop.

Big Red spoke out loud, "Looks like I might hafta kill him myself someday, but..." his soliloquy changed pace mid-sentence. "He's the kinda man I could ride the river with, thets for shore." He reentered the saloon.

Had anyone overheard, they could well have thought his words sounded more like a prophecy than a spur-of-the-moment afterthought.

As for Dan, he was acutely aware that he had been adroitly questioned, and while he had shunted off most of the inquisitive attempts to pump him for information, there remained the assumption that Red's banter and jousting was not all innocence and sociability. Briefly, he mulled over the information he'd gained in the saloon—Red's stamping ground had been in around the border of Texas and New Mexico. But that knowledge prompted no more information, and he discarded further thought of it when the blacksmith informed him that the black needed shoes. Leaving his horse in the blacksmith's care, he stepped out into the late-afternoon sun and lengthening shadows. Thoughts of putting up for the night were beginning to crop up in his mind when he caught a glimpse of his female friend from the water pump. Half-hidden at the end of the alleyway, she beckoned to him. At first, he was prone to disregard her signal, but on second thought he decided it might provide an opportunity to give her a piece of his mind. A glance at the saloon showed no one watching, so after a word to the smithy, he ducked around the corner to thread his way through the narrow passageway and up to a doorway through which the girl retreated. He was about to change his mind when she stuck her head through the doorway, a finger on her lips, shushing him to silence. A quick gesture to follow took him inside.

He felt surprised and disgusted as he found himself looking into the determined face of a young woman holding a Winchester on him. It was as steady as a rock and pointed directly at his middle.

"Got him, Major," she called, bracing on a step, as Dan moved closer, calculating his chances of getting his hands on the gun barrel. The rifle nosed up a trifle to cover his chest.

Realizing that such a sudden move could mean a bullet, he stalled for time.

"Now look here..." he raised his hand to brush the barrel aside but was cut short by the click of the hammer to full cock. "Now what?" he asked, deciding that it was a lot safer to stand still than rile this unpredictable, trigger-happy young woman.

"Send him in," a voice beckoned from somewhere in the rear, "and for heaven's sake, put that gun away!"

"I don't know, Major, He's pretty mad an' he's still some wet."

"Amy! You cantankerous female—do as I say!"

"Shall I take his gun?" she called backing away, the rifle wavering somewhat.

"No, damn you! Mr. Randall isn't about to shoot anyone—

unless it's you, and I wouldn't blame him a bit if he did."

Reluctantly, she lowered the Winchester and stood it in the corner behind her, an apprehensive look in her eyes as she flattened against the wall to let him pass.

"The major is expecting you."

"After you." The relief in Dan's voice was evident as he followed the girl down a short hall leading to a closed door at the far end. Not knowing what to expect and wary, he kept his distance, his gun hand poised for an emergency.

Normally, he would have been reluctant to pursue the matter had it not been for the fact that the major, whoever he might be, had used his name with enthusiasm making Dan think he had knowledge of Jace Randall and that the meeting might be well worth his while. The feeling persisted that here may be an opportunity to learn about the unknown parts of Randall's life.

Coming up behind the girl, he stood to one side as she knocked on the door.

"Come in," said a big voice, and Amy, pushing the door ajar, stood aside to allow Dan into the room.

A glance about showed a lanky, well-set individual by a window, the shades of which were half drawn to soften the sun's glare. Looking somewhat uncomfortable, he sat upright in a straight-backed chair, one trouser leg pulled up to accommodate his right leg bandaged from knee to toe. Another chair, cushioned with a soiled and rumpled bed pillow, served as a support for his injury. Tousle-headed and with several days' growth of beard, the man returned Dan's gaze with scrutinizing blue eyes.

Affably, he leaned forward to extend his hand.

"Howdy! Jace Randall, I am Major Tom Sterling, United States Cavalry. Won't you please sit down and let me apologize for Amy's very unusual method of getting you here?" Almost before he had finished, the door slammed shut. Dan saw his host wince as the building shook. An uncustomary smile appeared on his host's weathered-looking face.

"You see what I mean—Amy just can't take constructive criticism."

The humor of the moment struck a responsive chord in Dan, and he found himself grinning at the man's frustrations with Amy. His wariness eased as he recalled his recent unhappy introduction to this high-spirited lady.

Dan returned the handclasp and found it to be warm and strong despite the unusual circumstances for this first meeting. He took an immediate liking to his host. His puzzlement grew, though, as he noted the brown belt hanging from the chair back, partially hidden by a rumpled army tunic. The brass buttons and epaulets on the shoulders were that of a major in the United States Army. Having accepted the man's invitation, the springs squeaked as Dan seated himself on the edge of a bed—the only other available seat in the room—and felt a rifle underneath him. "Army Springfield," Dan commented, as he stood the rifle against the nearest wall well out of reach of his host.

"Yep!" the man nodded, "Latest issue." He raised the shade to peer into the street.

The major raised his hand as he continued, "I know—I know how suspicious you must be, but let me assure you, you are in no danger, and my only purpose in asking Amy to bring you here was to request a favor of you—a very important favor. If you don't like my proposition, you can ride out any time you choose with my blessings." Somewhat mollified by the apologetic expression, Dan searched the man's face for subterfuge and found none.

"How'd you know my name?" The bed squeaked again as Dan returned his weight to it. "Saw you ride in—would know that mare anywhere. She's a trademark with your name on it, and I recollect seeing you down Sonora way a couple of years ago. You've changed some—seems you're a mite younger up close. Recollect you shot your way out of a jam down there with two renegades. A simple case of self-defense, but you let out for the border hell for leather, like the whole town was on your heels, an' I don't blame you. You never can tell with the Mexican border patrol." The man interrupted his conversation to fumble behind himself to remove his coat and gun-belt from the chair.

"Would you mind..." he said, passing the holstered weapon to Dan, who had half risen. "I'm a little uncomfortable here." He changed his position of his injured leg, but a fleeting wince of pain darkened his face.

"Jace," he broke in, "let me come right to the point. When I spotted you in town, I decided to make you an offer. If it sits right with you, you'll get a chance to do something inside the law. I say that because there is no record of Jace Randall having killed a man except in self–defense, but you are still a hunted man. Someday they'll put a price on your head, and you know what that'll mean." The man again fluffed the pillow under his foot.

Meanwhile, Dan felt that a door was about to open on information concerning Jace Randall. But he had to be careful. He withheld the impulse to quiz the major for more details. Certainly, here was someone, at long last, who knew of him. That he was an outlaw was no surprise. The "Wanted" poster in his saddlebag confirmed that, but the gunfight in Mexico was news to him, let alone any knowledge that he had ever been there. A logical and safer approach dictated that he not reveal his real identity and hope for some inadvertent piece of information linking him to his past and take it from there. Conversely, he thought, *what could be lost by hearing what the man had to say?*

"Can we talk frankly?" the major asked. The answer came sooner than he had expected.

"I'm listening," said Dan.

"Good!" The army man shifted his position, his face lighting up, "I'll start at the beginning. It's quite a story, so make yourself comfortable." He adjusted his ailing leg once again. He then rolled a cigarette and passed the tobacco to Dan before settling back to talk.

"A few years ago, somewhere south of the Mexican border, a gang of rustlers was organized to sell guns and whiskey to Indian communities. These guns are responsible for the savage Apache attacks on the wagon trains rolling West in ever-increasing numbers. These tribes, paying for these guns in raw gold—from sources they cautiously guard—have spawned such a lucrative profit that it has all but halted the development and expansion of the West.

"The United States government is so concerned that it has built and is building a string of forts along the wagon routes to protect the homesteaders and help them reach their destination in safety."

The major paused and raised the window shade again to look out, then let it fall back in place.

"Some time ago," he resumed, as he handed Dan a drawing, "the army was assigned the job of locating the renegade organization responsible for this and destroying it once and for all. We think a man named Strom is working with them. In case you run into him, he stands almost six feet tall, has long features, and walks with a limp. You will know him, as he always wears black clothing. His hair lies down a good portion of his back. I guess he is trying to fit in with his friends."

"Where do they get the guns?" Dan took advantage of a pause, his interest increasing.

"I'm ashamed to admit it, but they are, for the most part, being consistently stolen from army supply depots. Furthermore, they are being transported to the Apache under our very noses.

Now we come to the heart of the matter and where you come in. Army intelligence has learned there is a traitor supposedly a member of the army, working with some renegade who arranges these thefts and acts as a go-between for the outlaws and their business partners."

The story continued to unfold, and Dan became more involved in the plot. Army intelligence had dispatched the name of the traitor via courier to the commanding officer in charge of a new outpost near El Paso, and the courier is enroute at this very moment. Dan learned that the man sitting before him had been assigned to meet the courier and provide him a safe escort to the fort.

But Major Sterling had just recently suffered a broken leg—when thrown by his horse—and was unable to carry out his assignment. He had been held up in his room, unwilling to risk a message to his superiors, when he'd spotted him, Jace Randall, who, while an outlaw, was known to be a trustworthy man. In a desperate gamble, he had hurriedly arranged to bring the outlaw to his room and enlist his services in his stead.

"Didn't you figure it was risky sending a girl to splash me with water just to get me up here? That female needs somebody to set her straight about her obnoxious behavior!"

"Sorry about that! The bucket of water was her own idea. In fact, she was mighty upset when I asked her to bring you here—she was half scared to death, especially after soaking you," responded the major. "Amy can be very creative at times—the girl's got a lot of anger. Both her parents were killed by outlaws when she was a child. She ended up marrying a man at a young age for convenience, which turned out to be a big mistake. Her husband treated her badly almost from the beginning of their marriage. She later divorced him, leaving her to fend for herself. She has been working for me for some time. She tends to do things in an out of the ordinary way. She does have a good heart if you can believe that."

The upshot of the plan was that Dan, in return for his participation in the forthcoming venture, would have an excellent—almost guaranteed—chance of having all charges against him dropped, along with an official lifelong amnesty.

Convinced of the validity of the plan and the personal integrity of his host, the clarion call was both loud and clear. He,
Jace Randall, alias Dan Morgan, stood on the threshold of not
only clearing his name but of being absolved of all charges. This
would give Dan the opportunity to clear a dead man's name,
live free from pursuit, and be relieved of any false crimes held
against him.

The major had finished, and Dan joined his host at the
window.

"Something out there bothering you?" Dan eyed the street.
The sun had set, and an early dusk was moving in.

"Oh, a worry or two," the major gave a small laugh. "Nothing to bother anyone too much," he said, thumbing his cigarette out. They both watched the blacksmith appear, momentarily, to fling several old horseshoes into a rusting pile outside
his shop. All was calm. Night fell rapidly, and soon the town
was strangely quiet, except for the saloon.

Dan turned to the major.

"You got yourself a deal!" he said, offering his hand.

"I'm glad to hear it! Mighty glad." Sterling's grip tightened,
a look of relief cracking his sober expression. "But first I must
tell you that it holds considerable danger for you. I heard that
one of our informants at an army depot was ambushed and
killed just recently, and I suspect the traitors will try to get
their hands on those documents. They'll kill the courier—and
you, too—if they think you're in on it. Does this change your
thinking?"

The pseudo Jace Randall shook his head to indicate he was
still in on the deal.

"Didn't think it would," his host said lowering his bad leg gingerly to the floor. "Let me have that army jacket." He pointed to the jacket Dan had hung on the bedpost along with the major's gun. Dan gave him the blue tunic and watched him rip the insignias of rank from the shoulders.

"You'll need this, seeing you don't have a coat with you," he said, handing it back to him. "It's just about your size and warm. You'll be riding some high country, and it'll come in handy. You won't be as much of a target without these." The major tossed the epaulets on the bed.

"Now, with your permission, I'll get Amy to arrange a room for you tonight. A hot bath and a good night's sleep will feel great—so will a good drying out. Sorry couldn't resist a little bit of humor there. Meanwhile, I'll prepare a map with instructions for Amy to give you at breakfast before you leave."

Dan nodded his thanks, folding the army coat over his arm. He stepped just this side of the door, his hand on the nob, and then turned back. "And my amnesty?"

Sterling nodded. "I'll deliver the recommendation by letter to headquarters personally, soon as this leg'll let me travel. You'll find your black in the corral out back. Amy's probably taken care of her by now."

"I'll take care of her myself." Dan opened the door. Sterling rose and stomped across the room. "Amy!" he yelled, sticking his head through the doorway, "Put Mr. Randall up for the night—and bring him enough hot water for a bath." Dan caught the barely intelligible answer down the hall. Sterling couldn't resist a final dart: "And he'd like the water *in* the tub, not *thrown* at him..." He got the door closed just before a heavy object banged against it.

Major Sterling grinned, and his eyes twinkled with humor. "She just said yes," he said as he stretched out his hand. "Good night and thank you, Jace; you'll not regret it—good hunting."

"Good night." Dan shook his hand and opened the door. "If there's nothing more, I'll look after my horse and pull out early in the morning." He was about to close the door when the major's voice stopped him.

"By the way, Randall—there is something, if you don't mind." Sterling had again settled in his chair and was looking at his corncob pipe. Dan stuck his head inside. "If you should ever hear of a man by the name of Jim Elkins, I'd sure appreciate your getting word to me."

"Jim Elkins," Dan came to quick attention. "Did you say Elkins! Jim Elkins?"

"That's right. Why? You know him?" Sterling was sitting straight up, his unlit pipe spilling half its contents onto his lap.

Dan shook his head with a mixed emotional response that intrigued the major.

"Can't say as I do. Where's he from?"

Tom Sterling laughed, settling back in his chair, side-stepping the question. "Just some personal business—just thought if you crossed his trail."

"What's the man look like?" Dan posed the question, treading on something too familiar and too close to ignore, cautiously withholding information as he questioned the major.

"Oh! He's tall and slim and talks with a deep Southern drawl. If you ever meet him, they tell me you'll never forget him. The army's been looking for him some four years, going

140

on five now—and haven't the slightest idea where he is. He may be dead for all we know, but we'd sure like to know, one way or another."

Dan nodded, closing the door softly. "Jim Elkins," he rolled the name over on his tongue. That description would fit any number of men, but it was a close description of Clay. Why, he asked himself, did the major make such a big deal about finding him? The feeling persisted that Jim and Clay were one and the same. There was so much he did not know about Clay. He pondered all evening about their conversation. Yet there was nothing he would be able to do, and he would never jeopardize Clay's cover, if that was what he needed.

An hour later he was in bed, scrubbed and clean-shaven. Amy had been nowhere in sight when he had returned after seeing to his horse. A lukewarm tub of water proved he was in the right room.

He did make note that his bed had been turned down.

Chapter 8

A Reckoning

The predawn hours of the next day found the pseudo Jace Randall, having been accepted at face value and now the trustee of a vital responsibility, well on his way. He had risen early and left quietly while the household was still asleep, having planned to have his breakfast somewhere along the trail. Passing through the kitchen on his way to the corral, he'd found a bulky envelope lying on the kitchen table with his name scrawled boldly to his attention. Pocketing the envelope and shouldering his saddle, he'd slipped away unobserved, leaving the town sleeping off the activities of the night before. Some miles west of the settlement—the sky was lightening— he'd stopped to gather greasewood for a fire and shortly thereafter, over his first cup of coffee, he'd settled back to read his instructions. A carefully drawn map detailed a place along the Pecos River as a rendezvous point to meet the courier. From there they would work their way southward.

To his surprise, the reverse side of the map showed an alternate route to be used at the discretion of the messenger. The map also indicated where Dan would layover for several days if this route was chosen. In the event of the latter, they would then swing southwest, crossing the Salt Flats under the Guadalupe, over the desert, and then on to the Ranger Headquarters.

A description of the courier, named John Walkingstick, revealed him to be part Navajo, raised by a white father, several years with the army, and readily identifiable by his left hand with two missing fingers—a misfortune of camp horseplay—

and long braids reaching down his back. He would be wearing an army blue and have the customary means of further identification.

To Dan Morgan, these events could not have been better timed. The mantle of the famous gunfighter bestowed recognition upon him as though it were a birthright. The sound of the name—Jace Randall—familiar now, the respect it engendered, the heavy forty-four strapped to his hip, and the snow-footed black all increased his confidence in being successful. Instinctively he knew more about the person he was pretending to be and that his gun was legend.

Day and a reddening salmon sky came crashing through the top of the world as Dan tucked his instructions away and rebuttoned his army jacket. His gear repacked, he swung into the saddle and was once again on the trail.

And so it was that, on this bright morning, there were vast stretches of sand and purple sage all around him as he rode into the broken wasteland that lay ahead. Crusted ridges stung by the scouring winds shone beneath a blazing sun. The brilliance of the underlying flowers against the muted browns of the earth framed the compensatory beauty of the desert, and the Chollas paraded in dress rehearsal across the gigantic sweep of creation. Moving leisurely through the chaparral, it was not long before the sentinel spires of mountains etched themselves against the horizon.

From a high point, Dan and his horse pulled up to take in the vastness of the land.

Monumental in significance, even by nature's harsh standards, it served not only as a beacon and guidepost for the traveler but also as a warning of the gateway to the homeland of the prevailing Mescalero Apache.

Picking the easier footing to the bottom of the obelisk, Dan threaded his way through the jumbled rock, negotiating the rise from the light encircling the marker. Dismounting on the shady side of the landmark, he rolled his first cigarette of the day, and as the match flared, its odor permeated the air. He spread his map before him for a more comprehensive look.

Satisfied as to his direction, he returned the map to his pocket, stepped into the saddle, and was about to ride, when he spotted the haze of dust rising along his back trail. Standing upright in the stirrups, he shaded his eyes as he watched the dust grow.

"Now, who in hell do you suppose that could be?" he muttered, scrambling down from the mare. "Couldn't be that damned dispatcher this far east—or could it?"

Yanking the Winchester from his boot, he sheltered behind a pile of red stone, having led the mare out of sight behind him.

The handle clicked as he levered a cartridge into the chamber, laying the rifle within easy reach. "Just in case," he said to himself, "Just in case."

"Whoever he is, he sure rides like hell and fury," Dan observed, noting the deft sureness of a seasoned horsemen. "Coming on like the hammers of hell, too," he jested as the horseman broke into full view below him, still some distance away.

"Could be the courier, at that—but what is he trying to do, kill that hoss?"

Quickly Dan stepped into the open, vigorously signaling his position by waving his rifle overhead. The rider, catching the sun's glint on steel, veered and changed his course, coming into the incline at breakneck speed. The need for explanation died abruptly as two horsemen in hot pursuit came into view. There seemed little doubt as to their purpose as they sharply kept on the heels of the first aggressive rider, now headed in his direction.

Reacting quickly, Dan lined up a shot that brought the pursuers to an abrupt halt, and a successive volley scattered them in retreat. They pulled up well out of range and after what appeared to be a council of war, were last seen riding off into the brush in the direction from whence both had come.

Hurriedly Dan moved to greet his visitor, who pounded up in a whirlwind of dust and came to a sliding halt.

"Howdy," the light-voice inflection held a provocative quality that he was sure he had heard before. Suspicion leaped as the rider slid from the saddle to join him. Sweeping back the rim of the black sombrero, a tousled mass of brown hair spilled into the sunlight, a small blue ribbon, somewhat askew, holding it from complete disarray. The worst was now confirmed. It was her.

"You!" he exclaimed staring incredulously at the rider. "Don't tell me..."

"Yep! Mr. Randall, it's me—and before you turn purple, maybe you had better look at my horse. I think she threw a shoe."

Humor twinkled mischievously in Amy's eyes as she faced him. A wide smile lit up her face. She stood arrogantly before him, brushing the dust from her riding habit, making futile attempts to wipe the grime from her face and tidy up her hair at the same time.

A cursory inspection of her horse revealed only a loose shoe.

"You're lucky," he said pounding a nail into place with a rock. "Now what's this all about?" he said, as he passed her the reins.

"The major's dead, Mr. Randall," she said, her face serious. "Just after you left, he went out to the corral to check on his horse—that's his horse here," she nodded, "and someone bush-wacked him. Before he died, he said to catch up with you and give you this." She rummaged in her saddlebag and produced an official-looking envelope. It was unsealed, and the address was blank.

"He said to tell you it was important that you deliver it to no one but, the commander at the army post yourself."

He took the packet from the girl and looked inside, then dumped the contents into his hand. A puzzled look knitted his brow as he stood holding the epaulets the major himself only recently had torn from the very army jacket that he was now wearing. Included was a letter explaining his mission to meet the courier.

He stuffed them into his inside pocket. "Sounds mighty strange. I am sorry to hear about the major getting killed. I suspected that he was on edge when I was with him. I can't understand why he didn't give them to me himself if he want-ed me to have them." He stared at Amy hard. "Knowing you, I think there's more you are not telling me."

"Well! Yu needn't get so all fired up about it, Jace Randall, and I don't give a tinkers damn what you think," her voice rose angrily, as she continued. "If you think those men were just having target practice—" Impatiently she turned and was in the saddle before he could reply. "Well! Why don't you mount up, and let's go." He'd barely caught her last words when she went on, "And don't be such an old stuffed shirt."

"Well, I'll be damned—of all the gall—I have a notion to chuck the whole deal." He started after her, catching up with her on his horse to come alongside. "Come on," he said. "I'm taking you home—the sooner the better."

"Oh! I'm not going back," she shot back at him, wheeling her horse only to cut him short. She adjusted her hat, tucking in several stray hairs. "You can drop me at the first settlement or wagon train we come to."

"You're what?" She saw his face darken as he spoke. "If you think..." he found himself inarticulate. "I'd rather be boiled in oil." Disgust choked him.

Amy kneed the horse ahead, ignoring his outburst. "You coming? Or do I have to go on alone?" And with that, she sank her spurs and lit out across the desert on the run.

Thoroughly frustrated at his inability to cope with this tigress, Dan went into the saddle with a vengeance. He brought the animal about. The girl was rapidly widening the distance between them and was already racing up the far slope, a swirl of dust at her heels. Briefly, she appeared against the hilltop and then vanished over the crest.

"Women!" he snorted as he led the black out in pursuit. He found her standing by her horse just over the knoll, overlooking a sluggish stream below.

"What the devil are you trying to do? Get us both killed?" He flung himself down from the saddle, grabbing for her bridle strap. Anger glinted in his eyes, and his words flayed her. "Don't you know we are in Apache country, and we haven't got a chance if we're spotted? Now! You stay close to me—understand?"

He looked hard at her and felt the fire go out of him as a long tear smudged her cheek.

"Are you crying?" He fumbled for his bandana.

"I am not!" Amy went back at him defiantly. "You mind your own business!" A slight quiver crept into her voice.

"I didn't mean to be rough with you, but we don't need any more of that kind of nonsense if we're going to get through this alive."

The girl nodded, "I know," she said, suddenly surprisingly meek. "Look!"

Dan stared into the distance. A column of grayish-white smoke billowed upward against the blue sky. Swiftly he gathered the reins, and a few minutes later he was leading both animals to cover in a nearby woods. Amy, now pensive and contrite, followed at a distance. Once under cover, Dan was about to secure the animals when her horse became agitated. His first thoughts were of a possible rattler, but a look around revealed no such danger.

Cautiously, step-by-step, moving with extreme care and quiet, he left the girl to explore the undergrowth. Something was there, *that* he knew. He was too old a hand with horses to be mistaken...but what was it? Quickly his thoughts turned to

Amy, and he was about to retrace his steps when he suddenly froze.

During the next few minutes, Dan, spellbound and horror stricken, reeled under the lurid impact of a gruesome Apache assault.

He had met the courier, John Walkingstick. Standing there, frozen, he tried to control the convulsive retch in the pit of his stomach. The man was dead. Stripped naked, the body of the scout sagged to his knees, his braids covered in blood, an inert lump of tortured flesh. His left hand revealed two missing fingers. A heavy Mescalero war lance, stained blood-red was driven through his stomach pinning the corpse to a tree. A tomahawk, still embedded in the tree trunk, had split the man's face in two, crushing it like an eggshell. Arrows plunged deep into the man's chest wrote a finish to the bizarre game of Indian cruelty. The scene around him was havoc.

An army dispatch case, ripped apart, hanging from a limb, left no doubt as to the identity of the messenger.

A search of the paper litter strewn about failed to turn up anything of significance, and it only took a quick glance to know whatever documents it once held were gone. Someone had evidently informed on the courier, and his life had been forfeited to prevent the messages from getting through to their destination at army headquarters.

How long the dispatcher had been dead, Dan had no idea, but the freshly congealed blood warned him it had probably happened only a short time before. Dan knew he had to get Amy to safety as soon as possible.

Racing from the scene of carnage, it took him only a moment to reach the place where he left Amy and her horse. She was gone. Movement across the shallows on the far side of the river brought his attention into focus. Casting the mare loose and fumbling for the cinches, he rammed his knee into the black's midsection, knocking the air out of her to bring the saddle tight. The mare was already in motion when Dan hit the saddle on a dead run. Rampaging through the thicket, a cold dread clutched at his heart as he cleared the far end of the undergrowth. Hardly had he come astride when he realized neither Amy nor her horse were anywhere in sight. He thought she had gone up a large hill to the west of his location, but when he searched the area, there was no sign of her. She had disappeared in an instant. There was nothing he could do— except get out of sight. Dan struggled to keep his emotions in control. He kept telling himself that she was smart, and if someone had been pursuing her, she would have gotten away safely. The other alternative was too painful to imagine, especially after what he'd just witnessed.

Hours passed, followed by an eerie quiet. Sick at heart, Dan decided to make his break and ride out. Amy might just show up unexpectedly. Or maybe she had ridden on and picked up a wagon train or found a mission where she would be able to find safety.

This girl had been difficult, but this unexpected twist of fate had shaken him. He had no choice but to keep moving.

He needed to reconsider the task Major Sterling had given him, knowing as he did that there was no carrier. But for now, he knew he needed to settle down his frazzled nerves. What else was in store for Jace Randall? Only time would tell.

Chapter 9
Jeb Smith Takes a Hand

The clang of the breakfast gong awakened Clay Elkins with a start. Indulging in one of those long, satisfying stretches, he brushed the sweet-smelling hay from his clothing, pulled on his boots, and headed for the bunkhouse and the washstand just outside.

Suddenly, the reality of yesterday hit him, and he wondered how John Morgan had spent the night.

"Heard about Dan?" one of the ranch hands addressed him as he approached. "Understand Mr. Morgan's all broke up, and Miss Elizabeth pretty shaken, poor gal. Things jest won't be the same without that boy roun.'"

As Clay threw away a washbasin of sudsy water, he nodded. He gave no reply but made a mental note to see Elizabeth first chance he had to offer whatever support he could. Before long, he rode to the boarding house where the men were having breakfast on the patio. Clay bit his lip as he watched Elizabeth, following her movements, as she served breakfast to the workers sitting at the table. Only a slight redness around her eyes revealed any evidence of grief as she went about her usual chores. She had ignored her father's suggestion that she take some time off from her usual responsibilities.

Five years ago, when Clay had first signed on as a rider, Elizabeth had been twenty. He had been struck with her beautiful dark-brown eyes, soft-spoken voice, and alluring good looks. He soon found that her engaging personality made life much more pleasurable for all the Boxed M riders who lived, worked, and sweated—even died—on the open range.

Through the years that followed, he'd found himself falling in love with her in mute silence but, for reasons of his own, had never declared his feelings to her. As time passed, they'd established a close relationship that had grown out of mutual respect. They spent a lot of time together, taking long walks and engaging in deep conversations about their hopes for the future.

It took Clay some time to feel like he was even worthy of her love. What right had he—a total stranger—to think she would even consider him over any of the other suitors that had tried to claim her for their own over the years? Clay also knew the place she held in her father's heart and that she had been the only mother Dan had ever known across his growing years. But now that Dan was no longer around, he began to consider the joy he was missing by withholding his true feelings. This great tragedy had brought about a new certainty. Clay would gladly give his life rather than bring more grief and pain to the rancher or his daughter.

So, he was awkward and ill at ease when he presented himself at the ranch house kitchen following breakfast to see Elizabeth.

"Miss Beth," he addressed her as he had always called her, "I am sorry about what happened." He hesitatingly added, "If ther's anything I can do. . ." The words died on his lips as he looked on helplessly, unsure of how to assuage her grief.

"Oh, Clay." Her lips trembled as tears dimmed the loveliness of her eyes. She came closer to him. Shaken by her nearness and her distress, Clay tried to fight the urge to gather her into his arms to comfort her and soothe the pain in her heart. But when she put both her hands into his, he responded by reaching out and pulling her closely to him. Responding to his tenderness, she accepted his arms around her as she laid her head on his chest, finding comfort in his embrace. She then broke through the barrier of self-restraint, and as though her heart would break, she spent herself in a paroxysm of weeping.

Clay had never dared hope for this moment. The sweet scent of her hair and the very essence of her being swept through him. He wanted to find the right words to tell her of his love but was not sure this was the right moment. It seemed like a very long time that they stood in the kitchen holding on to one another. As Elizabeth raised her head to dry her eyes on the rim of her apron and gain a measure of self-control, Clay held her face ever so gently and put his lips on hers. Their kiss became sensual and longing. They held each other until Elizabeth broke away, a faint blush rising in her face. "Elizabeth, I..." he hedged, "you should try to get some rest." Clay turned to pick up his hat. "You and your father must be plum tuckered out." He walked toward the front door but then turned back, looked at her, and quietly stated, "I have loved you for a long time. I know this isn't a good time to tell you, but I wanted you to know that if there is anything—remember—anything you need, I will be close by."

"Thank you, Clay," she said, composure regained. "You will never know what that means to me. We can talk later. I don't want Father to see me like this." Clay turned to go. Neither of them had heard the inner door close. John Morgan, who had started for the kitchen a few minutes earlier, had stopped short in the doorway when he'd seen Clay and Elizabeth discreetly withdraw from one another.

Now the rancher knew what he had suspected all these years—that his daughter was in love with Clay Elkins. It came as no surprise, for he had watched his foreman's eyes follow her around whenever they met, and it had always seemed that Elizabeth was acutely aware of the strong, silent reserve in Clay.

"Things sure have a funny way of working themselves out," he spoke out loud to himself as he saddled his bronco, and swinging into the saddle, he rode out to join his men on the range.

All through the long weeks that followed, John Morgan threw himself into his work with furious energy, and the nights found him tired and spent. He just could not make sense of what had happened to his son. Every now and then, Elizabeth would find him standing by the old, battered desk, looking at the picture of her mother. More than once, when he'd been late for supper and she had gone to look for him, she'd found him up on the hill at her mother's grave, just standing there, hat in hand.

Elizabeth knew her father was a changed man. The ranch felt it, too, as John Morgan pushed himself to the limit of his endurance. It seemed that with every passing day, he became more withdrawn.

As the weeks dragged on, there was little opportunity for Elizabeth to talk to Clay about his declaration of love. She knew he was busy getting things ready for roundup. She was delighted when, one afternoon, Sarah Smith rode in for a visit and a message for Clay.

As Sarah entered the front door to the ranch she began speaking to Elizabeth. "Oh! Gramps wants Clay to ride over when he has the time. He says it's important that Clay get the message right away—you know Gramps; everything's important to him. I honestly didn't want to face coming over, knowing that Dan was no longer here, but I came because Gramps asked me to."

Sarah Smith and Elizabeth Morgan were good friends of long standing. Sarah, from the time she was a little girl, had grown up almost as a member of the Morgan household. Until about a year or so ago, she had been a steady fixture at the Morgan dinner table, especially during the long summer months. Elizabeth had always enjoyed her effervescent friend and the fact that she and her brother were beginning to become more than acquaintances.

Standing in the living room, Elizabeth gazed at Sarah. It was difficult not to notice how smartly she was dressed. She was of medium height, and a good-looking Sam Browne belt set off her trim figure. Her blonde hair was tied back with a blue ribbon that matched a pair of mischievous blue eyes. She had a slightly upturned nose that was disposed to wrinkle when she laughed and bright, white, even teeth that lent contrast to a dusky tan.

Just a few short years ago, it was not uncommon to see Sarah up on one of her grandfather's thoroughbreds, pigtails flying, racing Dan to see who was a "gimpy-legged slowpoke." It went without saying that Dan, a shy grin on his face, was the good-natured loser. Once, she had taunted Dan for losing the race, and he had picked her up and unceremoniously dumped her into the horse trough. Sarah had been thirteen then, but for whatever reason, the water treatment hadn't dampened her ardor for Dan.

One afternoon, when he was on his way to the Smith ranch by way of the south pasture, Dan happened to come upon Sarah swimming naked in a secluded area of her grandfather's lake. She'd known he'd been watching her from the concealment of the thicket. He'd been unable to tear his eyes away. . . and dared not move lest he be found out. After that Sarah enjoyed watching Dan blush guiltily every time they met. From then on, he had given her lots of attention. No longer the freckled-faced skinny kid he had played with as a boy, even with all the aggravation she'd caused him at times; they had remained best of friends. Each time she came home for the summer, she and Dan would spend lots of time riding the trails together.

The years had gone by, and now she was a young lady. It was only recently she had graduated and returned home from an eastern school; a place her grandfather had handpicked, as he would say, in the hope it would make a lady out of a tomboy, not to mention a bit of a rebel. She was eighteen and determined to live closer to Dan. Now that school was finished, she was hoping for a long-term relationship.

"Won't you sit down, Sarah, while I put on the kettle?" Elizabeth said to her.

Sarah dropped her riding gloves on the large polished oak table and walked to the small mirror over the fireplace mantle to primp, fixing an unruly wisp of well-styled hair that made her no less attractive. "How are you getting along, Elizabeth?

I keep thinking about the day Dan galloped by me in town. He didn't even stop to talk. I mean, you know about the fight that led to his running away?" Elizabeth was about to respond when she saw Clay approach.

"You called, Miss Beth?" he asked, pulling up his horse. "What can I do for you?"

Sarah Smith, coming up behind Elizabeth, called out to him over her shoulder.

"My grandfather wants to see you...when you have time." Seeing the puzzled expression on Clay's face, she added, "He didn't say what it was about, though. Seems he is being very secretive."

Clay nodded. "Thanks! I'll try to make it sometime to-night," he answered, coaxing his pony into a walk.

"Clay!" called Elizabeth.

He pulled up the mare and half turned in the saddle.

"Dad's all right out there, isn't he? Look after him, won't you?" Elizabeth blushed slightly, as though she had planned to say something else.

"Sure will," was the response. The mare moved out as Clay, feeling somewhat cheated, returned to his chores.

"Let's go into the parlor, Sarah," said Elizabeth, turning. "Tea will be ready soon."

Both girls went into the big living room. The afternoon was full of sad conversation about Dan and the loss that they were both feeling. Elizabeth understood that Sarah was heartbroken that Dan would no longer be part of her life.

It was soon after the incident that Sarah had got news from John Morgan that he and Clay had gone looking for Dan, but sadly, they'd found his grave instead. She'd been overwhelmed with grief. She'd cried every night until her grandfather had suggested she apply for a teaching position away from their ranch so that she might gain a new purpose other than becoming Dan's wife. But Sarah was not ready to let go of the past. She needed time to adjust to losing Dan.

That evening, after supper, Clay cut across the southern section of the Boxed M to see his friend Jeb Smith. It had been a long ride to the Smith ranch, and dusk had spread its deepening mantle of gray by the time Clay rode up to the adobe hacienda.

The Circle S lay about ten miles southeast of the Boxed M and was the only ranch for miles around devoted solely to raising and training horses. Just west of Buffalo Gap, the stage road from Abilene to San Angelo ran across Jeb Smith's property. Sprawling across miles of good grazing land, the ranch bordered a small lake that provided water in plentiful supply, which Jeb Smith shared with his neighbors. It was a choice jewel among the larger ranches in the county.

Clay Elkins had ridden the distance to the Circle S in deep thought. He wondered what Jeb Smith had in mind. It had been every bit of six months since Clay had bought his mare from Jeb. He had not had a conversation with the rancher since then.

Clay had known and enjoyed Jeb Smith's company ever since their first meeting. The horse trader's friendliness and wit—not to mention his irrepressible energy—never failed to bring a warm feeling of welcome to Clay's heart whenever the two men met.

Jeb was known for his square dealing as a horse trader. It was pretty much public opinion that Jeb Smith could train a horse better than any man alive—and the Smith spread had become a favorite gathering point for horsemen far and near. Clay instinctively liked the man and trusted him.

As for Jeb, the welcome mat was always out for his stalwart buddies from the Morgan spread.

Clay knew that Jeb, as an ex-ranger, was very well informed—receiving copies of all notices and "Wanted" posters from Ranger Headquarters. More than one outlaw had been snared on account of some anonymous ex-ranger's vigilance.

Jeb Smith, an old timer in every sense of the word, was of medium height and build. He was slightly bald, with a fringe of greyish-white hair at the sides and an oversized handlebar mustache that drooped down at both ends. Somewhat bandy-legged from years in the saddle, he walked with a slight limp as though he was always in pain.

Clay understood Jeb to be one of the few ex-rangers who'd made good as a rancher after suffering an injury on the job. While Jeb never mentioned the cause of his affliction, Sarah made no secret of it. She seemed quite proud, in fact, of the bullet he still carried somewhere in his hip. Her story of it, however, varied considerably from time to time, and her eyes would twinkle in mischief when she would embarrass her grandfather by the telling of it to anyone who would listen.

Jeb Smith came out to greet Clay as he rode up and stepped down from the saddle.

"Howdy, Clay! Glad to see you."

Clay responded, "Sarah said to tell you that she is staying

overnight with Miss Beth and will ride in tomorrow sometime." Jeb nodded in agreement.

"Thought that's what she'd do. Well! Come inside, Clay. Just having supper. Will you join me?"

"Ate before I left—but coffee shore smells good." An hour later, Jeb passed the cigars to Clay and helping himself to one, bit off the tip and lit the end, preferring to provide a light to his guest. No words were spoken as both men drew deeply with satisfaction.

Clay rose from the dinner table to lean against the big hickory mantle as he found delight in the excellent Havana. He watched the bluish-gray smoke spiral slowly upward, dissolving in a myriad of shapeless impressions. The delicate fragrance of fine tobacco permeated the room.

The silence held. Clay knew Jeb would tell him what was on his mind when he was ready. He was content to wait.

Finally, Jeb spoke, comfortably ensconced in his big easy chair, both feet propped atop a worn hassock.

"Clay, I guess you're wondering why I asked you to come see me."

Clay nodded.

"Well, I ran across something last week that made me mighty curious, and I've been thinking about it ever since. I asked you to come over because you're John Morgan's best friend. I've just got a hunch. It's about Dan Morgan."

Clay felt a tremor run through him, but he gave no sign as he studied Jeb's face. Jeb continued, "Last week I took in a rider from out Lamesa way. And, as I was writing a bill and going through a pile of posters that routinely come across my desk from rangers throughout the Southwest, this rider—Will Brown—happened to see the one about Jace Randall, the outlaw. Well! This fellow leaned over to take a long look and said, 'Boss, that sure ain't the Jace Randall I seed gun a man down in Lamesa last month. It says here that Randall was in his thirties with blue eyes an' black hair. And the Jace Randall I seed had brown eyes an' black hair an' was aboot twenty or so. Them fellers shore do mess up a poster, don't they?'"

Jeb paused. He held a match to his half dead cigar.

Clay waited.

Jeb resumed, "The more I thought of what that rider said, the stronger my hunch got."

"What hunch?" Clay spoke for the first time.

"Let me finish," gestured Jeb, holding up his hand to defer the answer to Clay's question.

"I checked with headquarters, and they told me there was no mistake. In fact, they said that they are always careful to see that all the information on the posters is correct because it could get the wrong man killed if it is incorrect." Jeb shifted slightly. "Clay, I must ask you a very important question. Did you and John actually see Dan Morgan in that grave?"

Clay stared at Jeb. What was the man getting at? Did he think... No! It was impossible—hadn't they found Dan's horse, his saddle, and even his boots buried with him? Clay's thoughts whirled as he stood silently, at a loss for words.

Again, Jeb pressed the question.

"Think! Clay, did you in fact identify the body of Dan in that grave?"

Clay slowly shook his head.

"John was too broken up," Clay spoke for the second time. "We only went down till we found his boots...and didn't have the stomach for it...just filled in the grave and let it be."

"Then I could be right!" interrupted Jeb.

Clay was dumbfounded. His own cigar had gone out, and he tossed the dead butt into the fireplace as he spoke. "You think that was Dan in Lamesa?" Jeb nodded vigorously.

"I do—don't ask me how or why, but I do." Then he quickly reiterated, "You admit you didn't make certain at the grave it was Dan, and you and John could have made the wrong assumption?"

A weariness stole through Clay's body. "If Dan's not in that grave," he wondered aloud, "who is?" Jeb looked at his guest and exclaimed, "That settles it!"

Clay suddenly felt angry with himself that he had not been more inquisitive when he had first discovered the grave. "You propose we take another look at that grave?" he questioned.

"Absolutely! I sure do," answered Jeb. "I think it's worth a gamble...and if we're wrong, nobody need know anything about it. If we're right..." His words hung in the air.

Jeb lit a fresh cigar and sat watching Clay pace slowly up and down in front of the hearth. Clay looked at Jeb. "I need to make this right. When can we leave?"

"Come morning," answered Jeb, rising from his chair to discard his second cigar. "You'll stay tonight?"

Clay nodded and sat down heavily on the settee. He helped himself to a new cigar as Jeb joined him on the sofa.

Before the men retired for the night, it was agreed that not a word would be said to John Morgan unless they had definite proof that there was some new evidence about Dan's whereabouts.

That night Clay slept fitfully. He imagined he heard Jeb Smith in the next room also tossing and turning in his bed.

Both men were up at the crack of dawn and soon on their way. The ranch was just beginning to stir when they were about to cut across the open range. They decided to swing south of the Boxed M to avoid any early riders, turning westerly to take an oblique course to make better time. They traveled briskly, passing the Sweetwater turn-off. Before long they rode into the canyon, with Clay riding ahead of Jeb, who trailed behind.

Early evening found them entering the narrows, and some twenty minutes later, they swept into the glade.

Clay led the way in, and once across the greensward, he pulled up at the black remains of the campfire. Time and the elements had almost erased its evidence.

Clay dismounted first and immediately untied the short-handled spade from his pack. Jeb's saddle creaked as he followed suit.

"It's a beautiful spot." Jeb surveyed the scenery as he spoke.

He turned to Clay as though to continue, but Clay was already on his way up the north slope, his long legs making great strides as he covered ground rapidly. Jeb hurried to catch up with him but fell behind, puffing from the exertion.

Clay led him directly to the three graves. He couldn't have missed the three saddles serving as grave markers, a little worse for the slight rain that had fallen since that fateful day.

"Which one?" Jeb struggled to get his breath. Clay pointed with his boot.

"Let me have that shovel," Jeb reached across the grave as Clay reluctantly, although without protest, surrendered it. He stood aside, ill at ease as Jeb started to dig. They took turns digging until Jeb realized he was feeling his age and handed the shovel back over to Clay. Once the work was well underway, Jeb went down to look around the stream.

He studied the earth for signs of the horses that Clay and John Morgan had described on their recent visit. He was about to give up the search when suddenly a horse nickered, and a moment later, Dan Morgan's sorrel came splashing across the water. She came up short—inquiringly—within hailing distance. Jeb cupped his hands to call to her when he heard his name shouted from above, and he turned to see Clay gesticulating frantically for Jeb to join him.

Jeb ran toward Clay as fast as his heeled boots would permit. His heart was pounding like a drip hammer by the time he reached the slope and Clay's side. The old ranger saw that most of the dirt and gravel had been scooped out of the grave to expose the figure of a man wrapped in a gray blanket. A pair of old musty boots lay to one side. Clay again recognized Dan's boots.

How familiar, thought Clay, dropping to his knees to peer at the shrouded figure.

"Go ahead, take a look." Jeb leaned over and turned back the edge of the blanket to expose the face of the corpse.

Clay stared in surprise. The face of the dead man was not that of Dan Morgan. Who he was, Clay did not know. The only thing he cared about was that this was not Dan.

His spirits soared.

Instinctively the words fell from his lips. "Thank God," he said, as he looked at Jeb.

Jeb, by far the calmer of the two and looking as though he had known it all along, replaced the blanket over the man's face and straightened up. "That sure looks like the man in the poster to me, Jace Randall," he stated matter-of-factly, answering the question forming on Clay's lips. "Certain sure," he added with such emphasis that it left no doubt in Clay's mind. "Just like the poster says," Jeb restated, as Clay picked up the shovel and started refilling the grave.

After Clay picked up Dan's boots, he made his way slowly down the slope to pick up their horses, now grazing side by side. Gradually his mind began to take in the magnitude of their discovery, and he had an overwhelming urge to run to tell John and Elizabeth the wonderful news.

He felt like a man who had been rescued from some horrible bad dream, yet still unable to shake the fantastical feel of the moment. The reality felt too unreal.

Jeb Smith's coming down the slope snapped him back to the business at hand.

"Jeb," Clay addressed the rancher when Jeb had joined him. "I don't know what to say. How can I thank you? John is going to be so happy to hear that his son is alive!"

Jeb put his arm across the big shoulders of this fine, simple, honest person and grinned a happy smile.

"Let's go and tell him," he said.

"I'm taking Dan's horse along," said Clay, dropping his rope over the sorrel, which stood quietly nearby.

"The boots, too," offered Jeb, swinging up. "Might's well

bring the boy's saddle along. He might need it sometime."

The day was well along when the two men rode out of the glade, one leading a sorrel with a pair of dirty boots bouncing across the saddle.

"Looks like rain," commented Jeb as the horses bunched, turning into the trail. "Maybe we'd better make camp here for the night." "I'd rather ride on through," answered Clay. "If it's all right with you."

Jeb nodded his head. He understood Clay's urgency to hurry and tell John Morgan—and Beth and Sarah—as soon as possible.

"Right," he said, his face impassive as he settled down to ride.

The two men rode throughout the night, the horses picking their way safely through the canyon depths and narrows with consummate skill. The gray dawn found them emerging into the broad, familiar Sweetwater Valley road home. They were exhausted, but a sense of urgency kept them moving along. Neither man had eaten since the previous day, but neither of them felt the need for food.

Sometime later, they turned into the Boxed M, tired but happy.

Elizabeth was the first to spot them from the parlor window, and she literally flew across the porch when she saw Dan's sorrel. Close on her heels came Sarah, as she saw her grandfather dismount.

Clay slipped off his horse as Elizabeth ran straight into his arms.

"Clay!" Elizabeth's voice broke as she recognized the

dirt-stained boots hanging from Dan's saddle. "Where?! Oh, where..."

Clay's arms went around her holding her closely.

"Dan's not here, Beth," he said, his voice choked with tenderness. "But hopefully he's alive...somewhere."

Clay Elkins, standing there with Elizabeth in his arms, was no longer tired. He felt as though fatigue had dropped from him, magically, and that he could move mountains. It was unbelievable, but it had happened. Elizabeth, the golden girl of his dreams, had come flying out of the house and had flung herself into the shelter of his strong arms—as though it had always been this way. He closed his eyes, oblivious to those around him, and hoped this was not part of a dream. If it was, he hoped it would never end.

Jeb was speaking.

"Well! When you gals feel like asking a couple of hungry gents to breakfast, we'll sure oblige."

"Oh, forgive me. Come in, please!" said Elizabeth, blushing as she hurriedly withdrew from Clay's embrace. Sarah, with tears in her eyes, took over the chore of cooking breakfast while Elizabeth went to find her father.

"Come, Clay," she said. His name had never sounded so good. She grabbed his hand and literally pulled him along as fast as she could go. He found himself grinning from ear to ear like a foolish schoolboy. He tried to suppress his emotions, but it was impossible.

They found John Morgan mending the corral gate. In response to his daughter's hail and the sight of her pulling his foreman—whose grin belied his usual reserve and solemn mien—he broke into a run to meet them, wondering what was going on.

"Dan's alive! Dad!" shouted Elizabeth before Clay had a chance to speak.

Clay nodded, his reserve reasserting itself.

"Is it true?" stammered John.

"It shore is, John. I don't know where, but..."

The rancher's face went blank at the incredulous news. Visibly shaken, he stammered, "How? Where?"

"Jeb Smith's inside having breakfast, so why don't we go in and hear the whole story?" stated Clay. "Jeb can tell yu better'n me."

Puzzlement showed in John Morgan's face as he struggled to grasp the impact of Clay's words. Once he heard the story in completion, his outlook suddenly began to improve. Within a short time, the news that Dan was possibly alive spread quickly among the ranch hands, and the ensuing burst of light-hearted bunkhouse chatter chased the gloom that had hung over the ranch like a dark cloud.

Breakfast lasted a long time as the two men answered many questions. The story lost nothing in the retelling.

"You'll be my guest and stay over," invited the rancher, looking from Jeb to his granddaughter.

"Thanks, John, but I'm wide awake now after that coffee. Anyhow, we'd better be getting along. Clay can tell you anything more you want to know."

They rose from the table, and the cattleman said goodbye to Jeb while Sarah got her things together for the ride home with her grandfather.

Jeb Smith stepped into the saddle with ease as he pulled his mare around, waiting for Sarah to mount her pony.

John Morgan held out his hand, and the two men met in a strong handclasp of camaraderie and affection.

Sarah waved as she followed her grandfather, cutting across the south pasture toward the Circle S Ranch. Clay and Elizabeth watched them go, waving them out of sight.

"I'll take Dan's horse to the corral, John," said Clay, stepping down from the porch.

"No!" answered the rancher, an excitement in his voice that Clay hadn't heard for a long time. "I'll take care of her myself."

Chapter 10
Clay Rides Out

Life at the Boxed M ranch crawled on as summer sped by and the days shortened. Almost imperceptibly, the hot dry day took on an accent of coolness in the early evening. With the arrival of the changing season, the foliage began its slow transition from lush greenness to autumn's brown and gold.

The mood around the homestead began to change. A restlessness had infiltrated the entire ranch family since Dan had not come home. The horseplay that made the ranch a happy place had diminished. Men moved woodenly through their chores. Several hands quit, and even Cookie the chef's infectious good spirits, which had always lit up the place, seemed to disappear. Everyone seemed to be missing Dan and John Morgan's sullen mood only served to bring down everyone's spirits even more.

Clay made several half-hearted attempts to snap the ranchers out of the doldrums but without success. He was acutely aware of the effect all this was having on Elizabeth and conscious of its implications on the ranch's future. He found himself standing by helplessly. Of course, he could not blame either Elizabeth or John for lamenting over Dan's absence, but he was convinced that unless something changed, the apathy now characteristic of the Boxed M would continue to spread like a disease.

It was one evening, after roundup was over, when Clay went into the bunkhouse to search for a new bridle strap. Supper was over, and a hot game of blackjack was in progress. Several men lounged around, talking and smoking as they performed the minor repairs necessary to keep their gear in good shape. The conversation crept around to the subject of Dan Morgan.

"Wouldn't be su'prised," said one hand, "if he headed west. Sure hope he stays two jumps ahead o' that sheriff. I heard he sure looked awful mean when he got back to town without Dan, after losin' two deputies. Someone said they was both shot in the back by Morgan. Hear he turned in his badge and left. Said he was gonna find Dan no matter what an' kill him. Clem, the barkeeper, tole me that Crawley still blames Dan fer his brother's death. Yu think tha't whut's worrying the ole man?" He laid aside the lariat he was braiding and reached for the tobacco pouch string dangling from his shirt pocket.

"Hard tu tell, an' he don't say much," replied the first cowboy. Nobody spoke as the first man rolled his smoke and a match rasped into a flame.

Clay listened as the conversation resumed. It was no news to him that Jud Crawley had quit his job, and he was going after Dan as a personal vendetta.

The game broke up shortly as the men, tired from the rigors of the day, withdrew one by one to their bunks, leaving the table to a young cowboy with a yen for solitaire.

That night, Clay Elkins lay in his bed staring at the darkness that was punctuated only by the glow of his cigarette. From afar he had watched the transformation of two people he loved. John Morgan was growing apart from the men and seemed to have crawled into a shell of depression. Elizabeth was finding it difficult to have a meaningful conversation with her father. His mien had become one of somber long silences and deep recollection. Clay twisted and turned in bed as he developed a plan. His decision was final. Extinguishing his cigarette, he fell asleep.

The night passed quickly, and Clay arose at dawn, had breakfast alone, and headed for the corral. A short time later, his horse saddled and ready to ride, he went to the bunkhouse to start packing his personal gear. Carefully, he weighed and evaluated the choice of every item, and after a last-minute survey, he picked up his thirty-thirty, shouldered his saddlebags, and headed for the door. With his gear in place, his forty-five Colt tucked in his holster and the rifle in his boot, Clay led the bay across the yard to the ranch house. Leaving the animal ground-line hitched, he stopped on the porch to take one final look around. Cookie, wiping his hands on his greasy white apron, was watching him from the kitchen door, not letting any move go unnoticed.

Dismissing Cookie's close attention to his actions, Clay entered the house and passed through the deserted dining room to the kitchen, where Elizabeth was having her morning coffee. Dressed in a becoming blue gingham dress, she looked up in surprise as Clay's big frame filled the doorway. A pleased expression lit up her face, but her smile quickly faded as she saw his grim look. Her gaze traveled apprehensively down the length of his tall figure, noting the heavy brass-studded cartridge belt and tied-down holster. A shiver went through her as she sensed something was different about him this morning.

"What's going on, Clay?" She brushed back a stray strand of hair. "What's with the serious look?"

Just then John Morgan came through the back door of the

kitchen, slamming it behind him. "Morning, Clay," he said as he rummaged through a kitchen drawer. "Elizabeth," he continued, intent on his search, "where is that wire cutter you borrowed last week?" He looked up and saw Clay standing alongside Elizabeth and sensed the tension that seemed to permeate the air.

"Anything wrong?" he asked, closing the drawer. "You both look like you've seen a ghost."

Elizabeth started to say something, but Clay held up his hand.

"John," he said, "I am ridin' out this morning' an' was jest about to tell Miss Beth here when you came in—now I might's well tell you both at the same time."

The rancher, taken up short, stared at him with a look of disbelief.

"Why, Clay? This is your home as much as it is mine. At least I've always considered it so. If it's money or anything you need, say so, man, and it's yours for the asking. That goes for just about everything I've got."

Clay's focus was on Elizabeth's expression. She had turned pale, and her smile was gone as she silently faced him. He had not anticipated her strong response. More than anything in the world he had wanted to spare her any unhappiness. It had seemed such a simple idea to search for Dan when he had first thought of it. Now, suddenly, he wasn't so sure.

The rancher glanced at his daughter.

"I was kinda hoping...," he stopped in the middle of the sentence. "Won't you reconsider, Clay? You are more like a son to me than a foreman. I'd do anything to get you to stay," he stopped for a moment. "But if your mind is made up, then I suppose you must go. Whatever happens, Clay, you know you are always welcome here with us, don't you?"

Clay stood without answering, his eyes fixed on Elizabeth. Awkwardly but gently, he put his arms around her and drew her to him. He sensed her emotional struggle as tears welled up in her eyes.

"Beth, if I could only spare—" His arms dropped to his sides when he felt her stiffen as she seemed to regain a measure of self-control.

John Morgan stole away unnoticed from the kitchen. Disturbed and visibly shaken by the sudden news of Clay's departure, he was at a loss to say or do anything that would change the situation. Ever since that joyful day in June when Clay and Jeb had returned with the news that Dan was possibly alive, he had increasingly depended on Clay and his expert judgment in ranch matters. He knew Elizabeth would be heartbroken.

John Morgan went straight to his moneybox. He counted out Clay's wages for the month. Then adding an additional several hundred dollars, he slipped the money into an envelope, sealed it, and in a bold hand wrote Clay's name on it. This was a hard thing for John Morgan to do as it was the end of a dream. Envelope in hand, he leaned back in his favorite rocking chair, waiting patiently for Clay to come from the kitchen. He tried not to listen to their conversation, although the muffled sound of their voices carried over and fortunately, he was able to hear the entire conversation. He now had a better understanding Clay's reason for leaving.

"Must you go, Clay?" asked Elizabeth as the first shock of

Clay's leaving passed. "I don't understand...I must admit, I am very surprised. Is there some reason you have suddenly decided to leave, or have I misunderstood your intentions toward me?"

"There is something I must do that will be important to you and your father—I think you know that this ranch hasn't been the same since Dan's departure. I need to find him. God willing, Beth—I will come back." Clay's voice was saddled with emotion as though the effort to speak was draining. "You have not misunderstood my feelings toward you. Beth, I fell in love with you the first moment I saw you. That has not changed." He pleaded with her, "Trust me—please—I need to do this."

"Then you will come back?" Elizabeth whispered, the words gathering strength from an inner source. She put her hands on Clay's shoulders, her eyes probing his for signs of assurance.

"Thet I will, an' when I do, I will be able to settle down permanently."

Elizabeth dropped her arms, and Clay turned to leave. She felt like a person in a bad dream. First, there was the loss of Dan, and now—Clay. She walked a trifle unsteadily to the window and looked out over the beautiful pasturelands that were bathed in the shining rays of an early morning sun. She fought for composure. For a moment, she stood looking into space, seeing nothing, and feeling her heart break. Then, with a tremendous sigh, she followed Clay into the sitting room to join her father.

Clay was folding the envelope the rancher had handed him and was placing it inside his shirt pocket when Elizabeth entered the room. Knowing John Morgan, Clay knew it was all there to the last cent.

John's voice shook a little as he clasped Clay's hand.

"Come back to us, boy, come back to us when you can... and if you ever need help, let me know." Clay nodded. His misery was complete.

"Thank you, John, for all you have done. I won't forget it. We will see each other again." Both men walked to where Clay's horse stood. There seemed to be an unspoken understanding between the two men as they shook hands for the last time. The saddle creaked as Clay swung up.

"Take good care o' Beth for me, John," he said in a low voice. "I love her."

"Hasta luego!" he added, touching his hat in farewell. He nodded to Elizabeth as she stood in the doorway watching his every move.

She waved to him, unashamed of the tears that fell.

"Goodbye, dearest Clay," she whispered. "Come back to me. Dear God, let him come back to me."

Then, in a whirl of dust, Clay Elkins pulled his bay around, and with a touch of his spurs, the animal sprinted toward the open range. A deep weariness worked through him. He had turned his back on five of the happiest years of his life and even more so on the one person who was the epitome of all his hopes and dreams—Beth Morgan. When he had made his decision to leave, he hadn't expected to feel so shattered.

Perhaps there was another purpose to his venturing away from the ranch, he thought. He would be able to experience the call of the wild and the thrill of living on the trail one more time, something that had mesmerized him in his earlier years. He loved Beth Morgan. Of this, he had no doubt. He had only to close his eyes to see her standing in the doorway, waving farewell, tears in her eyes.

And there was the inescapable fact that there would be no contentment at the Boxed M for anyone until Dan Morgan was back where he belonged.

As he rode away, he decided it would be best to shake the guilt from his mind and proceed to his task.

Clay snapped himself out of his self-reproach, kicked up his horse, and decided a course of action. First, he would ride over to Abilene and if the ex-sheriff was still there, set him straight on the death of his brother Ed. If he failed at this, there remained only one other thing to do. He would goad him into a fight and kill him. The second step in his plan was to visit the Texas Rangers, where he would look for any official information regarding Dan's whereabouts.

Clay rode rapidly, joining the valley road and turning over the mountain trail into town. He rode up the main street and dismounted in front of a weather-beaten shack, its dirty, broken window crossed with iron bars. An almost illegible sign hanging askew to the right of the door read "Sheriff's Office." The door, sagging from a broken hinge, was slightly ajar. Clay hitched his gun forward and stepped inside. The jail was empty except for a drunk who was snoring loudly in one of the open cells, his open-mouthed burps adding to the foul smell. There was disorder everywhere. The floor was littered with old newspapers and filthy coffee cups. Several official-looking envelopes lay on the desk, unopened and gathering dust. Clay picked up the overturned old swivel chair before leaving. It was apparent that the office had not been swept or cleaned for weeks. The door remained stuck as Clay went outside and pulled it shut. His next stop was the Silver Dollar Saloon, where he hoped someone—possibly Clem the barkeeper—could give him information on the whereabouts of Jud Crawley. It took Clay no more than five minutes to get the real story from two men who had nothing better to do than to sit idly and play two-handed stud. It seemed that Sheriff Jud Crawley, or rather the *Ex-Sheriff* Jud Crawley, had had a falling out with the town fathers after losing two of his deputies. This time he'd lacked the ability to convince them of his capabilities as sheriff and had quit—or was fired; the men did not know. He had packed up and cleared out, openly swearing he was going to get Dan Morgan, whom he blamed for all his recent misfortunes.

The card players also told Clay the real facts about the killing of the sheriff's brother Ed. The truth about his death had come to light after Jud had left town. He had pulled out quietly one night a couple of weeks ago and had taken some of the town's reward money with him—no one knew how much.

Clay questioned them about the absence of the barkeeper, Clem, and they said he was across the street getting a haircut and shave. Yep! He was still the barkeeper.

Clay thanked the men and made his way back to his horse. Leaving town, he rode west, taking the old stage road. It was his intention, having completed his business in Abilene, to bypass some of the local ranches. From there he could travel southwest as the crow flies toward Big Spring and eventually north to Lamesa. During his first stop, he could check out the authority's information about the gunfight that Jeb Smith had described to him and John months ago. This might give him more insight into Dan's trail.

The hour was late, and the sun began to turn crimson on the western hills. Off to his right, a stand of timber along the sluggish waters of a shallow creek reminded him of his need to rest. Sparse vegetation afforded some screening shelter as Clay rode up creek. He stopped, dismounted, and within minutes had a pot of coffee going over a brisk fire that kept him warm in the chilly air.

Good ole Cookie, thought Clay when he found some food in his pack. He remembered the cook watching him getting ready to leave and surmised Cookie must have slipped in extra food while he was inside the ranch house saying his goodbyes.

Eating sparingly, he made himself comfortable, rolling a smoke with his back to a dead cottonwood. He inhaled the sun-ripened tobacco deeply as he watched his horse roll around in the cool grass edging the stream. Gradually he felt the tensions of the day fall away. He was reaching for his Bull Durham to roll his second smoke when the action of the bay caught his attention. She stood motionless, her head poised, testing the breeze with quivering nostrils. Her ears flickered forward.

Clay froze into immobility, not moving a muscle as he watched the mare resume feeding. Almost immediately, she raised her head again, her ears cocked forward.

A sixth sense snapped Clay into a tenseness he hadn't felt in a long time.

Rolling over on his side, he lay with his ear to the ground.

"Hosses," he muttered, springing to his feet. Quickly, he stepped to his saddle and drew his rifle from its sheath. Levering a shell into the chamber, he stood well back from the light of the fire and waited. He checked his gun to make sure it was fully loaded.

A moment or two later, four riders turned off the road and pounded up. The group pulled their mounts to a halt a safe distance from the fire.

"Howdy," came the greeting. Clay stepped into the circle of light. He nodded as he replied, "Howdy."

"Seen any riders cross the creek while you been here?" asked one of the men.

"Nope," answered Clay, standing tense and vigilant, aware of every detail of the four men. He guessed they had been traveling and seen his fire, but it wasn't likely they were just curious. All four men bore the look of nightriders. If so, they spelled trouble. The fact that they were interested in someone crossing the creek appeared to him to be pure fabrication, since it seemed unlikely that they would be trailing someone at night. He made no comment.

The spokesman, a stout man with coarse, pockmarked features, swung down from his saddle and was about to approach the fire when Clay's voice stopped him in his tracks.

"Nobody invited you to stay!" snapped Clay.

The man halted almost in mid step.

Instantly, the other three men dismounted to move up behind their leader.

"Thet's far enough," came Clay's quiet drawl.

Trouble was shaping up fast, and Clay knew it. Four to one,

but there it was. Nothing he could do now except play out his hand.

Years on the trail had taught Clay Elkins one thing—never bluff; it could cost you your life. He'd also learned that few men are big enough to swallow their pride and back down—even with death as a paymaster. It was not apparent to Clay at this point what their next move would be, except that he had a hunch these men were the type of border ruffians who preyed on lone travelers and defenseless people. If he'd read them right, they were like most cowards, who found safety in numbers.

"Now, don't git riled," answered the leader, shifting his chew from one side of his mouth to the other. "Yu can't buck all four o' us, yu know—so why don't yu let us have a look at yer saddlebags there. Yu won't git hurt if yu don't do nuthin' foolish."

"I said that's far enough." Now the words were ominous and edged. Clay shifted his weight as he spoke, legs spread out, his hand close to the ivory butt of his forty-five.

"Now, yu ain't aimin' tu take us all air yu?" grinned the round one.

"You first," snapped Clay. "An if that iron's not an ornament, maybe yu'd like tu try your luck."

Now that the play had been called, silence held as the four waited for the challenge. Each knew the test had come. Usually, it never came to this. They got what they wanted without a fight. This was different. Something of the steadfast inflexibility of the stranger gave them a feeling of uncertainty. Four to one—and he had called their bluff. The spokesman, the heavy-set man, ran his tongue over his lips, perhaps to size up his adversary, unsure of his next move.

"Wal, Rolfe! What're yu waitin' for?" spoke the dark, thin-faced man standing to the right and slightly to the rear of the leader. "Your always tellin' us what a big man ya air. He's called yer bluff, air yu gonna use that hogleg an blast'im? Yu ain't afeered o' him, air you?"

Clay sensed the animosity between the two and waited. The slim, dark man continued to entice the leader.

All eyes were centered on Rolfe. They waited.

Clay watched the ringleader carefully. If a fight developed, he decided his best bet would be to get the man he felt was the more dangerous of the two. The remaining two men some distance behind, did not constitute an immediate threat.

"Now! No offense, stranger," said Rolfe, pushing his sombrero back on his head. He rubbed a hand over the stubble on his face. "We don't mean no harm, now do we?" The silence continued with no one answering.

Clay studied the smaller, more dangerous-looking man. He seemed to have an axe to grind with his leader, Rolfe. Clay decided both would bear the closest surveillance.

"Any coffee left?" asked Rolfe, shifting his eyes to the coffee pot.

"Nope," Clay's answer was succinctly abrupt as he took a backward step to offer less of a target in the firelight.

"He ain't very perlite, now is he, boys?" The ringleader stepped back as he spoke.

Clay watched him, always keeping the thin-faced man in the threshold of his sight, but Rolfe made no move. Though his hand was opening and closing near his gun, he seemed unable to force his muscles to do his will. Desperate and now seeming thoroughly frightened, he laid himself open to a renewed assault by his right-hand man.

"I knowed it," his words flayed Rolfe mercilessly. "I allus knowed it. Yore a yellow son-of-a-bitch! The first time yu come face tu face with a real man, yu lose yore nerve. This man had the guts to call yu, an' yore scared. Now you make yore play, or I'll bury you in hell myself."

"C'mon, Pope," spoke up one of the men, a Mexican in the rear. "He ain't got nuthin' we want anyway."

"We're staying right heah," snarled Pope, "until I see the color o' our leader's backbone." He caught Rolfe by the arm and spun him half around. "Air yu gonna make yore play or not? I'm countin' tu three, and if yu ain't drawed, I'll cut you down like a dog."

Clay watched with uneasiness as he began to surmise that this was a long time coming between the two men, and there was going to be a showdown. Pope had thrown caution to the wind. His words tore into Rolfe, cruel and vicious.

Rolfe, now a sweating hunk of flesh, appeared broken in spirit. The firelight revealed him to be a haggard, beaten man.

Rolfe turned to Clay. His voice trembled with emotion.

"I pass," he mumbled and stepped out of the circle of light.

"Yu coward! Yu stinking coward!" Pope spit the epithets at his chief and, completely ignoring Clay, turned his back on him to confront Rolfe.

"Now, Pope," Rolfe held up his hand in a gesture of supplication. "Don't git all riled up."

"One...two..." Pope started the chant, his hand hovering over his Colt. He was totally ignoring Clay's presence. "Three..." Rolfe, realizing for the first time that he was going to be gunned down in cold blood, reached for his Colt, but he was far too slow. His six-gun had barely cleared the holster when Pope's bullet caught him dead center. He staggered, stiltedly erect, only to pitch face forward, now a corpse at his executioner's feet.

From across the fire, Clay witnessed the gunplay remaining poised and ready should Pope turn his gun on him. The small man holstered his Colt and without a downward glance at his fallen chief, stepped over his body and faced Clay.

"Wal, stranger, I'm standin' pat, and I'm callin' yu."

Clay caught the tremendous intensity in Pope's voice. He had gotten himself to a point where he had to kill—or be killed. He was no coward.

"Call it when yore ready," he said, as he dropped into that familiar crouch that Clay had come to know so well.

"I'm waitin'," answered Clay, his hand steady, his fingers claw-like over his gun butt.

For the space of a second, the two men stood frozen. Then it happened. Like a striking rattler, Pope's hand darted downward and all motion blended into one as his gun came out of leather. But fast as he was, Clay Elkins was faster. Over the crashing report of his six-gun, he saw Pope shudder as the forty-five tore into his body. Pope's shot screamed off into the night as Clay's second slug hammered him backward. Severely wounded, Pope desperately tried to get off a second shot. He struggled for control but collapsed over the body of the man he had just defiled.

Clay, his gun covering the remaining two men, watched him die.

"Anybody want tu back his hand?" asked Clay, holstering his gun.

"Not me," said one of the riders.

"Then get them out of here!" ordered Clay, nodding toward the dead men. He watched the men heave the two carcasses across their saddles and ride off in the direction of the road the bodies flopping grotesquely.

Chapter 11
An Unexpected Twist

The mare broke into a sweeping stride across the natural roll of the prairie as the miles fell away. Distance soon swallowed Dan up, and it was somewhat of an awakening to see swirls of smoke in the sky ahead. He stopped to get his canteen and look at his map when suddenly, he heard a someone holler "Help!"

Sweeping back the rim of his black sombrero, he quickly turned around to see a young Indian woman peering out from behind a pile of rocks. She was wearing a cotton calico dress and knee-high boot moccasins. Her hair was long and braided, decorated with bright strips of cloth and shells. Dan was captivated by her beauty.

With a command of authority, he responded. "Come out from behind that rock and tell me what you are doing here." With a sense of urgency she hollered out to him, "Ya'ateh"

Alyana was tired, hungry, and noticeably distraught. Most of all, she was seriously thirsty, as the day's temperature had hit the triple digits.

Dan knew he was in Apache country and wouldn't stand a chance if he were spotted. But when he looked at the girl, his trepidation changed from fear to empathy as he noticed she looked disadvantaged and exhausted.

He put down his gun and fumbled for his bandana. She looked at him awkwardly. Dan stared into the distance at a column of grayish white smoke, billowing sporadically upward in the sky. Quickly, he gathered the reins, asking the girl, "Can you understand me? What can I call you?" To his surprise she replied, "Alyana. I speak English."

Dan knew he needed to find cover and fast. He quickly spoke, "My name is Jace Randall." She responded by stating that she would be glad if he would help her find a safe place. She was relieved when he offered to have her ride with him. Dan reached out and assisted her to climb up on Lady.

As they rode, Alyana held tight. She explained as best she could the event that had taken place that had brought her into hiding. Days ago, Alyana had barely survived an assault on her tribe. A troop of white marauders had entered her village and slaughtered everyone. She'd been down at the river nearby, getting water, when she'd heard the commotion. She'd seen smoke and known something was wrong. In a panic, she'd run away as fast and far as she could, something her mother had taught her to do if there were ever an attack on her reservation. She'd reached a canyon, where she'd been able to hide. She'd been hoping someone from her tribe would come find her, but to her dismay, no one came. Her voice became shaky as she explained that her family was probably gone, and she was frightened and alone

"That smoke signal's a long way off now," Dan said, trying to ease her fears. Once they came across a small stream, they stopped to rest. "We'll wait here."

The girl stood quietly, her back to a tree, watching him check his saddlebags. Feeling somewhat protected, she proceeded to go to the stream for some water. As he turned his attention to the black, he noticed the animal tense up. Then he heard Alyana yelling out to him. Instantly, he jumped on his horse and ran ahead as cleared the far end of the undergrowth.

There was Alyana, running straight for the open plains, her long black hair streaming in the wind. To his right, a white man who was riding too fast to describe, his mustang in full stride, was making for the girl. Behind him was the Mescalero Apache thundering toward him.

Knowing full well what would happen if the Mescalero got his hands on him, Dan tried for the man with his rifle, but the shot missed.

He quickly realized that he needed to get out of there fast. One of the renegades might have been stalking them all along, searching for Alyana.

A quick appraisal showed his charge had brought an entire semi-circle of foes into view. The Apache were everywhere, but ahead of him. Whooping and hollering, they were strung out on both sides of him, closing in fast as he goaded the mare for speed. Dan knew that his only hope was to grab the girl and run. Another Apache who was gaining speed slung to one side of his pony, about to make the pickup, when Dan's six-gun spoke. It was only when the brave tumbled to the ground, almost knocking the girl from her feet, that Dan knew the shot had gone home. Cutting his pace, he swung by and caught Alyana around the waist.

"Hang on," he yelled as he pulled the panic-stricken young woman up to ride behind him.

The white man seemed to be the leader of the pursuit. The Apache were close now, and it was apparent that nothing short of a miracle would save them. The mare stumbled on the uneven terrain. The Apache circle was closing in on them and both sides were getting closer. He felt the two arms around his body tighten, giving him the confidence he needed to keep going.

The half circle around him was smaller now but close enough to make out the Apache war paint as they shouted and barked for the kill.

Any hope he had of escaping died quickly. Ahead, not more than half a mile, a lake blocked his way. The trap was complete. They had formed a three-quarter circle around him, forcing him to ultimately come to a stalemate—planned and executed with the precision of a military maneuver.

Riding directly towards the lake, he made up his mind. They would die at the water's edge, drown in it, or by some miracle, get across—if only to die on the far side.

The black was racing downslope to the water when Dan felt the animal falter.

Close on their heels now, as they both hugged the saddle, arrows whistled about. A rifle cracked. It was a miracle that they were not hit. Suddenly, they were at the lake, and the horse hurtled into the water with an explosive splash. Plunging and lunging, she stoically fought free of the muddy bottom, and her motion smoothed. She was swimming, but her breath was coming in tortured gasps as her energy seem to drain away quickly. Dan looked back. The Apache were bunched on the shore, making no attempt to follow. He turned his attention to the mare. She was coughing and fighting to keep her head above water. Something had to change, or the mare wouldn't make it. Slipping from the saddle, he shouted for the girl to let go and hold onto the horse's tail. Spitting and choking, Alyana began to sink under water. Dan struggled to swim alongside the girl, and he was able to support her so she could hold her head above water.

Now the mare began to make steady progress.

Spent from his exertions, Dan was hard pressed to keep his strength up by the time they had reached the shore. His boots felt like lead weights and hampered his efforts to get the girl ashore. Alyana was able to grab on to the bushes and grasses and pull herself to safety. Breathing heavily from her ordeal, she collapsed onto the bank. The trauma of the last few days hit her hard. She felt the gentle nature of this young man. He could have let her drown but had done everything to save her from the ravages of the rough waters. She knew his quick responses had saved her life. She was now reliant on him for survival.

Dan helped the exhausted mare gain the bank, where she desperately fought for breath. They had all made it, despite the odds stacked against them.

Across the lake, the Apache raised their arms in a silent tribute to their courage. Almost immediately, there seemed to be some sort of discussion or disagreement between them and the lone white man standing near them at the shore.

To Dan's surprise, the Apache turned their ponies northwest against the horizon, dropping out of sight. The white man rode north along the lakeshore and eventually disappeared.

"Safe," Dan's voice was little more than a grunt, "for now."

Convinced the girl was unharmed and conscious of their need to rest, he summoned his will to do the things he knew had to be accomplished. The mare's need for attention was obvious. Knowing any delay would not be good, he spent the next hour walking and rubbing her down with dry grasses, administering to her in any way possible.

"Good ole girl," he whispered to her, and the animal quivered as the warmth of the message seemed to permeate her body. Her breath was easier now, and gradually her shivering ceased, and she relaxed under his touch. He knew she was alright when her ears perked up at the sound of his voice.

He turned his attention to Alyana, who was now quietly settled on the grass, wringing water from her clothing. Dan knelt beside her. "You all right?"

She nodded, too exhausted to speak.

Dan, struggling unable to find the right words to comfort the girl, felt a pair of inquisitive eyes looking at him. He became suddenly aware of the strange softness in their depth that he hadn't noticed before. Shaken more by what he felt than by what he perceived by her gaze, he literally had to tear himself away.

The sun, deep now in the west, copper toned in color from the reflections of the lake, stained the heavens a reddish gold. Dan disappeared into a stand of timber when he noticed an object standing near him. But a second later, a sheepish grin lighted his face. He bolstered his gun and rose; an Indian totem pole was before him. He now knew why no one attempted to follow him. He was in an ancient Indian burial ground, and it was common knowledge that no Indian would dare violate the sanctuary where the spirits of their ancestors hovered. This land was taboo to all warriors.

When Dan got back to the campsite he noticed Alyana had

recovered her moccasin boots and stockings and had hung them over a branch to dry. She had drawn her feet up beneath her, making an unsuccessful attempt to hide the revealing contours of her body beneath the clinging wet undergarments.

Dan, busily engaged in bringing up the fire, avoiding watching her, sensing her embarrassment. He made a special effort to concentrate on what he was doing, but it took control to ignore her attractiveness. Her appearance was distinctive. She had striking features. Her skin was flawless and she had long black hair that looked like silk.

"Sorry about what happened back there," she said. "So many villages have been attacked. Some of my people want to kill any white man they see except the ones that offer them a reward. You have been more than kind to me. If I find any of my family, I will make sure they don't hurt you."

After a final poke at the fire, he rose and looked down at her.

"It was more my fault than yours. I walked right into a trap. I took a chance helping you. You probably would have been discovered by someone from your tribe."

They shared a meal. Afterward they sat by the fire, watching the early veil of dusk move in grayish mists across the river. A fish broke the water offshore, the concentric circles ever widening in its wake. Alyana shivered in the half-light as the calmness of the evening breeze began to affect them both.

Alyana watched Dan intently as he refurbished the fire. She shivered again and moved closer to the flames. She waited patiently for him to speak. Instead, he rose. "Better get you set for the night. It never occurred to him to discuss the fact that they were on the burial site for Apache warriors. He was sure she knew this, but she never mentioned it."

Alyana broke her silence, "I know of that white man. He is an enemy of my village." She refrained from admitting that she also knew some of the warriors that had befriended the man for the wrong reasons.

"You are kind." She stopped and looked toward the ground. "I no longer have a home. Not all white men are bad. My father was a white man and fit into the tribe's way of living. He loved my mother and would never leave her." Dan listened closely with compassion to Alyana's story.

Alyana continued, "My mother was Chiricahua. We lived on my father's farm when I was young. But before too long my father was tormented by the townsfolk, because of my mother. We were all forced to flee for safety and then moved in with my grandfather and became part of the Chiricahua nation. Shortly after the move, my father had gone into town for some supplies when he'd been followed, shot, and killed without warning."

Dan was fascinated by her story. He thoughtfully approached the girl to wrap a blanket around her. When Dan was leaning over Alyana, she reached up and touched his cheek. Half dressed, she opened her blanket to Dan. He accepted the invitation and lay down next to her experiencing the warmth of her body.

The events of the day drifted off, and their thoughts of doom were replaced with a spirit of euphoria—something neither one of them had expected. Alyana explained that she had been promised to one in her tribe, Lone Star, who was known for his gruff behavior. She had held off the marriage as long as she could. She had dreams of one day finding her father's family. She said nothing to Dan, but earlier, she'd noticed that Lone Star had been riding with the group of Apache and the white man who had tried to grab her. She would have done anything to get away from him, and unbeknownst to Dan, he had rescued her.

Dan was about to speak when her prolonged silence caused him to peer intently at her as the brightness of the stars lit up the night. He reached over and caringly covered her.

Dan's mind was spinning. He imagined he heard something...but outside was the sound of blowing winds. He concluded it was only the usual night noises.

Dan lay next to Alyana thinking about tomorrow's plan—to find a way out of this dilemma. But his thoughts would not jell; he was too exhausted. He couldn't help but notice the balmy essence of pine that filled the air. Around him, the shadows danced in the firelight.

He glanced again at Alyana. The rhythmic rise and fall of her breathing told him she was in a deep sleep. How strange, his coming to this woman. Inexperienced as he was where women were concerned, he had become galvanized by a mixture of confused emotions. She tossed lightly in her sleep and turned, the blanket falling away and exposing her shoulders and the provocative contour of soft, well-rounded breasts. He chastised himself for the thoughts he was imagining. An amber flared in the fire to light the features of her beautiful face as she stirred in restless slumber. Hastily he averted his eyes, lest she awake and find him staring.

A light fog was moving in, and there was a dampness to the ground. He rose to break the tension and poked the fire. He couldn't keep away the thought that was uppermost in his mind: they were one man and one woman along in the wilderness.

He closed his eyes. Gradually his anxiety abated. Slowly the fire died, and the summer night soothed him. He slipped into slumber.

He dreamed that Alyana had come to him and was trying to rouse him from sleep. Startled, he awoke. Alyana was adjusting her blanket as best she could as she huddled closer.

"Here, let me," he said turning towards her. What happened then was beyond them both. Lying on her side, she put her arm around him and spontaneously pulled him close. Instinctively, he kissed her. The last vestige of restraint deserted him. Excitement raced through him as he held onto her tightly. Caught up in the moment, her warmth and softness overwhelmed him. Their bodies came together so naturally—but he suddenly caught himself before they were both swept away into a night of mindless passion. He had too much respect for the young girl, and it was not the way he wanted this to happen. There was too much at stake, and he needed to focus on the reality of their situation.

Deep night tiptoed in, and a nesting bird fluttered restlessly. A firefly, winging its way offshore, blinked its lantern. Wrapped in each other's arms, they stayed together throughout the night, sleeping off and on, briefly waking to be sure the other was safe.

Chapter 12

An Unpleasant Reunion

Dan woke with a start. Something was amiss. A twig had snapped—or had it? Not a muscle in his body moved. There it was again, this time unmistakable. A glance at the mare confirmed his suspicions. Her restlessness was obvious. Dan's skin crawled as the tension grew and with it the question: Who or what was it? Ever so slowly, his fingers closed around the Colt that he had been careful enough to place within easy reach. He lay still, with his ear to the ground, and listened.

Out of the corner of his eye, he noticed Alyana had rolled slightly away from him. Her arm was thrown up under her head to form a pillow.

The minutes passed. Any noise he had heard—real or imagined—had ceased for the moment. He rose swiftly, gun in hand. Quickly, he retrieved his still-damp footwear and blended into the cover brush. It was still too dark to see any distance, making it difficult to remain quiet as he walked slowly through the thicket.

He thought he heard a horse heave but wasn't sure. Moving closer, he recognized the high creak of saddle leather. Dan stood silently, peering through the night, probing the swirl of early morning mist for a glimpse of the invader. Someone was out there. He quickly ruled out the likelihood of a stranger merely stumbling onto this place. No, it was someone who knew exactly where he was and what he was after. The intruder undoubtedly would first circle the far northern tip of the lake to come up behind his quarry. Was he the white renegade acting alone, or had he persuaded some of his die-hard Apache friends to join him? The Apache might wait on the outskirts for their friend to flush out their game from hiding before making their move. Certainly, they knew there would eventually come a time when their prey would have to leave the burial grounds.

The only thing Dan could see now was a horse, saddled and ready to go, that had been tied to a nearby tree, but no rider in sight.

His uncertainty brought him to an inevitable conclusion. White men with rifles constituted a far more impending threat than the Indians themselves. They would sweep the thicket with gunfire and either kill both him and the girl or drive them into the open. And what of the girl? If she fell into their hands, he knew what to expect. It was common for these renegades to hold Indian women in captivity or sell them on the slave market, to gain favor with unscrupulous strangers.

Dan quietly approached the horse, untied it, and led the animal to his campsite. It was still an hour before light. He knew timing was important. If he sent Alyana out on Lady, she would at least have a chance. His plan was to use the intruder's horse and run for it, getting rid of the threat presently pursuing them. To the south or even east, she might find someone who would assist her. He knew there were several settlements that would support grieving Indians, especially women who had survived some of the most brutal killings in the Southwest.

Lady was fully rested, and Dan knew there was nothing on four legs that could outrun her, especially with so slight a weight on her back. This may be the one way to guarantee the girl's safety and his escape. Should he manage by some miracle to get away, he would find Alyana. Something in his very being was prodding him to put his plan into action quickly. There was no time to sort out his unexpected feelings for Alyana. He thought about his commitment to Sarah, his childhood girlfriend. Yet he couldn't explain his attraction to this woman. Was it due to his loneliness? He put his confusion aside and proceeded to the task of saving both of their lives.

Alyana was still sleeping when Dan approached the camp. He slipped across the opening and knelt beside the girl, shaking her shoulder gently. "Alyana," Dan's voice penetrated her consciousness. "Wake up," he whispered.

Alyana turned, opening her eyes. Dan thought she was about to scream and put his hand over her mouth to silence her. "It's me," he said.

Slowly she relaxed. "We've got visitors," stated Dan quietly. She gathered the blanket about her shoulders, striving to be calm as Dan explained his plan.

"I want you to take Lady and ride out of here. It is still dark but will be daylight soon. Ride to the south, and it will take you out of danger. Watch for wagon trains or maybe find a mission, they will take care of you. There will be food and water for you. The letter in my army jacket is important and needs to be delivered to an army headquarters. Give the letter to someone in charge. I should be right behind you shortly."

Alyana sat up straight. Her eyes were round and questioning.

She rose and disappeared into the thicket while he busied himself.

She emerged from the brush with the army jacket, several sizes too large, deftly tucked into her still-damp clothing. Dan helped her as she struggled into her boots. Fear was evident on her face as apprehension halted her movement.

The mare, bridle in place, was standing ready. "How will you...?" Alyana started to say something but changed her mind. "Why must I go without you?"

Dan searched for a simple answer. "Somebody is on our trail and knows where we are. Figure if I will use their horse and make it out easy...and Lady will carry one of us real fine."

Spontaneously, he scanned her face one last time and picking her up, helped her onto the mare. "Ready?" Alyana nodded. Putting the reins into her hands, he led the black through the thicket to the southern fringe of timber to an obvious path out of the area. Faint streaks of light were fingering the sky. Dawn was not far off.

"Alyana, if you yell in her ear, she will run like a scared rabbit. Not too far south, you will hit country flat as a pancake. Ride straight. Don't forget what I told you—take care of Lady."

Dan knew their parting would be difficult. He went up on his toes as she leaned over to touch his face with her soft hands. Dan nodded, and with a sharp smack on the rump, started the mare on her way. Dan watched the black with her single burden move into the open. A dark shadow in the graying light, she soon became a speck against the discolored sky, and then disappeared.

For a moment, he stood watching. Suddenly a cold air draft began to pass through the mesa, twisting and flattening the tall prairie grasses and rustling the treetops. A flash of lightning jettisoned across the darkening sky. The thunder struck and rolled to stun the valley and shake the world with defiant growls. The storm was a moving curtain of rain sheeting across the land as the downpour pelted against his face. The drenching deluge swept over him, soaking him to the skin.

Dan ran for cover as the storm broke with feral savagery. Huddled beneath a tree for what little shelter it offered and aware of the brief respite offered by the storm, he planned his next move. Somewhat oriented to his adversary's position, he took advantage of the storm's fury, leaving his cover to use the stranger's horse to prowl the perimeter of the thicket, partially obscured in the mist-shrouded graveyard. The hiss of rain on the leaves covered his sounds as he moved stealthily through the grove with nerves on edge, his gun poised. Concealing himself, he waited. A moment later, clear of the thicket, Dan was racing through the downpour.

He swung south in pursuit of Alyana. He was happily aware that the horse under him was strong and sound, and things had worked out better than he had expected. He grinned as he visualized the ruffian's return to find both his horse and his quarry gone and the bitter humiliation at having been abandoned in this remote and lonely place with only the dead as company.

Stepping up the gray, Dan rode through the morning shadows over the wide range, searching, but the storm had wiped out all traces of any trail. The constant rainfall forced him to stop and find shelter until the storm abated.

Now some miles south of the lake, he discovered a cave near the rim of a gully that suited his needs. He led the horse inside, where he unsaddled the creature and settled himself, cold and hungry, to await the storm's passing. It was daylight now, and he seemed to have a new and vital purpose. Something profound had happened to him. Old perceptions had been brushed aside. He knew he wanted to find Alyana and his horse. She had conjured up feelings in him that he had not experienced before. He didn't question his own motives and was driven to persist.

The rain continued to fall and several feet below, the water in the cavern continued to rise as the gully neared flood stage.

The horse nickered. Dan rose and quieted the animal, rubbing warmth into her with his hands. He searched the saddlebag and found, in addition to a small supply of food, some dry tobacco and matches, both of which were promptly put to good use. Emptying the contents, he frowned as he pulled the rifle from its scabbard and hefted it.

"Hm!" he exclaimed aloud, "a new army Spencer. Where do you suppose he got that?" Then he remembered the purpose of his mission and his discussion with Major Sterling. But now he was questioning himself. The messenger was dead—and whatever documents he'd carried were gone. Alyana had his jacket now and if he didn't find her, would she feel safe enough to report to an army headquarters?

As the hours passed, Dan became impatient as he watched the swirling, muddy waters imprisoning him begin to subside.

It took a few minutes to saddle the skittish gray and lead her to solid footing. Clear of the wash, again in the saddle, he rode south under a clearing sky. Several times he spotted small, isolated herds of buffalo, and late in the afternoon, he noticed some horsemen riding along. They were too far off in the distance for him to distinguish whether they were Indian or white—nevertheless, he kept away from them. The wastelands rolled endlessly all around him as the hours sped by. He discovered several settlers' cabins that appeared to have been hastily deserted. Dan surmised that the recent Indian uprisings had something to do with the people fleeing. Dusk forced him and his horse to halt, and the cabins provided shelter and food for the night. He built a roaring fire to dry his clothing and to rustle his supper.

The night passed and as soon as light permitted, he was back in the saddle. The weather was finally clear. Chrome yellow, magentas, pinks, and dashes of brown clustered on the desert floor in a symphony of colors. Plant life surrendered to the arid summer in one last display of vigor. Below a brilliant blue sky glowed a pink mist on the purple hills. Amethyst and saffron grew abundantly. He watched the mesa broaden and the buttes break apart. The horizon rose majestically, and the probing light chased the terraced walls to dress the chasms and crevices in crimson.

Toward high noon, Dan's spirits rose at the discovery of tracks that he envisioned to have been made by the black. But soon after riding through a mile-long canyon, they vanished. Days of hard riding and diligent searching followed. Ranging throughout the sand desert wastes to the foothills, he questioned those on wagon trains and probed the settlements for word of the girl, but the answer was always the same and left him hoping the next train or perhaps the next settlement would have some information. Alyana seemed to have gone astray—and the desert kept its secret only too well.

In the days and weeks that followed, Dan grew exhausted.

Stranded and alone, he began to wonder if he would ever see Alyana or the black again, and if she was still alive. That night, in the flame of his campfire, he struggled with the thought of giving up, but something inside of him told him to keep to the plan and continue looking.

It was along midafternoon the following day, and the sun was well behind him, when signs of civilization rose in front of him. He quickened his pace. Sometime later, he was on the flatlands approaching a wagon train camped in the open desert. The tops of the wagons formed a uniform crest of white as their coverings snuggled together in a circle for maximum security.

Almost immediately, a rider who must have spotted him rode out to meet him, a long rifle cradled in his arms.

"Jest sit, Mister, an' state yere business." A hammer clicked as a Winchester pointed directly at him. Before Dan could answer, the man was joined by another long-haired plainsman.

"What is yere brand, Mister, an' what is on yere mind?" The second man's face was grim. His sharp blue eyes probed deeply, staring at the newcomer with a glare that missed nothing. With both hands glued to the saddle horn, Dan sat on his horse quietly listening to the solid authority in their voices. One of the men was much older than he had first appeared at a distance. In his early sixties or thereabouts, he extruded a boundless but well-controlled energy. He had a jet-black mustache handle barred downward at the corners of his mouth as he chomped on the tobacco pouched in his cheek. Dust and grime stained his buckskins, and a beaten pair of army boots marked him as a brusque, hard-bitten trail master who probably knew his business and the dangers of Indian country. A heavy Colt and bowie knife rode high around his waist.

"Well?" the man's gaze never left Dan's face. A group of curious bystanders gathered to see what was going on. Dan looked over at the unsmiling faces of the men before he spoke.

"Did you see a young Indian woman come this way—say in the last fortnight? Riding a horse black as midnight with four white feet?" He stood in the stirrups partly to stretch, but mainly to look at the horses tethered inside the circle of wagons.

The plainsman said, "Kinda curious, ain't you? Maybe you'd better step on down stranger, an' careful like. Joe, take his horse. I'll send Marty to take your place. Now, Mister, suppose you hand over yer gun an' come with me?" Dan cooperated and followed the man through the wagon space to the campfire. The tantalizing aroma of stew simmering in a big black pot made his mouth water. The plainsman indicated a wooden crate by the fire.

"Sit," he said, settling himself across a makeshift table. "Now what is all this about an Indian woman with a black horse? But before you get too comfortable, let me warn you. There is fever and death in this camp." Seeing the concerned look in Dan's eyes, the old man continued.

"Yep!" he nodded, a faraway look in his eyes. "They's fever here, but it is might near gone now. Who'd you say you was?"

Dan shot back. "I didn't. Don't waste my time, man. If that woman's here, say so, and I will tell you what you want to know. I have been in the saddle—I can't remember how long—every day searching for her. She has my horse."

"Hold on. Hold on," the plainsman raised his hand to silence the outburst. He looked hard at this big, broad-shouldered man who'd come riding in so fearlessly and whose eyes were hard and cold. "Nope! She ain't here. She was, but she ain't now."

"What do you mean she was but she ain't now?" Dan repeated his words and rose from his seat, his eyes searching the plainsman's face for an explanation.

Men were gathering around as the plainsman continued. "She came asweepin' 'cross that prairie a couple o' days ago riding like crazy—woulda gone right by iffen Joe here hadn't spotted her along that river yonder. We boxed her in so she couldn't get away. Might surprisin' to find an Indian ridin' out of nowhar alone on such a fancy horse. She strongly resisted 'til she saw our womenfolk. As was, took some simmerin' down to git her in tow, at that."

The speaker paused and filled his corncob pipe, carefully tamping down the tobacco.

"Told us her folks were dead, and a man named Randall let her take his horse to get away from some renegades that were after her. Jest told her to hang on and ride. She shore as hell did just that and thinkin' how she almost get by us. She—," the words stopped, the wagon leader evidently in a quandary.

"Where is she?" Dan interrupted, frustrated by the plainsman for the delay in answering his last question.

"Wal—she left a day or so with one of the fellers that came ridin' intu camp a couple days ago. There was a red-headed one, him being a big, good-looking man with curly hair an' a way with Indian women. They peared tu hit it right off at the start. Afore dawn the next day they lit out together, an' we ain't seen hide ne'r hair o' them since."

Dan felt his stomach turn. He knew Alyana was in trouble and the man was lying. No white man would have easily taken up with a young Indian woman lost in the wilds unless he was looking for a good time. His thoughts about Alyana numbed him. Anger replaced the useless hope that things were simply misunderstood. Torn and twisted by the agony of uncertainty and days of searching, he forced himself to face the probability that Alyana had been taken advantage of with a promise for a better life and had been told lies that a young, innocent Indian girl would never have recognized. Worse yet, she may have been killed. Dan's emotions hardened. This awakened a hatred, not for Alyana, but toward the man who he now knew he could not trust. A gathering inner force reconstituted him as his emotions began to swirl. He had a mission to complete, but now it included vengeance.

The plainsman continued, "Recken you're the young man that she was talking about? Serta like she described you." He rose, sensing Dan's frustration as he handed back his gun.

"My name's Warren. They call me Major around here. Not really a' army major—jest Major. I run this shebang an' I don't like any monkey business on my trains. Yer welcome to stay 'cause we can always use another gun across this godforsaken hell hole right straight through tu Californy."

The major handed Dan a tin cup of coffee. Selecting one for himself, he filled both cups.

"Boiled away tu nothing, but it's wet an gives us somepin tu do while we're layin' over for repairs." Dan's eyes peered over his tin cup as he took his first swallow.

"Maybe the men yonder by the corral can help you more," suggested the major. "They rode in with the red-headed man; a fellow named Luke and his brother Pete."

Dan nodded, downed his coffee in several gulps, and rose, returning the empty cup to his host. Fear began to take over as he recollected his encounter with both a Luke and Pete not too long ago in the town of Monument.

"Think I will do just that," he said. "Thanks for the coffee." A few last words from the major caught him going away, and Dan halted to hear him out.

"Think I should tell yu, she musta been a good friend of your'n cause someone heard the red-headed guy arguing with her about leaving the black. But she would have none of it. She would not go unless she took the horse. Settled it, too—for she was ridin' the mare when they left." The major rose, placing his empty tin on a barrelhead.

"By the way, keep a keen eye, could be trouble for yu—understand?"

The major finished, turning to join his men, inwardly aware that Dan was only half listening to this last admonition. He sensed trouble but kept his counsel. Out of the corner of his eye, he watched Dan ease the Colt in his holster and head for the corral.

Dan walked slowly. He was frustrated, yet he knew he would find the answers he sought in time. Certainly, these past few months had taught him to trust his own instincts.

At long last Dan Morgan, alias Jace Randall, was no longer the yearling but a hard-riding outlaw, a gunman who sought no favors and gave none. Cool, confident, and assertive, he had discovered he could stand alone when needed.

Almost at the end of the makeshift corral, he sought out a man nearby to ask him a question. The man was bent over with a brush in his hand, dressing down his mare, when he spotted Dan from below the horse's underbelly. When he straightened, to Dan's surprise, there was a six-gun in his fist menacingly pointing at his chest.

"Well! Mr. Randall, so we meet again."

"Hold it, Mister," Dan responded. "I am looking for a fellow named..." He stopped short as recognition hit him like a punch in the stomach.

"You plumb looking at a familiar face aren't ya? Glad we could meet up again, Randall. Don't make no sudden moves er you're a dead man. I oughta put a bullet in you fer makin' a fool out of me and my brother back thar at Monument." The Colt wavered somewhat as Pete realized he had an audience listening to his remarks.

He continued, "I want you to meet someone, Mr. Randall. Luke!" he shouted, backing off a few steps. "Got a friend of yours who is anxious to meet up with you again."

Luke's response was to ram himself into Dan's backside with all the fury of a wounded grizzly. The force of the attack swept both men across the clearing, crashing their heads into a stacked cord of wood. Flailing and twisting, the men fought their way out from under the toppled heap.

Once on his feet, Dan ran into Luke with a punishing kick to his stomach that caused him to cave at the middle. But by maneuvering a quick roll away, Luke avoided a second blow.

Now back on his feet and blinded by the pain racking his body, Dan was caught with the big man coming in hard on his mouth. Dazed momentarily by the blow, he shook his head to recover enough to then drive his fist into Luke's mouth. Blow after blow, Luke's face split into a bloody mass, but he wouldn't give up. Hurling his weight in close, he used the tremendous power in his big hands and heavy arms to wrap them around Dan's throat. Writhing with pain, Dan's body bent under the punishment, gasping for breath.

Dan, fighting for his life, managed to get his hands under Luke's chin and, mustering what remained of his strength, clinched his fingers onto his throat and jugular vein and clawed until his own fingers were red with blood. Almost at the end of his rope, he suddenly felt the hold about him loosen and inhaled fresh air into his tortured lungs, which gave him renewed hope.

Luke shrieked, clutching his bleeding throat stumbling on his feet. Instantly Dan was on him, his sledgehammer punches finding their mark time and time again. Bewildered by the assault, Luke retreated. Dan, sensing victory, and aware of the throbbing pain in his chest, set himself for the final attack.

A jolting left hook snapped Luke's head back, followed by a terrific right uppercut. He quivered like a felled ox and went to his knees. He was down, but the glazed look in his eyes showed no fear—only wonder. Minutes later, still on his knees in the dirt, his eyes closed slowly as he realized he was beaten, and his head fell forward on his chest.

Dan, reeling under the punishment he had received, nevertheless acknowledged the terrible ordeal to which this simple soul had been subjected and in an act of mercy, moved to raise the beaten man to his feet. He hoped others would attend to the bloody giant, now placed on blankets under a nearby tree and left to lick his wounds, all alone.

The spectators, awed by this courageous stranger, whose name may have been familiar to some, milled about, craning their necks to get a better look at him.

"What's up?" the terse voice of the major broke in. The men parted to let him through. "What's going on here? I won't stand for any trouble in my camp. So break it up." He looked pointedly at the outlaw. "If they's any fightin' to be done, save it for the Injuns when they come looking for their lost family. See that smoke yonder? Well!" He addressed the men, "That's Apache talk for trouble, so git back to your chores all o' yu—an' keep yore traps shut—I don't want the womenfolk to know yet."

The hour was late when Dan, still smarting under the medicines applied to him by the campers, settled himself under the Conestoga Wagon for the night. All but a small fire had been doused, and the camp was fast asleep. The major had doubled the watch. The afterglow of cigarettes punctuated the night shadows as the guards made their rounds, softly calling to one another as they met for a cup of strong coffee to help keep them awake. Gradually the camp sounds died, leaving only the disgruntled sleeper to slap at an errant mosquito or pull the blankets over his head against the cold night air and to muffle the cacophony of snoring sounds.

Dan, nestling under his blankets, dropped off to sleep, too exhausted to dwell on the enigma of which he was a part. Only for the briefest of moments did he allow Alyana to enter his thoughts, and he dreamed of her sharing a moment of passion with him; something that was still fresh on his mind.

Just before dawn, he was roused from sleep by one of the guards, who apologized for waking him. The major was right behind him as he rolled out of his blanket.

"Anything wrong?" he asked, reaching for his boots.

"One of the men you had trouble with rode out about an hour ago," he replied. "Our guards saw him go—didn't want to alarm the camp trying to stop him—followed him on foot for a spell, but lost him on the trail."

Dan pulled on his boots, shivering in the cold predawn, and was handed a cup of hot coffee that scalded his throat as he drank it. He and the major both sat by the fire, the guard having returned to his post.

"What do you know about those men, Mister?" asked Dan, leaning forward to warm his hands by the fire.

"Only that when they first showed up with the big red-headed guy there were mighty suspicious things happening—stealing out o' camp in the middle of the night. Like I said, couple of us saw him and those guys with that Indian woman and that black horse you was talking about. Seems like they knew each other."

"Major, I have to follow that man," Dan stated as he threw his bedroll over his shoulder and headed for the mare. It was a while later that he returned to thank the major, the gray saddled and ready to ride.

After shaking hands with Dan, the guard watched him disappear as he was swallowed up by the thick ground fog.

Chapter 13
The Long Trail

Clay Elkins was not unaccustomed to the rugged life on the open plains. He was not surprised by the riders attempting to rob him. He was slightly disturbed at having been caught off guard but quickly dismissed the incident. He immediately broke camp and moved upstream for the rest of the night just in case his visitors decided to return. He slept lightly. It was sunup before he was on the trail, and his horse clattered over the rickety wooden bridge, bringing him into the town of Lamesa where small houses and adobe huts lined the sides of the street. A saloon, a general store, and a barbershop constituted the larger buildings. Clay rode down the main street that was all but deserted, with the exception of a lone pony tied up at the far end. A man in an apron appeared in the door front of the general store with a broom in his hands. He watched Clay ride up. The man nodded and said, "Good morning." Clay shifted his weight in the saddle and acknowledged the greeting. Inquiry brought to light that the sheriff's office was at the end of town.

"That's his hoss outside," the storekeeper indicated, pointing the broom handle toward his office.

Clay thanked the man and moved along. The storekeeper leaned on his broom for a moment, eyeing the stranger, and then returned to his chores.

In front of the sheriff's office, Clay dismounted. A small sign with peeling paint read *Mortimer Gross-Sheriff*. Clay knocked on the door, and a deep voice from the rear boomed an invitation to enter. The door squeaked on its rusty hinges as Clay pushed his way inside. Sheriff Gross appeared from the jail section in the rear of the office. A blanket was draped over his arm. Clay estimated him to be around fifty years old, lean, tall and muscular in stature.

"Howdy," Mort Gross greeted his visitor with a friendly smile. "What can I do fer you?"

"My name is Clay Elkins, and I am looking for a man."

"Clay Elkins—Clay Elkins!" the sheriff studied him as he repeated the name aloud. "Now where have I heard thet name before? Seems familiar. But dern if I can place it. What's the man look like an' what's he done?"

"He's a young lad just turning twenty or thereabouts. Tall, not much meat on him, has black hair and brown eyes. Might have passed this way say, two, three months ago—and he's not wanted by the law, if that's what you're thinking, although he thinks he is."

Clay watched a frown knit between the sheriff's eyebrows. A moment passed before he spoke.

"You say two, maybe three months ago?" Again, his brows wrinkled. "H'm, would you say this gent was some handy with a gun?"

"'Tolerable," answered Clay. "Why?"

"You know what kind of hoss he was riding?" asked the sheriff, ignoring Clay's question.

"Don't rightly know," Clay asked. "Why?"

Mort Gross scratched his head and draped the folded blanket over the back of his old swivel chair. The answer came slowly.

"There was a man who came through here about that time. But this feller rode a big black an' packed his gun low and tied down. We got a saddle tramp buried on boot hill to prove he warn't jest tolerable with an iron."

Clay's face revealed nothing as he digested this bit of news. The reference tied in with Jeb Smith's deductions, and the fact that Dan's sorrel was found bore out the strong possibility that the man to whom Mort Gross referred may well have been Dan Morgan riding Jace Randall's horse.

"Lit out west of here, if that's of any interest to you," the sheriff volunteered.

"Someone took a potshot at him, but he was moving too fast, an' they missed." The sheriff picked up the blanket. "If thet ain't your man, I can't help you."

The sheriff turned to resume his chores. He paused at the entrance to the cellblock.

"Anything else?" he asked.

Clay shook his head. "Thanks," he said. "Hasta luego!"

The sheriff followed him to the door. "Tell that runny, if you see him, that Lamesa has no call on him."

The information was almost too old to be of value, but it did indicate the direction the lad was traveling. It left Clay little choice but to follow the stage road to Seminole. He lifted the bay into a canter, and gradually the miles fell behind him. It was a bright, sunny morning. Strong hues and numerous light-brown mesquite trees surrounded by cactus flowed by innocuously as he rode, indicating the end of the summer season.

The days passed quickly. For the present, the world was new, and it felt good to be alive, especially in the big, wide-open country. Clay rode along feeling somewhat as though he finally had a direction. There was no one on the trail except for a cowhand who happily waved, his pots and pans rattling as he whipped his horses through a billow of dust. He passed through Seminole, which proved to be not more than a stage depot. He stopped only long enough to find that no one could supply any information on Dan's whereabouts. Unable to turn up anything pertinent, he was sensing there was no point in continuing further west, so he headed southwest toward the Pecos River country.

It was almost midnight when Clay crossed into the border town of Hobbs. He went directly to the stable, where he put up his horse, and registered at the only hotel. Having settled himself, he had an early evening meal at the hotel restaurant and joined several of the local townspeople on the porch rockers to smoke and enjoy the day's local gossip. Clay received little response to the questions he asked regarding Dan's possible presence in the town.

The town had quieted by the time Clay turned in for the night. He dropped into a dreamless slumber in the middle of an attempt to consider the information he had gotten from the sheriff in Lamesa. His last thought was that Dan had dropped from sight somewhere between Lamesa and Seminole. But where? If he failed to locate any trace of the lad, he would ride into El Paso and inquire at the ranger station.

The hotel clerk roused him early the next morning. Clay rose to a hearty breakfast with lots of hot black coffee. As he lingered over his meal, he pondered that Hobbs, situated on the Texas border, was the jumping-off place to the wild, uncharted frontier country. The only law west of there was Fort Apache, a remote military outpost, hundreds of miles in the heart of the Apache hunting grounds.

It was into this hell hole in the town of Carlsbad, a town on the bend of the river that Clay Elkins rode several days later.

An outlaw retreat, it was one of the wildest, if not the roughest, place in New Mexico. It was said that every conceivable type of bad man, border ruffian, and renegade eventually came there. Your survival there depended on your skill with a gun. The law only visited the town in an extreme emergency. Moreover, the town boasted of the largest boot hill in the southwest and had little trouble maintaining their reputation.

A replacement troop of Calvary passed enroute to Fort Stockton. The town was absorbed with the news that Little Fox, a chief of the Chiricahua, had sparked a general uprising through the five Apache nations. Rumors were that Fort Apache itself was under attack. Two men who rode in from the settlement of Albuquerque, New Mexico, verified the news of widespread burning and pillaging by both Indian and renegade whites all along the frontier.

Keeping to himself, he made inquiries discreetly and only as the opportunity permitted.

Clay gleaned from their conversation that the Indians were streaming out of the hills in full war paint and regalia. They were being supplied with new Spencer army rifles—rifles that lined the pockets of certain unscrupulous gun-running interests with gold. Stories of horrible atrocities filtered in from time to time, each more lurid than the one before, until it became impossible to separate truth from fiction.

After leaving the town of Carlsbad, Clay continued to ride along for several weeks, making inquiries along the way, but to no avail. There was no word of Dan. He decided to hold up for the night at an Inn a short distance north of El Paso and move on the next day.

Late that evening, lying in bed wide awake, staring through the semi-darkness, he took a last draw on his cigarette before pinching it out. Through the thin walls, he heard a drone of voices in the next room. He was able to distinguish some words from the deep, booming voice of a man. The lighter voices only added to the confusion, but they seemed to drop out as the heavy voice dominated the conversation.

Clay could tell that a meeting of some kind was under-way. Matters of great importance were most likely being dis-cussed, because once or twice he heard the heavy voice calling for order, but slowly the sounds faded from his consciousness as sleep took over. After that, an occasional word penetrated, only to be lost in muffled inconsequential tones.

Suddenly, the word "Little Fox" jolted him awake. He turned on his side and listened. He heard the words *Laredo, army,* and *rifles.* Quietly, Clay crept out of bed. He found a heating duct directly under his bed through which the sounds were amplified. Gradually, the content of the meeting became clear.

These men represented a combine, supplying army rifles to the Chiricahua, and they were in the process of planning an-other delivery soon. As the talk continued, it became increas-ingly clear that these men delivered the rifles to Indian tribes. They acted only as middlemen for the combine, who operated from somewhere near the Texas boarder.

They worked hand in hand with a group operating out of Mesilla. The guns were being crossed into Texas somewhere near Laredo. The ambitiousness of the plan astonished him. Most startling was that they were transporting the guns over hundreds of miles through rugged wild country, with little or no interference from the law.

The meeting broke up amidst the scuffling of feet and the scraping of chairs. Clay had heard enough to know that somewhere in Mesilla, New Mexico, and one day soon, there would be a designated meeting place of the entire conclave to plot further gunrunning activities. They well knew how to keep the Apache on the warpath.

As Clay got back in bed, he realized he now had a double mission in going to the Ranger Headquarters in El Paso. First, he would ask the rangers to be on the lookout for Dan, and second, he would inform them of the gun-running plot to supply arms and ammunition to the Chiricahua.

The next morning after breakfast, Clay left town taking the southwest trail to El Paso. He skirted the area to avoid loss of time, constantly changing his course wherever the terrain permitted. The only time he rode into a town was to renew supplies and make an occasional inquiry concerning two men—Dan Morgan and an outlaw, Jace Randall.

A week after leaving, Clay approached the outskirts of El Paso. This was not Clay's first visit to the town—he was fascinated by the changes that had taken place over the last five years. Situated at the foot of Mount Franklin and on the Rio Grande opposite Juarez, Mexico, it was one of the largest Texas towns and the busiest on the international boundary.

The homes of Spanish design, which dominated the landscape, intrigued Clay. He rode down the main street of Ysleta, the oldest community in the state of Texas, where the ancient tribe of Pueblo Indians lived in peace and harmony with the whites. Clay stopped to read a weather-beaten sign at the side of the road: El Paso Del Norte. A smaller sign was nailed to the bottom of it. Clay bent low to read the words: Population 380.

Clay lifted the reins and the bay moved forward. It had been a long day, and both he and his horse were hungry. The sun sank over the horizon, casting purple shadows as they rode through the town. Lights gleaming in the windows heralded the early evening hour and the clip-clop of the bay's hooves made pleasant thudding sounds. At the far end of the street, Clay turned his bay through an archway to enter a hacienda set well back from the road and walked his horse to the fountain and swung down. The horse drank, and when she'd had her fill, he led her over to the hitch rail. Securing the reins, he stepped onto a wide stone porch. His spurs jingled as he strode to the door, where he knocked and waited for an invitation to enter. Once invited in, he stooped a little to step inside a large room that was exceptionally well furnished. The floor of random oak was polished to a high luster. A massive fieldstone fireplace, the focal point, was balanced on both sides by bookcases extending to the full length of the room. Heavy oak furniture was placed around a large center table. A multi-colored rug exuded elegance. Clay doffed his hat and walked over to the fireplace. Above it, and almost as wide as the fireplace itself, hung a beautiful painting of a New England winter scene.

A man in his early fifties entered from a side door. At first, he didn't notice Clay until he had divested himself of his gun belt and had hung it alongside Clay's Stetson. Startled, he faced his guest. Clay caught the lightning glance of appraisal.

"Well! We have a visitor, I see. My name is Trent—Captain Waring Trent." His voice had a sharp, authoritative quality. The captain advanced and offered his hand.

"Name's Clay Elkins," offered Clay, shaking the proffered hand. "Are you in charge here?"

Captain Trent studied Clay for a moment, not missing the slightest detail of the tall Texan. Satisfied with what he saw, and noticing something familiar in the name, he nodded cordially. "I am. Won't you sit down and tell me what brings you to Ranger Headquarters?"

"Captain, I have information that could interest you and a request for a favor."

Captain Trent beckoned Clay to a chair and then sat comfortably in another facing him. He helped himself to a cigar and passed the box to Clay. Captain Trent remembered that the army was looking for a man named Elkins and wondered if there was some connection between this man and the one being pursued. He sat back and let the man tell his story but said nothing.

Clay leaned forward to take a light from his host and drew deeply. He crossed his long legs and settled back in his chair, exhaling a cloud of blue smoke. He was grateful for the few minutes of leisure. He began his tale with Dan's episode at the Silver Dollar Saloon in Sweetwater, leaving nothing out of the telling—and with special emphasis on Jace Randall. There was a flicker of interest from the captain at the mention of the famous outlaw's death. As he began explaining that he overheard a conversation about a meeting that was to take place in Mesilla, New Mexico, the front door opened and a lanky, rawboned individual—who seemed in a hurry—burst into the room. "Captain," he started to say—then noticing the captain's visitor, he stopped short. An expression of surprise crossed his face as he stared at Clay.

"As I live and breathe!" He rushed to shake Clay's hand; his eyes wild with excitement.

"Captain! Do you know who this is? This is the man we have been wondering about for five years, Major J. C. Elkins, head scout and special agent for the First Cavalry at Fort Quitman along the Rio Grande." He paused, breathless.

Captain Trent was somewhat relieved to know his recall of the name "Elkins" was correct. The ranger continued, "You remember Colonel Watson, who has been asking us all these years to locate a Jim Elkins? Well, this is that Jim Elkins." "Hold on, man," interrupted the captain, looking hard at his ranger. "Are you saying this is the man the army has been looking for all these years?" "Sure is, Captain, one and the same," came the response. "And boy, is he a sight for sore eyes!" Ross nodded with enthusiasm. "How about having dinner tonight with me and my family, Jim?"

"Well, Ross, I sure did not expect to see you here," said Clay, a grin spreading over his face. "You ever settle down and marry that little girl you used to tell me about?"

"Sure did, Jim, an' got a fine young son to prove it."

The captain interjected again, "Now simmer down, Ross. I

221

want to talk to Mr. Elkins if you don't mind—you can arrange your social chitchat later."

"Yes, sir," answered Ross, regaining his composure. He turned to Clay, "See you before you go, won't I?"

Clay nodded. "Sure will," he said and turned his attention to the captain as the ranger left, closing the door behind him. The ranger turned to Clay. "Jim, you ole hunk of dynamite, where have you been all these years?"

"Working as foreman at the Boxed M spread in Sweetwater, just east of Abilene," answered Clay.

"Could I ask you why you left the army after doing such a fine job for them?" He added quickly, "You don't have to answer that question, of course."

"Don't mind at all, Captain." A trace of a drawl crept into Clay's voice. "Just wanted to get away from everybody and everything after that last fracas down on the border, so I resigned."

Clay had followed the killer as far north as Buffalo Gap near Abilene before he had completely lost his trail.

The captain sensed that Clay's brief explanation would be his final statement on the matter.

"Jim," said the captain, "they tell me yours is the fastest gun north of the border. You figure to use it again?"

"Perhaps," answered Clay, sensing there was more to come.

"Well, I'd like you to wait here while I send word to Colonel Watson. I am sure you will be more interested in what he has to say to you. The story from Colonel Watson will relate to what you overheard last night."

Clay nodded. "I will wait," he said, and got to his feet.

"You will be at Ross Weir's for supper?" Captain Trent asked.

Clay nodded again. "Then the hotel," he said.

"Thanks, Jim," the captain extended his hand. "I will send a message at once, and I guarantee Colonel Watson will be here posthaste when he gets the news."

The men shook hands, and Clay bid the captain goodnight after getting directions to his friend Ross Weir's house. He walked slowly to his horse, mounted, and rode out as he heard the ranger captain shout for his orderly. He stopped at the livery and ordered his horse fed and stabled, and then he headed for his friend's house just down the street.

That night Clay relaxed in the friendly atmosphere of Ross Weir's home. He felt a nostalgic touch of homesickness sweep over him. Perhaps it was because the happiness he saw on Mrs. Weir's face reminded him of the lovely face of Beth Morgan. Clay had been preoccupied and restless about the meeting with the captain. But he finally was able to enjoy his first home-cooked meal since leaving the ranch, followed by an escape into sleep that night at El Paso's oldest and only hotel.

The following morning, Colonel Watson, Commander of the United States First Cavalry; James Clay Elkins; and Captain Trent met in the ranger's office.

That the colonel was delighted in renewing an old acquaintance went without saying. When the men settled down to talk, Clay learned that the colonel had uncovered evidence of the theft of army rifles by an outlaw gang operating somewhere on the north side of Rio Pecos at Horse Head Crossing. A Texas ranger working out of the Texas Panhandle had found the bodies of two dead men in a creek on the outskirts of Lamesa. On one, he had found papers identifying him as Frank Rolfe. Certain other papers had indicated that he was to attend a gang meeting that would be held in Mesilla, New Mexico at the end of the month.

Colonel Watson said that information had reached him concerning a well-organized gang who supplied guns and ammunition to Little Fox and the five Apache nations. Further, he believed he had several of the culprits under surveillance. They informed Clay the army had reason to believe it was the old Laredo gang that had been rejuvenated and was back in business. They were reputed to be financed by a group of unscrupulous businessmen north of the Texas border who promised them gold. There was a well-laid plan to set up an army supply transport pretending to carry gold bullion over land to Mesilla, New Mexico. It was disguised as an arms and ammunition shipment for transport to the area army posts throughout the southwest.

"That's where you come in," the Colonel wound up his story. "That is, if we can persuade you to take this one last assignment." Clay listened carefully. The colonel continued, "That's why we asked the rangers to be on the alert for you—and when Captain Trent told me your story, I was anxious to talk to you."

The colonel, clearly agitated, paused to wipe his brow with his handkerchief. "I have to tell you Clay. "The army was actively looking for you until just a couple of years back when Jeb Smith asked me to get rid of the poster that had your picture and information listed on it. We have an allegiance to Jeb," said the colonel so I withdrew the poster as discreetly as possible.

But, I was later plagued by second thoughts, as I questioned my wisdom in doing so. I realized soon after that knowing your location could have helped you rather than hindered you. Especially if you would have gotten into a tight spot with some members of the gang that had managed to escape after you wiped most of them out."

"What the colonel is getting at," interjected the captain, who had remained silent to this point, "is that you are the one man we know who can get to the bottom of this gunrunning business and smash the syndicate behind it."

The captain rose and walked across the room to stand, momentarily, looking out of the bay window. Then he turned and fixed his gaze directly on Clay as he waited for a response.

Clay's mind raced as he thought about his friendship with Jeb Smith, the old ex-ranger. Had he known all along that the army was looking for him and never mentioned it out of deference to him and his history with the army?"

"Poster! What poster are you talking about?"

Clay watched the colonel disappear through a doorway at the far end of the room, only to reappear a moment later with a flyer in his hand. "This," he reiterated, a smile on his face, as he handed it to Clay.

An inquisitive expression crossed Clay's face as he read the discreetly worded poster that included a drawing of him and a message that the army was requesting his assistance. He handed it back to the ranger without comment.

"Continue," stated Clay.

"We need your help desperately, Jim," added the colonel, leaning forward to place his hand on Clay's knee. "If you agree to help us, anything you want is yours for the asking. You can travel incognito if you want it that way."

"The assignment carries a special decree from the governor as an undercover agent with full military and ranger backing. I guess I don't need to tell you that Fort Apache is isolated and just hanging on by the skin of its teeth, not to mention the hundreds of men, women, and children that are paying a terribly high price to settle in the West."

Deciding not to belabor the discussion about Jeb Smith, Clay studied both men, then spoke slowly, "If I go, please understand that it'll purely be for personal reasons."

"How so?" added the colonel.

Clay answered, "I have a score to settle for one Lieutenant Nelson. You remember him, Colonel?" Clay didn't mention that the young officer had been bushwhacked and fatally wounded. He must have fought desperately for his life, his uniform ripped to shreds, his body bloodied and slashed as though by a wild thing, and he had died in Clay's arms as he kept repeating the killer's name. Clay had learned that the identity of the assassin was Gnome, and he had followed him as far north as Buffalo Gap before losing his trail completely.

The captain and colonel listened to Clay's explanation, knowing the lieutenant's father had been Clay's best friend. They sensed the brief report was Clay's final statement and went on to matters more pertinent.

Clay rose to speak, "One more thing, gentlemen." "What's that?" asked the colonel. "When I catch up with the man who shot Nelson in the back, I am going to kill him like I would a snake in the grass," he asserted. Colonel Watson and Captain

Trent exchanged worried glances.

Colonel Watson spoke, "Just be careful you have the right man, Jim—we won't interfere." "I will be sure," came Clay's reply. The two men rose, indicating the meeting had come to an end.

"We'll get the bulletin out on your friend Dan Morgan and/or Jace Randall at once. Don't worry—if he's alive and anywhere in the Southwest, we'll turn him up," the captain confirmed.

"When should I start?" asked Clay.

"Right now," answered Colonel Watson as he handed him a plan that involved his presence in Mesilla on October 27 at the Double Eagle Hotel. "Raise your right hand." After having been sworn to the allegiance of the United States, Captain Trent swore Clay into the ranger service under a special gubernatorial decree.

Clay accepted the coveted Silver Star from the rangers in silence and transferred it to the inside of his breast pocket with the necessary papers.

"You will hear from me soon," said Clay.

"Don't forget to contact the rangers as soon as you get to Mesilla, New Mexico. We will get word to them as soon as we can." Clay nodded to both men and left the room. "Good luck," said Captain Trent, "and Godspeed."

He crossed the patio to pass through the archway to the street. He didn't look back until he had reached his hotel, then only for a moment he glanced at Ross Weir's little white house by the side of the road. Again, nostalgia hit him when he began dreaming of a future life with Elizabeth. He paid his hotel bill and walked to the livery stable, where he tossed a dollar to the boy who had saddled his bay.

Clay tied on his bedroll and swung into the saddle.

James Clay Elkins rode out of El Paso on a beautiful fall day, halcyon and serene. There was little wind, and the white cloud scatter hung high against a tapestry of azure blue. All about him, the countryside was in a state of change. The trees were starting to shed their russet foliage, and Mother Nature was making her usual preparations for the coming winter.

Even as far south as the Rio Grande, coolness tinged the air. The sun felt good against his face. Having charted his course, the restlessness of the past several months vanished. Most noteworthy was the sense of purpose that came over him. Once more, he was Jim Elkins, hunter of outlaws, with a strong sense of duty and devotion to maintaining law and order. As he rode, he mulled over the drastic change in his plans growing out of his meeting with the ranger captain and Colonel Watson. Perhaps it would be better this way; if anyone could locate Dan it would be the rangers. For the interim, he had a job to complete, and he needed to concentrate on his next steps.

Elkins rode north for several hours, taking a somewhat northwesterly direction. He had negotiated the more treacherous miles before night closed in on him and was glad not to have encountered any mountain lions. Staying on the most heavily traveled trails for the next few days, he passed through the Guadeloupe Range and cut across the southeastern tip of the Territory of New Mexico.

As was the custom of men who traveled alone, he talked to

himself, "Reckon we are somewhere headed near the majestic Organ Mountains that rise out of the desert east of Mesilla—wouldn't hurt to have a look-see on the way."

He headed northwest, shortly crossing into the lower end of the canyon. gunfights. Both sides of the arroyo walls ascended sharply, making admittance to its narrow confines difficult. The floor pitched precipitously downward at the point of egress, leveling off in an expanse of hot sand. Scattered tumbleweed crouched, tufted in the sparse soil, and a sprinkle of barrel cactus spread throughout the area. A withered cottonwood writhed and twisted in contorted loneliness, angular and barely alive.

Seeking a sequestered spot, safe from prying eyes, Clay finally found a place to settle for a fireless meal. The moon rose, a silver ghost in the star-filled heavens. Their brilliance, like diamonds against the black velvet sky, seemed almost close enough to touch. A shooting star flamed into oblivion as he pulled his blanket close around his shoulders.

Clay paused to roll a smoke and take in the scene.

The first rays of false dawn were lightening a salmon sky when Clay rose to face the day, and the rising sun found him again on the trail.

"Hasn't changed much—still the same old hellhole," he mused. His bay flickered her ears forward at the sound of his voice. Clay checked and reloaded his forty-five.

The morning shadows were still hiding in the canyon depths when the drumming sound of hoofbeats brought him up short. "Hosses, lots of them," he muttered heading the bay up an offshoot ravine. "Apache, most like," he added, stepping down to quickly lead the bay a short distance up a nearby wash. "Won't do to let them know were here." He muzzled the mare none too soon, as the rising crescendo beat against the canyon walls, and a bevy of riders swept by his hiding place. Craning his neck to look through the shrubs, he saw some dozen or more horsemen, all heavily armed, some with bandoliers and what looked like army carbines in their saddle boots. Clay watched them bunch at the narrows, fan out behind their leader in straggling pursuit, and then disappear in a cloud of dust.

"White men," he uttered, surprise tinging his voice. "Now what's a band of armed men doing in this hellhole?"

Swinging into the saddle, the point of discovery now past, he resumed tracking, only to find his first clue. Broad marks of wagon wheels cut into the red, sandy shale. He followed their course some distance up the cut. He felt his emotions stir as he followed the tracks along the main canyon floor. Every passing moment confirmed what seemed the only plausible explanation. It was the trail of a gunrunner's supply route to Apache territory.

He headed for the ravine when the clang of iron brought him up hard. Ear to the wind, he listened, certain the sound had come from deep within the arroyo.

The ravine had widened to what looked like a dead end ahead. To the extreme left and part way up the slope, a ramshackle cabin hugged the gully wall. It was supported by large timbers cross-nailed for stability. Clay took note of the ledge-rock solid foundation under the rear of the structure. The shack boasted no windows, and one of its doors opened to a pathway sloping downward along the cliff wall to the ravine floor. Men were lounging about, talking and smoking. Clay strained but could not make out words. An iron triangle hanging from a nearby post swung rhythmically. Dull-gray smoke spouted from a stovepipe chimney, the sparks soaring high on the updraft.

"Come an' git it," hollered the cook as he threw down the horseshoe he had used for a hammer. "Gnome ain't gonna wait fer any o' yu lousy skunks."

Clay backtracked to hide, heading unobserved for a spot on the gully rim above the cabin and watching the activity below.

After breakfast, the men roped and saddled their broncos as they milled in front of the shack. One man, holding the reins of the saddled mare, stood near the doorway. Suddenly, the voices and confusion ceased. A man appeared in the doorway, turned to say a few words to someone inside the cabin, and then quickly moved to his horse.

As though by signal, the horsemen started to move out. They huddled at the narrows to let one of the men take the lead, then fanned out behind him. Clay watched the men string out and disappear in a cloud of dust as they turned north.

The coast being clear, Clay returned for his animal, lariat in hand, and raced across the open space for the cabin. He had not quite reached the shack when the cook came through the doorway to throw out a dishpan full of water, narrowly missing him. The bay came up short as both men stared at one another.

"Jud Crawley," Clay's surprise showed as he recognized the man.

The ex-sheriff, caught off guard, dropped the dishpan, which crashed noisily on the rocks before he scurried back into the cabin.

It baffled Clay to find Crawley here. Nevertheless, he went right to work. Darting under the building, he looped the lariat around the main support timber, taking a tug or two to secure the knot. Dust showered on him as the post gave slightly. Once clear of the building, he gave the rope a turnabout, hooking it onto his saddle-horn and wrapping it around his shoulder. As he tugged on the rope, he felt the timbers give way and heard Crawley shouting as the cabin started to topple. A shriek reached him, over the wall of lumber collapsing, as he flung the line clear. There was a giant whoosh as the roof caved in and the cabin came down in shambles. Crawley's body hurtled through the doorway, and he landed behind the wreckage. His cry for help brought Clay to his side.

"Don't shoot! I ain't done nuthin," moaned Crawley, his eyes glued to the forty-five pointed at him. "Can't yu see my leg's broke? I can't move it no how, an' it hurts terrible."

Clay, ignoring his plea, asked, "What happened to Dan Morgan?"

"Honest to Gawd, I don't know. We lost his trail that same day an' I ain't seen him since," Crawley's words tumbled out.

"I ought to kill you, you rotten skunk, an' I've got half a mind to do just that for pleasure of watching a viper die," said Clay, holstering his gun.

"My leg," whimpered Jud. His fat jowls sagged, and his eyes rolled.

"Who's Gnome?" Clay shot the question at Jud.

"Never heard o' him," he whimpered. Beads of sweat stood out on his forehead and tricked down his unshaven face. He licked his lips.

Clay grabbed his gun, and Jud's face drained white as he stared at the heavy weapon pointed squarely between his eyes.

"Don't, for God's sake," the man pleaded, shuddering in pain.

"Who's Gnome?" Clay repeated. His eyes stared intently at Jud, making no attempt to help him.

"I ain't never seed him," Crawley's repeated, his voice shaking. "Yu gotta believe me."

"I'll kill you if you don't talk," warned Clay, the steel in his voice hammering as the Colt came to full cock. "Who's the ringleader?"

"Gnome..." Crawley gasped, "he's meeting the gang...Mesilla...Double Eagle Hotel. That's all I know. I swear it...for God's sake...don't kill me." He nervously continued, "An' I'm plenty sick of being stuck in this damn rockpile cookin' for the whole lousy outfit. Gnome wouldn't let me go along an' I'm thinkin they aim to cut me outa my share o' the loot."

"Loot?" Clay wet his lips, hoping Crawley would keep talking.

"Yeah, gold! They got inside information about a gold transfer comin' through. That's what the meeting's all about— the gold bullion" ranted Crawley.

Clay let out an involuntary grunt. Crawley, sensing he had already said too much, clamped down on divulging further information.

"So the gang had swallowed the bait, just as Colonel Watson had predicted they would," Clay mumbled to himself. Quickly, he realized that if the information divulged by Crawley had any truth, and he had no reason to think otherwise, then there was an urgency, and he had to move and move fast.

"*Meeting in Mesilla*." The words rang in Clay's brain. Knowing Crawley could fend for himself, Clay gathered wood for splits and helped him into a sitting position—then handed him some rope.

Clay left him lying there, moaning and cursing his fate but alive. He ran for his horse. The animal reared in surprise as Clay threw himself into the saddle and took off. The bay lurched into a run and pounded into the main canyon.

Clay's thoughts raced as the miles sped by. Soon the canyon widened, and the floor rose as they crested the northern tip. A covering of cumulus clouds had drifted across the bright sky in lacy, odd-shaped configurations. He swung down from the saddle to stretch his legs and take stock of the beauty surrounding him.

Chapter 14
An Awakening

Dan, suspicious of Big Red's actions, decided to play a hunch. He wondered why he was in a hurry to leave his friends. He thought if he talked to him, maybe he would learn something about Alyana.

Dan hunted his quarry north along the river, following the deep tracks embedded in the mud. The fog was lifting, and daggers of light cut through the clouded sky in a pink dawn. For a moment, he was able to relax. He was climbing now, and ahead, the foothills seemed to get bigger. Winding and turning, he was still on Big Red's trail, and it would not be long before he made his way through some rough territory. Hours later, somewhere above the timber line, he eased his weight in the stirrups. Stepping down from the saddle, he rested the mare while checking out the trail. He was about to remount when he heard sounds of a gunshot. Standing quietly, he searched the horizon for evidence of someone close but saw nothing. Sounds of shots rolled through the mountains. Then, shot after shot sounded. He jumped into the saddle.

"Gonna be pretty rough, old girl," he spoke to the mare, slapping her flank. "Let's go." They raced toward the noise of rifle fire. Skirting the ravine, a new burst of rapid shooting built up a crescendo of sound, then stopped. Having ridden as far as he dared, he dismounted, leaving the gray tied to a bush. Once at the top, he saw he was on a wedge of rock and shale formed in the shape of an arrowhead. In spots, it was hundreds of feet above the floor of the ravine. From the tip of the arrow, which indicated north, the main canyon split into two diverging ravines and climbed the jutting ledge several hundred feet above. He had almost reached the apex of the triangle when he saw the Mescalero camp below him.

Women and children milled around, going about their chores. As he lay on his belly to watch, he saw a group of warriors who were deep in conversation with two white men, both of whom carried carbines. He was not surprised to recognize Strom from the Major's description as one of them, a tall man dressed all in black with long dark hair falling down his back. There was no question that the man had a definitive limp further confirming his identification. Dan watched the other white man hand his rifle to a big warrior. The Mescalero threw the rifle to his shoulder in mock firing position. One by one the gun was handed from one brave to another, and each in turn held the gun in the same way.

Now the big Mescalero took back the rifle, making motions to the white man. Dan read the Indian sign language without too much difficulty. The Indian wanted a live cartridge in the chamber.

Strom took the rifle from the Apache, shaking his head "no." At this point, the second white man, silent until now, stepped forward. He pulled a pouch from his shirt and shook it upside down. The inference was clear. No gold—no guns—no bullets.

Dan watched the Indians while the white men argued. Whenever the Indian would reach for the gun, one of the white men would back off a step or two and hold the gun out of the Indian's reach.

Finally, the Indian shrugged his shoulders and turned to the braves in the group. Dan saw the big Mescalero convey the white man's message. Strom's presence again confirmed Major Sterling's explanation regarding the exchanging of firearms with the Indians. He was one of the negotiators for the gunrunners, and Dan had stumbled upon one of their infamous transactions.

The Indians were nodding vigorously in agreement. With a wave of their leader's hand, they picked up their bows and arrows and followed him into the thicket. The two white men slapped each other on the back in a gesture of satisfaction, and both disappeared.

Dan jumped to his feet and scrambled to the edge of the mesa. Half sliding and jumping, he shimmied to the canyon floor in a shower of gravel and dust. Suddenly a shot sprang against a rock, and a yell from the lookout above him confirmed he had been discovered. He had no time to lose. Knowing his horse was in a canyon somewhere on the far side of the rockslide, he didn't hesitate. He frantically slid, and hauled his way over the mountain of rock and shale, crossing the very mound of debris under the peak where the lookout was shooting at him. He climbed desperately, with sweat pouring from him as he topped the rubble barrier to reach the far side. Following down and around the base of the escarpment, he ran hard, gasping as he swung in the direction of his horse. A pain grew in his side, and his lungs felt like they would burst. Scratched, bruised, and exhausted, he broke across the remaining open space. He turned into the gully where he had left his horse and within a matter of minutes, was in the saddle. He looked back and saw that the Mescalero were rounding the base of the cliff to the north. Their yells and shouts prompted him to wait.

A rifle boomed behind him, and half a dozen arrows whistled by as he bent low over the saddle. The mustang settled down to run, and the sudden burst of speed carried them out of range. He forced the pace, but his pursuers were familiar with every nook and corner of their camping grounds and hung on relentlessly. Suddenly, the mustang's ears cocked forward, and she whinnied with a vigorous shake of her head. Dan sliding off his horse pulled out the thirty-thirty from his belt and waited.

Dan knew he had to leave. He knew the Apache would be goaded by the two white men to keep on his trail until they caught him. He had seen too much.

To get to him, the Mescalero would have to cross the last twenty yards of the gully in open view of his rifle, and he intended for them to pay dearly for his scalp. His sharp eyes scrutinized every inch of the draw and everything that moved. He was satisfied that his position was well chosen. Silently, he watched the far side of the ancient one-time watercourse. The noise of his pursuer grew louder. Then, suddenly all movement ceased. Dan riveted his eyes on the rim of the wash opposite his position and hunched down behind a log.

Dan burned with anticipation but was steadfast as his thoughts hammered at him insanely.

Dan waited until the Apache had lined up abreast and carefully drew his gun, noticing the white renegade. When Strom spotted him, he raised his rifle and began to shoot at Dan. He triggered shot after shot in rapid succession. But it took only one shot for Dan to reach his target. Strom fell quickly to the ground. Mustangs squealed and reared in confusion as the Mescalero braves threw themselves from their horses to escape the fusillade.

"Not bad shootin' for the range." The voice, casual and unhurried, brought him about on his back, his weapon at the ready. Relief swept through him as he located the buckskin man leaning on his rifle. His sharp blue eyes twinkled with humor. Moccasins and army pants set off the tailed jacket, with most of the fringes missing. Medium tall, with powerful shoulders, he moved rhythmically with the chew bulging from his bearded mouth. Dan eased the hammer down and scrambled to his feet. His face creased into a smile as the men approached one another.

Cautiously, the man stepped away from the thicket, his left-hand palm held outward in a gesture of friendship. "My name is Monty Hayes, Head Scout for the United States Army, Fort Bliss," he said by way of introduction. Dan grabbed his hand and welcomed him with a full embrace.

"If I had known you were behind me, I'd have sweated less. Didn't know whether I was gonna make it or not."

Both agreed it was best to vacate the area before the Apache returned with a vengeance, especially after Dan had killed their collaborator and source for weapons. According to Monty, they needed to get out of there fast.

"We should ride by moonlight tonight," Dan said, leading the mare. "Don't aim to let them Indians cut us off this side of the creek." He and Monty rode away from death's trap until they found a safe place to rest so that they could talk and plan. Almost immediately, an instant camaraderie emerged, as Monty began to offer Dan some reassurance.

Relieved to have made a friend, Dan found himself recounting to Monty his experiences of being on the rugged trail; nearly dying; meeting two old, kind men who'd saved him; and then his brief encounter with a beautiful Indian girl and how it had changed him. Dan decided to keep his meeting with Major Sterling and Amy private for the time being until he knew he could trust his new friend.

The morning light made visible the vanishing skyline and mountains ahead. Giant buttes lay in the distance, half hidden in the predawn light. Most welcome was the sight of the great saguaro cactus that Dan knew yielded a cool, succulent liquid that provided moisture for the animals.

That morning seemed to Dan to be of exceptional beauty. He rode slowly as he watched the eastern light become stronger. Perhaps it was the taste of freedom, the satisfaction in what he had just experienced, because for the first time in months, he had hope. Monty had quickly become a companion, and he was alive. His spirits lifted as he watched the sun sweep the horizon. Monty, a short distance ahead, waited for his companion to join him. He squinted long into the distance.

"We'll rest the hosses heah," he said dismounting. Dan slid out of the saddle with a sigh of relief and hit the ground hard.

Dan rubbed the seat of his pants and noticed that his friend was doing the same. The horses blew in release. They had been on the run since yesterday and were weary.

"Quiet—too quiet," Dan's terse statement was succinct and abrupt.

"Hot, too!" Monty gazed at the sky. After a short while, he asked, "Ready?" His companion nodded and mounted; they had lingered as long as they dared. Briefly, Dan scanned the horizon. Monty was watching him and remarked, "So, do you see it?" Dan nodded. Far ahead, he could make out the faint clouds of smoke against the sky.

"What do you think?" The question seemed to catch Monty as he was about to ask the same thing. Neither spoke for a moment, each waiting for the other to reply, when finally, Monty answered.

"It ain't the smoke that worries me. It is that whirl of dust yonder. Could be a squall sweeping across the desert kicking up on the flats. Jest about make it out from heah." Monty squinted into the sun. Below them were the lowlands, bright with the haze of a new day.

"Look ahead," Monty replied. He chewed hard on his cud, pushing back his cap to briskly scratch his head as he noticed the Apache pouring out of the hills like ants out of the woodwork. From the canyons below, at least fifty cavalry men emerged to face the Indians head on.

Monty continued, "When I say go—hang on to your scalp and ride like all hell is after you. We best make for the river across at the shallows. I am hoping them braves are too busy ganging up on the army to pay us no mind. It's downhill all the way, an iffen we can make the water, we got a chance." Dan nodded in agreement. "Ready," he said, taking a firm grip on the reins.

"Let's go!" And both men crashed out into the open, bent low in the saddle, riding pell-mell down the boulder-studded decline, cutting for an open stretch of level terrain directly through the scattered groups of startled warriors.

"Let's get out of heah!" Monty shouted, and both men hit the trail. The open expanse of water was too dangerous for the Mescalero to cross with the calvary on their back. They rode away, ignoring a dead man who had been floating face down in the river.

The two men traveled steadily throughout the day, taking time only to share food from Dan's meager supply. At times, they were forced to hide when they spotted roving Apache, some in full war paint and battle regalia. They were grateful indeed to hear the mission bell resonating in the distance. Sometime later, they entered the Reserve Mission yard and were met by wide-eyed children and startled women, who seemed to quickly disappear as they approached. A moment later, the padre appeared to welcome them. Both riders dismounted.

"You are here again, my son," stated the priest. Monty handed the reins to a servant who suddenly appeared, then shook hands with the priest.

"Howdy, Father," he said. "Never thought I'd be back so soon. Had trouble getting here at that. It's a long way an' we are all in. This is my friend Jace."

"Greetings! Señor, you must be weary, for you came over a laborious route—and I know it's danger all the way." The padre offered his hand. "Pancho," he said, turning to a short, mustached man, whose face was almost hidden under a large sombrero, "take the horses to the stable for food and water."

"Come in." The padre led the way around a fountain surrounded by a low, circular stone wall, leading to a pitched and spectacular centerpiece statue of the Virgin Mary—still standing and in good repair—surrounded by a garden filled with beautiful flowers.

The two men followed the padre indoors to a dimly lit study with meager furnishings. He beckoned his guests to sit while he remained standing. Dan rose to offer his seat. The padre waved aside the courtesy with a smile. He instructed his servant to set extra places at the dinner table for his two guests.

"Perhaps you would like to freshen up before we say the blessing," he offered. "The food is almost ready, and you will join me in our simple repast. I must see to the kitchen if you will grant me leave."

Later that evening, in the safety and warmth of the heavily walled mission—and feeling more relaxed than they had felt in a long time—the two men enjoyed the hospitality of their host. Night came to wrap the ancient monastery in tranquility. The geniality of the padre lulled them into a welcomed feeling of peacefulness. The servant entered the room to blow out one of the lamps.

"You must excuse us, but we try to conserve our oil here. It is hard to come by, and it's a luxury we cannot afford to waste," said the padre apologetically. "It is long past my bedtime, so if you excuse me, I will see you, God willing, in the morning. Goodnight, my sons," he said and slipped quietly out.

Dan and Monty followed the servant to their quarters. Placing the lamp on a plain wooden stand, the old Mexican turned the wick down and closed the door behind him.

In the quiet of the night, with exhaustion looming over him, Dan thought about almost getting killed and again running for his life. *Was this all a bad dream? Was there a resolve in all of this?* He calmed down when he remembered that Monty was at his side. His eyes welled up as he lay in his bed.

It seemed to Dan they had just fallen asleep when the clanking of the breakfast bell awakened him. Monty was already dressed and making up his cot.

The sunshine was streaking over the eastern mountain with a cloudless vermillion sky of melding tones of oranges and pearl. After being led to the stables, both men thanked the padre for the night's lodging and hospitality.

"Oh!" the padre addressed Monty, "I almost forgot. I have something for you to return to army headquarters. I wonder if I may impose on you for a favor?"

Monty nodded. "Glad to be of service, Father," he said and stepped aside to allow the padre to pass.

"It will only delay you a moment," the priest said. Then he called to the peasant woman weeding the flowerbed that bordered the courtyard. "Would you get the army coat hanging in my study, child?" The priest turned to his guests as she scurried away. "It was left with me," he explained. It didn't seem important at the time—but for some reason a young Indian girl, very much distraught, gave it to me, asking me to promise to pass it on to the right people. She said it belonged to army headquarters but was not sure she should return it herself without the man who gave it to her."

Dan stopped short. He noticed that it was his blue army coat given to him by Major Sterling. His emotions began to stir knowing that Alyana must have found her way to the mission, and she was alive. "Padre," he said, "Where is the woman who gave you this coat?"

"She is gone, my son," he responded. "She was only here for a short time. She was one of many who have come through here, but she seemed to have somewhere to go.

Cutting through a small cemetery, they passed along a narrow footpath between the graves and crudely sculptured headstones. Both men were struck by the meticulous care given to the small burial plots with its flowered borders.

The padre halted halfway through the graveyard and crossed himself. "The one small doorway, my sons, through which all of us must pass." He gazed at the gardened plot with reverence. "You are young, and such matters are not of your concern yet." He hesitated, then decided to go on. "But I have lived my three score and ten years—and seen—," the padre turned off the pathway to walk among the neat rows of graves to pull a weed.

"My son," the padre put his arm out to hold on to Dan as they left the cemetery and walked on toward the barn. He motioned to the lad. "Come along," he said, walking toward the servant who carried the blue army jacket over her arm and handing it to Monty.

"You look troubled, amigo?" stated the padre, fingering his rosary as he noticed a haggard look in Dan's eyes. "Would you like to tell me what it is that bothers you?"

"The Indian woman, Padre; she was riding a big black mare, wasn't she? You know, the woman who left the jacket." It was more of a statement than a question. The padre replied, "Yes, a magnificent-looking creature. However, after only one night's stay, the woman and her horse disappeared, and we never saw her again. Poncho trailed her the next day and lost her tracks among those of the wild horses that come this way several times a year."

Dan nodded, thanked the padre, and had just pulled his animal about, when the priest spoke, "The lady did tell me, my son, that the black belonged to a man who would some-day come for her. The senorita's voice was too soft to hear the name—but I do know she cared deeply about this man. Many come through here for many different reasons, my son. I offer them a warm bed and food for their journey ahead. It is a step-ping-off point where a person can feel safe in God's house, if only for a short time. All is part of God's plan."

Dan recaptured his thoughts as he turned to the Padre and spoke one last time.

"There is something else I think I should tell you, Fa-ther—I killed a man...and I am not sorry." his confession now complete.

In silence, the two men saddled up and led their horses out into the sunlight.

Dan kicked his mare and moved out slowly. Under the stone archway he paused to look back, taking in the lovely set-ting and the tiny cemetery.

The last thing he saw as he rode off was the lonely figure of the padre standing there, his hand raised in a blessing.

"Forgive me," he whispered and caught up to his friend, who was patiently waiting.

Chapter 15
One More Misadventure

It was high noon when Monty and Dan reached the fort post in the southeast territory of New Mexico. The trail had been treacherous. They concealed themselves in the brush to escape the eyes of an Apache warring party several times. They were somewhere near the timberline, overlooking the stump-strewn clearing around Fort Bliss. While they were watering their horses at the creek, Monty said, "Thought you might be glad to have this jacket, seeing you ain't dressed too warm fer this time o' year. Figure it's more yore's than anybody I know."

He untied the tunic from behind his bedroll. "Purty well ripped apart seeing how the shoulder straps are missin'. Shore ain't no use to tarn thet old rag in and be asked more questions than I can answer." Monty went into his saddle, watching his partner search the inside of the jacket before slipping into it. He backed his mare from the water's edge.

Dan, grateful for its warmth and knowing full well the jacket was the one given him by Major Sterling back in Monument, had refrained from asking the scout for it sooner to avoid an uncomfortable explanation.

As they crossed the clearing, Monty hailed the gate until the big timbers swung inward.

"Gotta report to the old man, or he'll have my head on a chopping block. Wouldn't put it past him if he did one o' these days." Monty guided his mount toward a square-shaped building off to their left. Nailed to the banister, a sign read "Headquarters." A smaller sign below, still legible—probably the wit of some jokester—scrawled in crayon said "Wipe yer feet damn it."

At the hitch rail, Monty swung down. Walking around the back of his mount, he picked up the conversation as Dan dismounted.

"The colonel is a tough hombre when he is sober—ketch him with a few under his belt, and he will find you in contempt of just about anything."

Together the two men moved toward headquarters and were climbing the steps when

Monty snapped to salute a large, heavy man coming through the door. Fumbling, attempting to button his collar, he stepped onto the porch.

"Well!" the colonel exploded. "Where the hell have you been?" His keen blue eyes glared at his scout from under his bushy eyebrows. "Don't you know those blasted hills are swarming with Apache on the warpath—and you come riding in nice and easy like you don't have a care in the world." He paused, then continued. "And wipe that smile off your crummy face, or I'll have you shot for insubordination."

Monty started to explain, but the colonel interrupted him. He suddenly diverted the tongue-lashing, looking toward Dan standing quietly behind the scout. "Maybe I ought to have you both shot, but before I do, come in and wet your whistle—no sense in dying with a dry throat."

The colonel turned on his heel to enter the office, pausing to jab his index finger into Monty's bulging stomach. "And you—you'll clean the stables, young fellow. If I catch you spitting tobacco juice all over that porch railing—it will look like hell and smell worse."

"Yes sir, Colonel," said Monty, his sigh of relief noticeable to Dan as he followed the officer indoors. Inside, the soldier wasted no time in getting down to business.

"Now! Let's have it—eh! Who did you say this was?" The colonel's attention turned to Dan.

"Wal I don't rightly know much aboot him, Colonel. His name is Jace Randall—but he ain't no tenderfoot when it comes to throwing led. Pulled the string on Strom, the feller we been a trailin'. Figure he's got more gun smoke in his veins than blood, so I brung him along."

"Glad to know you, Randall. Colonel Watts here," he stated as he shoved out his hand. "No time to think about it now, but the name is familiar. I see you're wearing an army jacket— kinda messed up—you an army man?"

Dan was caught up in the rapid-fire barrage and hesitated. Seizing the opening, Monty began to speak, but the colonel was interrupted by one of the scoutmasters.

"Colonel," he said, "them Apache are in full war paint, and they are moving in on Murdock, just south of the Apache pass. It looks like this time they jest might shoot the buttons off his suspenders."

"Lieutenant Murdock!" The colonel's correction was pointed.

"Well—Lieutenant Murdock then." The scout grimaced as he came to order.

"I know, I know," the colonel mumbled, as he tugged at his collar, scratching his three-day growth of stubble. His balding head glistened with sweat. Wiping his neck with his none-too-clean handkerchief, he went over his head in much the same fashion that one would wipe the dust off a chair. "If that young whippersnapper lets Little Fox get his murdering fingers on that ammunition, we'll all die like sitting ducks before snow."

"So, that's it," the scout looked about for a spittoon and moved it slightly with a direct hit.

The colonel looked directly at Monty as he angrily blurted, "And while you were up in the hills playing hide and seek, these pesky injuns were scheming to take our men apart at the seams."

"Now, Colonel," Monty tried to fend off the onslaught.

"Don't 'Colonel' me!" bellowed his superior, making a dash for the door. Noticing the scoutmaster was lingering outside of the door, he belted out, "Guard! Now what the hell are you doing on that banister? Get off your ass and sound assembly! I want every man jack here and ready to ride in five minutes. You heard me! On the double—git!"

Acknowledging that the peace and quiet he'd enjoyed lingering outside the door was too good to last, the scoutmaster lost no time in hightailing it in search of the bugler.

The colonel closed the door. "Now both you fellows go get something to eat while I go over a few things. Guess you've got a square meal coming to you. I'll see you later, Randall, when things quiet down around here—if they ever do. We'll talk then. Monty will show you the way. Good day, gentlemen!"

Outside, amidst the hustle and bustle of the troops assembling for action, both Monty and Dan took their horses and headed for the mess hall. An hour later, the cavalry left. The two men satisfied their appetites and mused over the events that had brought them together and finally to the station.

Suddenly, a voice rang out loud and clear: "Hoss soldiers with wagon train coming fast!"

The colonel immediately appeared in the doorway of the headquarters, his tunic half open, a napkin still tucked into his collar. "Man the stockade, men, and open the gates!" he shouted, ducking inside for a moment, only to reappear, his uniform in a semblance of order, buckling on his army accouterments.

Instantly, Monty was on his way out of the mess hall, his companion at his heels. "Somepin's up!" he shouted back at Dan.

Outside, the stockade gates were swinging wide as men scrambled up the ladders to man the ramparts. A few minutes later, a cheer went up to welcome the first of the new commission of cavalry. At their head, smartly erect but showing the dirt and grime of a rough trip, rode their intrepid leader, his white stallion stepping high, as though on parade.

Facing the colonel, who was waiting on the top step of the porch, the troops came to attention in orderly formation as the command to halt was sounded.

"Lieutenant Murdock reporting, Sir." An orderly stepped forward to hold the white horse as the lieutenant stepped down.

"Welcome to the post, Lieutenant." The colonel advanced on him with his hand extended. "At ease." The lieutenant appeared to relax as he nodded to his sergeant and sent the word rumbling down the line.

"Had a rough time of it from the looks of things. Many casualties?"

Murdock nodded. "Too many," he said, pulling off his

gloves. "Thanks for the help."

"Sergeant!" the colonel shouted the command. "Take care of the wounded and see that the men are fed and cared for— lift your feet, man, and look to it!"

"Come in, Lieutenant. You look bushed. Orderly, take the lieutenant's things and show him to his quarters, then set an extra plate."

"That's Murdock," Monty's undertone sounded in Dan's ears—as though he hadn't already guessed. "The best damned soldier in these heah parts—an' a swelled head to go with it."

Murdock, approaching the porch, turned for a last look at his troops gathering at the mess hall. He nodded in satisfaction. It suddenly dawned on him that they had not eaten since the morning before—nor for that matter, had he.

Across the parade grounds, he heard the sharp bark of the mail carrier. He was about to join the colonel when he saw two men outside the mess hall.

"Colonel," he pointed toward them. "That man with your scout, over there near the mess hall—who is he?"

"Oh, that's a fellow named Randall. Came in with Monty this morning. Why?"

"Randall! Jace Randall the gunfighter?" The colonel looked at him.

Murdock followed the colonel inside. "I would like to talk to that man later, Colonel—with your permission, of course." The door closed behind them.

"That's odd," Dan turned to Monty. "You'd think the lieutenant knew me, the way he looked at me—or maybe he was looking at you; you are an old friend of his, I guess."

"Wal I know him, shore, but it ain't anythin' special. Scouted for him couple times—ain't really got acquainted; nobody does. He is sorta a lone wolf—goes by the book too much. Seems like he writ the army manual—personal."

Monty, dismissing the incident, hooked his heel on the lower rail of the fence and reached for a fresh chew. His fingers burrowed into the pouch, bunching its contents into a solid wad that he stuffed into his face. "Chew?" he asked Dan, working the ball into one cheek. "Kinda old, but plumb sweet—if you don't mind."

Dan shook his head to indicate he was not interested in tobacco chew as he relaxed a little leaning against the fence, his arms crossed under his chin, enjoying the warm sun on his face.

"You know, Monty, I didn't tell you before, but I was due to come here sooner or later. I'm supposed to deliver a letter to the general, but," Dan squirmed in discomfort, "the truth is that it was somewhere in this jacket."

Monty, his jaw hung mid-motion, resumed his chew. "It ain't me to pry, Jace, seeing it's none o' my business, but it has sompin' tu do with that gal back at the mission—ain't it?" The man's keen insight into his friend's affair was uncanny. Dan delayed responding by reaching for his tobacco, studiously tailoring the golden leaf into its slender paper cylinder. A deft twist at the ends and the smell of sulfur rose as it lit into flames. They were interrupted by the orderly, who informed Monty he was wanted in the colonel's quarters at once.

"Be thar, pronto," Monty responded. "Gotta go, Jace," he drawled, half turning. "Maybe I can larn somepin—can't keep that bobtailed soldier waitin."

Dan nodded as Monty took his leave, inwardly relieved; his confidence was still intact. Mulling the matter over in his mind as he strolled toward the corral to have a look at the compound, he was soon lost in thought. There would be time...plenty of time...to tell his story once he'd decided how to present the facts in such a way as to not incriminate himself. His intention to avoid any complicated issues (or telling it like it was) would be a challenge, but he would have to take his chances. If he chose the latter course, any possibility of amnesty to the name of Jace Randall, of which Sterling had spoken, would go up in smoke, unless the major had managed to get such a request off before his death. Of the two courses open to him, in view of the sudden demise of the man who had sent him, his best chances seemed to be in keeping his mouth shut and going about his business...and with any luck, the whole venture would be forgotten. At the corral, he climbed astride the top rail to watch the movements of the restless mustangs. He stood up on the second rail to better see a man on the far side of the grounds moving among the ammunition wagons that were ready to be unloaded. Two things held his attention—he looked familiar, and he was acting suspiciously. Dan watched the man furtively peer into each wagon, after which, his curiosity apparently satisfied, he walked into the open and paused to wipe his brow. Dan jumped off the fence hard, the nerves tightening in his neck. The man's hair was red. Could it be Big Red? His imagination went wild, but the need for caution forced him to calm down. After all, there must be hundreds of men in the West with red hair besides Big Red. His being here at the fort seemed most improbable. More than likely he was one of the dozen immigrants that had straggled in under the protection of the army, who was crossing hostile Indian territory and merely wandering about for something to do while waiting for a wagon train to come through. Stooping to tie down his gun, Dan crossed the yard. He had to know for sure.

Rounding the string of wagons in the direction of the redhead, Dan skirted an open space between two empty buildings, hugging the side of the one wall to follow him at a safe distance.

A sound caused him to duck out of sight behind a loose board in one of the shacks just in time. A tall, thin man passed his hiding place without as much as a suspicion that someone was there, hiding out of sight. Dan had a good look at him. He whistled softly as he passed by. The man was Pete Jukes, the brother of Luke with whom he had had the fight at the wagon train. Now he knew the identity of the redheaded man beyond any doubt. Dan slipped out of his hiding place and cautiously pursued both men. At the end of the shack, a glance revealed the red-haired man and Pete standing under a shed talking, their backs to him.

Dan stepped into the clearing.

With a loud voice, Dan called out to Red, "Turn around."

Both men whirled to face their foe, astonished. Pete's face whitened and he moved backward, his escape blocked by a rusting iron wheel. Trapped, he stood there biting his lips, looking from one man to the other, careful to keep his hand away from his gun.

Dan watched the look of surprise quickly leave Red's face

as he stepped from under the shed into the sunshine.

"So! We meet again, amigo," he said, scowling, anticipating the approaching ordeal. "I know why you're here, Randall, so let's get on with it." He went on to say, "Your Indian friend was sure fun to be with. Too bad you left her, but good for me."

Dan was fuming. He suddenly felt an overwhelming urge to destroy his opponent.

Red made no pretense, no effort to evade the confrontation. He showed no fear, no contrition. To him it was business, and killing was part of that business. "I knew from that very first day we'd meet again, and when we did, it would be to cross guns. We would have been a great team together." With a flourish, he brushed his coat clear of his holster.

"Stay out of this, Pete. It's not your fight," he said, his long fingers hovering over his gun.

To Dan he threatened, "Hombre! You better be as good with that iron as you think you are. We'll both walk out of here over your dead body if you're not—"

He struck with devastating force, his hand flashing downward in a perfect draw as Dan's hand moved like the lightening thrust of a rapier, to come up smoking black powder. The explosion of heavy guns shattered the quiet of the golden afternoon.

Then a strange thing happened. Dan, with the heel of his hand suspended over the hammer of his forty-four, saw Red quickly holster his gun. Wondering how either man could have missed at so short a distance, he held his fire, waiting his adversary's next move.

Red took a step forward and started to speak when his

knees bent, and he fell forward on his face. Pete ran to turn his friend over. Dan knew from the look on his face that Big Red was dead. Slowly he slid the six-gun into his sheath, when he was overcome by a sudden weariness that seemed to drain all his energy.

Pete, stunned by the death of his leader, looked up with hate in his eyes and a bitterness in his voice that was compelling enough to tear a man's soul apart. "Someday I'm gonna get you, Jace Randall, and when I do, you are gonna be buzzard bait." Walking to where Pete huddled, Dan saw a tear stream down his leathery face and suddenly felt compassion for the man, yet he walked on without a word.

Soldiers who'd heard the shots ran toward them, and soon the place was swarming with men gathered about the corpse and his mourner. Conjecture was widespread as to what two renegades were doing snooping around an army camp and the fact that Jace Randall somehow had caught them in the act.

Dan, making his way slowly back to the corral, suddenly stopped. The last thing he saw was Monty running toward him. In the next moment, he was tumbling down a small rock filled ravine. Before Monty could get to him, he had fallen hard, hitting his head on a nearby shelf of rock.

"Jace! You're hit." Monty knelt down beside his friend as he touched what appeared to be a gunshot wound. His hand came away from his side covered with blood.

"He was fast," Dan could barely hear his own voice over the roaring in his ears as he fought the darkness sweeping over him. "Too damn fast," he mumbled as he passed out in the arms of his friend.

Chapter 16
The Trial

Back at headquarters, breakfast over, the colonel and Lieutenant Murdock lingered over the last of their coffee.

"You were saying, Colonel, that the man with your head scout—his name is Jace Randall—is a friend of Monty's?" questioned the lieutenant.

"I didn't say that," the colonel hedged the question. "He was with Monty when your brigade was spotted on the other side of the river. They both verified the Apache attack shaping up and rode in to report it."

"I understand one of our old enemies, Strom, will no longer bother us, thanks to Mr. Randall."

"How so?" The lieutenant leaned forward in his chair.

"Killed him in a gunfight back in the mountains." The colonel motioned to the orderly to hand the cigars to his compatriot, then selected one for himself. Passing it under his nose, he tested its aroma and bit off the end, leaning forward to offer a light to his guest before lighting his own. "Why, Lieutenant, you interested in the man?"

The lieutenant settled back in his chair. "I request you place him under arrest immediately."

"Under arrest!" Why in heaven's name?" The colonel had his cigar clenched in his teeth as he suddenly stood up in bewilderment. "What charge?"

"Orders from Headquarters—both the army and ranger services have been searching the countryside for this man. It's a long story, Colonel, and I'm bushed—haven't slept for two nights. But this much I know, the rangers reported that Major Tom Sterling, army intelligence, who was close to divulging some big cover-up, having to do with the theft of army guns is dead. That outlaw, if he is Randall, was reported to have been talking to Sterling the day before his death. Oh! I'm sure you'll have no trouble charging him if you'll take the time to open those sealed orders on your desk. Now, if you'll excuse me." The lieutenant rose, placing his napkin beside his plate with precise care. "I'll leave the matter in your capable hands, Colonel." He couldn't resist tempting the colonel. "You might even get a citation for merely handling the matter according to army regulations." The lieutenant saluted, then followed an orderly to his quarters, where he could be heard rummaging about, getting ready for bed.

His confidence shaken by the lieutenant's claims, the colonel busied himself with reading his orders with fervent interest. The instructions contained were lacking specific charges, but stressed the detention of and, if necessary, the arrest of one Jace Randall, gunfighter for the death of Colonel Sterling. In addition, he was wanted for questioning in the disappearance of Daniel Morgan, also a fugitive from justice. Further details were vague and uninformative.

"What the hell?" The colonel tossed the document angrily on the desk. " I'll never know why that mealy-mouthed lieutenant doesn't know it's their job to capture bad men—not an army post out in some God-forsaken country. I wish the general was back—he sure picked a helluva time to go east."

"Now Colonel," the orderly said, as he returned. "Watch your blood pressure. You know what the doctor said—you're not to get excited."

"The doctor be damned—that old crocker." The colonel's face turned red as he raged at his aide, "Get the hell out of here! No! Wait! Find that no-good scout Monty and tell him to get in here on the double." He flopped into a chair, mopping his perspiring face, and continued. "And stop fussing around me like you're my mother. You're worse than that old sawbones ever was—vamoose!"

The door banged behind the orderly as he dashed out in pursuit of the head scout.

"Doesn't anybody around here ever just close a door?" grumbled the colonel. "I'll have that tin soldier Murdock's scalp—someday." He straightened his tunic.

"Strange about Randall turning up here—at the fort—just about this time," he mused and reached for a fresh cigar.

Sick bay was especially quiet for the time of day that Dan Morgan regained consciousness to find himself in a strange bed in a still stranger place. The strong smell of medicine, mostly liniment, pervaded the whitewashed room amidst the unnatural hush, except for the bark of a drill sergeant carrying through to the open window. He turned his head slightly to see a row of beds next to his empty and neatly made up, each with its own washstand, washbowl, and pitcher.

For a moment he lay still, then raised himself on his elbows, quickly falling back on the pillow when a sharp pain shot through his body. His head was pulsing. Gingerly he felt the bandage strapped about his chest. Ignoring his discomfort, he managed to stand up to reach for the water pitcher. A sudden and inexplicable thirst consumed him as he got the pitcher to his lips, and he enjoyed a deep, long drink, oblivious to the overflow running down his chest.

Suddenly, a professional-looking man in a white coat came into the room and took the water from him. As he placed the pitcher on the stand, the man's voice was authoritative and firm. "Back in bed for you, young man. You're not well enough to get out of bed yet."

"Who are you?" Dan made a feeble effort to defy him but soon realized the wisdom of taking what sounded like good advice.

"I'm the doctor at this post," the man said, shaking down a thermometer. He looked hard at his patient as he inserted the tube between his lips.

"I don't blame you for being wary. That was quite a jolt you took. Luckily the slug struck a rib, or you wouldn't be here to talk about it. That egg on your head is another story. Must have some headache—but a little rest, maybe a week or so, and you'll be up and around. Meanwhile, no more talk." The doctor's brisk tone quelled further conversation as he reached for Dan's wrist to take his pulse.

"Hm," he said releasing his hold and withdrawing the thermometer from his patient's lips. "Hm," he said again, slipping the glass tube into his breast pocket. "I'll look in on you in an hour or so. And stop guzzling water—you understand?" His eyes twinkled. "You're a lucky man, Randall—a very lucky man."

Just then the door opened, and Dan saw a lanky, bewhiskered individual stick his head through the doorway.

"How is he doing? Doc?" Monty held the door ajar to let

the doctor pass.

"He'll live, if that's what you're driving at. He's pretty lucky—bullet bounced off him like a stone wall. But he does have a bad cut on his head. He's been dealing with a bad headache and seems a bit dazed. Must have fallen at some point." He added, "Not too long now—he's gotta get some rest, you know!"

The scout nodded, ignoring the doctor's admonition as he scraped a chair up alongside Dan's bed and settled himself.

"Wal Randall! I gotta say yu shore can handle a six-gun—yu catched that guy snooping around and got him with one shot plumb dead center."

Dan stared at his visitor, a perplexed look on his face.

"Wal! Cat's get your tongue or er you jest not talkin'? By the way, Jace, the general got in last night jest after everything went down. He's got your gun and stuff. Sez he wants to see yu when yu get outa bed."

"I don't know who you are or what you're talking about. The last thing I remember is being lost in the desert and passing out," responded Dan.

"Wal! I don't know nothin' about that; but that bullet in your ribs and that fall musta knocked everything outa you cause you shore are talkin' crazy." Monty stood up. "Maybe I oughta call Doc."

"Wait," Dan struggled to sit up. "How did I get here? Tell me, and maybe then I will start to remember."

Monty looked at him, suddenly aware that the man was confused. Further questioning convinced him that his getting shot and falling had done more than knock him out.

"I'm Monty," he said simply. "Don't you recollect the fight yesterday back at the woodshed? It shore whar a corker."

"Is that how I got here?" Dan asked.

"Thet's how you got here," the scout rose. "I'll see you later when you got some sense back." He rose and closed the door behind him.

Dan heard him talking to someone outside the door for a moment, then the voices died away as the footsteps receded.

Dan tried to reconstruct his thoughts. Some things just didn't make sense—no sense at all. Lying on his back, staring at the ceiling, he did remember the gunfight at Lamesa, catching a bullet in his left shoulder and quite vividly wandering about the badlands. His horse—the big black—he remembered her, too. He made a mental note. He would ask Monty about his horse.

He began to consider what Monty had told him. He had no recall of the gunfight yesterday, but there was a wound in his side and a big lump on his head.

Accepting the memory gap, he came to the frustrating conclusion that there was a time lapse between the healed shoulder wound and the recent one on his side.

He shifted his weight to his right side to ease the dull pain in his body. His head throbbed, and he couldn't think clearly. Nothing seemed to add up. Maybe tomorrow he could fill in the gaps. In the meantime, his body needed rest. He closed his eyes, and gradually his headache abated, as he fell asleep.

The ensuing days of convalescence dragged slowly under the watchful eye of the doctor and the periodic visits from the army scout.

The general himself, a tall, gangly, white-haired man with a cadaverous sunken face, had stopped in to specifically read the charge against him and advised him he was under military arrest. He was being accused of the murder of one Major Thomas Sterling of the United States Army and was told that court would convene at the fort as soon as the doctor determined he was well enough to stand trial.

Several days later, his rib was sufficiently healed under a light bandage, and he was transferred to the jailhouse. In the interim, however, he continued to receive periodic visits from Monty, which seldom presented a problem to the guard. His bribes of whiskey made it easy for him to be granted a modicum of privacy. Monty told Dan that a man known as Pete Jukes was restricted to the fort as a material witness to the shooting. He asserted that he could prove Jace Randall had bushwhacked Major Sterling. He had volunteered the information only after the death of his companion Reagan at the hands of the gunfighter Jace Randall.

The days awaiting trial dragged on; the morning of it came all too soon. The first light of day crept steadily through the barred jail window. Stretching, Dan could see the somber hills rising beyond the fortification walls and watched the shadows jumping up and down in the morning light.

Indeed, on this clear, warm day, the Indian threat seemed trivial.

Inside the fort things were beginning to stir. The hubbub of excitement, despite the colonel's demand for orderliness, did nothing to allay Dan's apprehension.

It was shortly after breakfast that the order for the prisoner came, and Dan was escorted, under guard, to the mess hall, where the courtroom trial would be held. As he entered, his hands unencumbered possibly in deference to his injury, he was escorted to a table stationed off to the left of the judge's bench that served the prosecution. A chair placed in front of the bench between the prosecution and the defense counsel completed the arrangement. The remaining seats were for spectators in the rear. A voice loudly spoke out, "They shore went by the book."

Shortly thereafter, the attorneys walked in to take their respective places, and Dan was surprised when Lieutenant Murdock came over to sit by his side. Positioning a sheath of papers on the table before him, he meticulously lined up several sharpened pencils and turned to Dan.

"Mr. Randall," he said. "I am Lieutenant Murdock, and I have been directed to represent you at this trial. I expect you to tell the truth and always the truth. Do we understand each other?"

Dan studied the lieutenant's face for a moment, taking in his well-groomed look, his directness, and his impersonal mien. The prisoner shrugged his shoulders. "I do," he said, helpless to say otherwise under the circumstances, and leaned back in his chair. He instantly rose with everyone else in court as the judges, three of them, entered to take their places on the bench. One was General Warburton, the commandant; the second was the Colonel Watts; and the last one was Ranger Jay Smith, a man he hadn't seen before.

The general banged on the table. "This military court will come to order," he said and nodded to the court clerk. "Read the charges. Will the prisoner please stand."

The court was extremely silent as Dan Morgan stood in stunned silence listening to the appointed clerk intone the crime that he, the prisoner, was charged with the premeditated murder of one Major Thomas Sterling of army intelligence, in or about Monument, a remote border settlement in the Territory of New Mexico.

To Dan, the trial was a farce from every conceivable angle. The only option for his attorney was to make an immediate motion for dismissal of the charges on the grounds that a military court had no jurisdiction over a civilian. Unfortunately, the third man on the bench represented the Texas Rangers—a nonmilitary organization—and under these circumstances, the court had no alternative but to deny the motion.

The prisoner, bewildered by this spectacle of court procedure, quickly realized he could offer no rebuttal as the evidence against him mounted.

The first witness called by the prosecution was Pete Jukes, of uncertain address, who testified he knew the defendant, Jace Randall. He identified the prisoner as such, stating he had run into him in a settlement called Monument, a small buffalo trading post, and that Randall had stayed overnight at Sterling's house. He had heard a shot before dawn the next morning and seen the gunfighter gallop out of town. On investigation, he stated, he had found the major dead in the corral behind his house—shot in the back. He went on to say that while the sheriff was getting a posse together, some servant girl from Sterling's house had followed the outlaw on the major's own horse. The posse, according to testimony, had caught up with the girl near Chimney Rock, but had been driven off by Randall's fire. He concluded by saying that Randall and the girl had ridden away together.

Mr. Jukes was asked to rise from his chair to answer a question from the prosecution as to how he had been able to identify the defendant. He stated that Jace Randall had a black horse with white markings, and he would never forget the horse. He knew that because he and his brother Luke, along with Red Reagan, had gotten to know him when they'd shared a drink together at a saloon in Monument. He testified that Randall and his friend Reagan had got into a fight when Randall had threatened him before leaving town. "He was wearing that army jacket," he said, pointing to the blue tunic crumpled on the prosecutor's desk.

"Looks as though Major Sterling put up quite a fight," the prosecutor stated declaratively, augmenting his remarks by holding the tattered jacket up for all to see. He requested permission from the court to place the apparel in evidence.

"Your witness, Lieutenant," he said, walking back to his table.

Murdock, leaning over, whispered something to his client. Then he straightened up. "No questions," he said, staring abstractly at the sharpened end of his pencil.

Dan Morgan, listening to the army scout's testimony, sat shaken by the masquerade playing out before him, trying to convince himself that he would shortly awaken and find this all to be a bad dream. He looked at Murdock making notes on a pad. He certainly looked real enough. Dan tried to calm himself by reflecting about his home. He pictured himself riding through the gates at the ranch and his family all waiting for him with open arms. The pleasant fantasy had lasted only a few seconds when his attention turned back to the drama that was unfolding before him.

Monty Hayes was called to testify by the prosecution. He stated that he'd met the defendant while fighting his way clear of an Apache attack back in the mountains. The prisoner had killed a renegade named Strom, and in their subsequent race for freedom, he'd been forced to seek refuge in an old mission. He informed the court, making quite a point of it, too, that the army jacket in question was one he had been given by the padre. Jace had been glad to have it because it was cold in the mountain passes, and the defendant had had no heavy coat of his own. He failed to explain the fact that a woman had left the jacket with the padre and directed that it should be returned to Army Headquarters, as he did not want to further incriminate his friend, especially since he was unsure about the circumstances of the situation. He ended his testimony saying that he had been talking with the colonel. During their conversation, he said he'd heard the shots that had prompted him to race across the compound to catch the wounded gunman as he fell. But he'd been too late. The defendant had hit the ground before he'd got there.

"Is this the army regulation jacket that was given to the defendant?" Murdock was holding the garment aloft.

"Hit shore air, I c'n tell it by—them epaulets that ain't thar," he said, squirming, glancing at the bench.

The prosecution, on redirect, seeking to discredit the scout's testimony, handed an army carbine to the scout. "You did see the prisoner with this in his possession back in the mountains, didn't you?"

"Yes!" admitted the scout. "Can't say for proper if thet's the one. Gotta say though, it was one of them toy pop guns the army is using—that's for shore."

"If you didn't give it to him as you claimed, isn't it safe to say it could be the gun owned by Major Sterling, and if so, couldn't you also be mistaken about the army jacket?"

Before the scout could answer, the prosecutor turned quickly. "You needn't answer that question, Mr. Hayes," he said. "I'm through with this witness, your honor."

From that point on, the prosecutor began to cast doubt on the veracity of the scout's account of the army jacket, as he proceeded to present damning evidence. He called the court's attention to the fact that the courier working as a messenger for the army had never arrived. In addition, Major Sterling had been found shot in the back. Jace Randall had deliberately picked a quarrel with Red Reagan, a friend of Pete Jukes, and killed him to prevent him from talking. Mr. Reagan was from the settlement where Major Sterling had been found slain.

The prosecutor, now in his glory, moved on with consummate skill. He held up the Colt forty-four, advancing to the table where the Spencer and army jacket lay.

"One last piece of evidence, your honor," he said, waving the six-gun in the air. "The defendant's initials are scratched on the butt of this six-gun. It was found on the prisoner and establishes his identity. It is beyond the shadow of a doubt that he is the infamous gunman and killer Jace Randall. Furthermore, the direct testimony of Mr. Jukes, freely given in the interest of justice, coupled with the subterfuge of no memory on the prisoner's part, proves the defendant guilty as charged." He closed over the defense's objection, returning to his table with a smug look on his face. He made no objection to the defense counsel's request for more time to prepare an adequate rebuttal to his accusations.

The tribunal, after conferring amongst themselves, granted Murdock's time to prepare a defense and agreed to recess eight o'clock the following morning, stating that witnesses for the defense could then be heard. All rose while the judges filed out, and shortly thereafter, the prisoner was led back to his cell for the night.

After supper was over and the lights went out in the barracks, Monty, having bribed the guard with his usual pint of whiskey, met with his friend Randall once more. With Monty standing on a rusted wheelbarrow beneath the cell window, the two men talked in low tones. Occasionally the scout checked with the guard to reassure him his supply of whiskey was limitless.

"Monty," the prisoner motioned the scout closer, until the scout's face was pressed against the bars. "It looked bad for me in there today, and the thing that worries me is that I don't remember a damn thing of what they're talking about—my mind's a complete blank. The doctor only half believes me when I say I can't remember killing Reagan—or even getting shot. Murdock wants to put me on the stand tomorrow—says it's my only chance, and if I can't think of something by then, I could be swinging on the gallows come sunup day after tomorrow. They are already building a scaffold," Dan stated nervously.

"Jace," the scout butted in. "Don't you recollect meeting the Padre at the mission—or what you was looking' fur in the blue army jacket he handed over to me? What about the Indian girl you saved on the trail or your encounter with her?"

"Sorry, Monty, the last thing I can remember is being lost in the badlands near Mustang Draw—the next thing I knew I was here in the hospital."

"Randall, Mustang Draw's in Texas hundreds of miles away—u ever think o' that?" Dan saw a shadow of disbelief flit across the scout's face.

"Well! I can see talking isn't going to help me now, but you are the only friend I have here, and I want you to listen to me—I'm not Jace Randall the outlaw. My name is Dan Morgan from Sweetwater, Texas. My father is John Morgan, who owns the Boxed M ranch there. My mother is dead, but I have a sister, Elizabeth, who knows I'm not a murderer." He continued, "I got into a scrap back in my hometown, and I had to run for it. The outlaw Jace Randall got killed helping me, and I buried him on the trail. That's how I got his gun and his horse. Someone mistook me for him in one of the towns, and I caught a bullet running. Look." Dan pulled back his shirt and pointed to the whitish mark on his left shoulder. "See," he said, "there is the scar."

Monty stared at the white crescent on his friend's shoulder, and for the first time, Dan saw that he believed him.

"You want me to let your folks know if you don't make it, right?" he asked, spitting to the side.

"Right," Dan nodded. "I'd sure appreciate it. I'll even write a letter you can mail to Clay Elkins, the ranch foreman."

"Who?!" Monty's attention picked up suddenly.

"Clay Elkins at the Boxed M—you're not listening, Monty."

"You did say Clay Elkins, didn't you?"

"I did," Dan said dryly, a wry smile on his lips. "Clay Elkins," he reiterated.

"That's what I done heard you say—write me that letter."

"Get me a pencil and paper, and you will have it in an hour."

Monty Hayes was not, by the widest stretch of the imagination, schooled in even the most primitive legal hocus-pocus, but no one could deny his tenaciousness once he had latched on to an idea, especially one that might benefit a friend—and this time he had a good one. Wasting no time, he tapped on Lieutenant Murdock's window and asked to borrow a pencil and paper so someone could write a letter. Murdock's ears perked up when he learned that his client was to be the recipient.

"I'd like to see that letter when you get it," he said, handing the writing material through the open window.

"Yu shore will, Lieutenant. I guarantee you have it in less-en' an hour."

I wonder what that damn fool is up to now? The officer returned to his reading. *I guess it takes all kinds.* He reached for a cigar. "This smoke is good for an hour," he remarked aloud, his brandy at his elbow. "If that interfering knot head's not back by then, I'll be in the hay."

The cigar was long since smoked and the whiskey well down in the bottle when the muffled knock sounded on his windowpane. He pulled up the window to admit the scout.

"That the letter?" he asked as the scout cleared the sill.

"Yep! And look at the name on it—Clay Elkins. That much I kin read—an I brung this," affirmed Monty. He unrolled a bundle from under his arm and draped it over the back of Murdock's chair. "I ducked into the mess hall and picked up the army jacket," Monty said guiltily. "Nobody seed me."

"What on earth for?" questioned Murdock. "We could both get shot for this!" Murdock raised his voice as he snatched the tunic up. "Get this back at once," he said, placing the uniform into Monty's arms.

"Hold on thar, Lieutenant. I got me a hunch, and that jacket ain't going' back till I am good and ready—so simmer down." The scout quickly stepped through the window and drew the blinds. "I think we need to search inside of the jacket. Now let's git on wif it," he added.

A moment later, the very proper lieutenant, for whom protocol was a way of life, was huddled over the contents of another man's personal mail, reading it aloud for the scout to hear. Throughout the long night, the two men talked, one a hard-headed, tobacco-chewing, rough-cut plainsman and the other a arrogant soldier, molded by military training.

When the two men disagreed, they shook their heads emphatically—each time more vehemently than the last—until they came to an agreement. It was a weary lieutenant and a still adamant scout that finally blew out the oil lamp at dawn when they parted company.

Chapter 17
A Legend's Clout

Dan spent a sleepless night, overwhelmed by the magnitude of the army's carefully prepared case against him. The testimony of the camp physician that the prisoner exhibited symptoms of amnesia had been ruled out as insubstantial and irrelevant. He knew he had given Lieutenant Murdock nothing to go on and read the look of defeat in the lieutenant's face when his motion for a dismissal was denied. He turned in his cot restlessly and was just starting to doze off when the call came for breakfast.

The second day of the trial moved swiftly. The court convened at the appointed hour, and the crowded room was noisy as the trial got underway. The defense's request for clarification of some of the previous day's testimony was nothing out of the ordinary, but when it pressed for cross-examination of the prosecution's star witness, it became apparent something was up. Peter Jukes was recalled to the stand and subjected to such a verbal barrage that only constant objections from the prosecution preserved the integrity of Juke's testimony. In short, the lieutenant-attorney's style of defense took a whole new direction.

"Your honor," Murdock addressed the court. "I am going to put my client on the stand. If he is to have a chance, he will have to testify on his own behalf." He turned to the prisoner. "Take the stand, Dan," he said. "It can only help."

Dan stared at the lieutenant. It was the first time Murdock had addressed him using his real name.

A voice sounded in his ear. It was Monty. "Don't give up on Murdock yet, Dan; he is a stubborn jackass until he has something to latch onto...and he has got it in his hand."

"You may take the stand, Randall," the middle judge instructed the prisoner. "Let it be understood that it is of your own volition—even though it is on advice of counsel."

Dan rose and took his place in the witness chair, glancing at Murdock, who nodded reassuringly.

Ten minutes later, everyone, including the prosecutor knew something big was about to happen. Having put his client on the stand, Murdock worked vigorously, tearing away at the fabric of the prosecution's case. The first question raised to the accused was a surprise.

"What is your name and where do you live?" The answer came promptly and without pause. "My name is Dan Morgan, and my home is the Boxed M ranch in Sweetwater, Texas."

The judge raised his gavel to quell the murmur from the rear. "I'll have no more noise in this courtroom!" he said, rapping sharply, eyeing the offenders among the spectators. "One more outburst and this courtroom will be cleared. You may proceed, lieutenant, but may I ask what you hope to prove by this line of questioning?"

"That the man on the witness stand is not the outlaw Jace Randall and could not be guilty of the charges against him." he stated with certainty. Instantly the prosecutor was on his feet. He had willfully built his entire case on the premise that the defendant was indeed the famous outlaw Jace Randall, and it was unthinkable for the defense to declare that they were trying the wrong man.

"Your honor." He reiterated, "Your honor."

"Mr. Prosecutor," the judge interrupted the objection that was in the offing. Turning to Dan, he said, "I remind you that you are still under oath. Will you tell the court in your own words what you can recall of your activities between the time you left your home and now? Speak up, Mr. Morgan."

A hush fell on the courtroom as Dan started to speak. Cautioned by his counsel of the gravity of the charges lodged against him, he recounted the affair at the Silver Dollar in Sweetwater, the death of the fatally shot outlaw Jace Randall, his burial, and Dan's attempt to delude his pursuers by masquerading under the name of the famous gunfighter. He told of his gunfight in Lamesa and the subsequent wound to his shoulder. His narration closed on the last incident he remembered: being lost in the desert wastelands near Mustang Draw.

"You remember nothing more? You never knew or saw the army officer of whose murder you are accused?"

"Sir, my memory is blurry since I was shot. I don't even remember meeting your army scout in the backcountry or the man I killed named Strom. Again, I can only say, if you have any doubt as to my identity, I suggest you contact my father at our ranch in Texas. If he isn't there, you can talk to Clay Elkins, our ranch foreman, or my sister."

Suddenly the room was electric. Calling for quiet, the tribunal whispered among themselves. General Warburton rose.

"Lieutenant," he said, "the court would like to ask the prisoner a question."

"By all means your honor," said the lieutenant, stepping aside.

"Mr. Morgan, you just said something interesting to this court. You mentioned the name of a Clay Elkins. Would that be the former Major James C. Elkins of the United States Army?"

"I wouldn't know about that, your honor," Dan addressed the general. "He's a cowboy my father hired short of a half dozen years ago."

The silence in the courtroom held. One could have heard a pin drop as the judge put another question to the witness, waving back the prosecution, who was about to say something.

"Objection overruled, Major," he said, turning again to the witness. "Before you go on, can you prove the existence of such a person?"

Lieutenant Murdock approached the bench and addressed the court.

"I have here a letter addressed to him at the Boxed M ranch in Sweetwater, Texas, your honor," he said, holding Dan's farewell letter to his people.

"May I see that, Lieutenant?" The general took the letter. The judges whispered for a few moments, examining the letter while the courtroom awaited some explanation.

"Your honor," Murdock walked briskly to the bench. "May I suggest a conference in your chambers? I have a concern for the security of the material about to be further divulged and the irreparable harm our additional evidence would do to the United States government if it were revealed in public."

The gavel came down sharply. "This court stands adjourned for one hour," ruled the judge, instructing counsel and the prosecution to come along with the defendant to his chambers.

Realizing the damage done to the prosecution's case, Murdock gathered up the army jacket—replaced by the scout early that morning—and motioned to the defendant to follow him across the parade grounds into the general's office. Once inside, he lost no time in advancing his case with the one thing he had been holding in since his session with the army scout the night before.

"With such understanding, that you will be expected to demonstrate the relevance of this new material, you may present your evidence, Mr. Counselor."

The lieutenant had the floor. "It's here in this jacket, your honor. While the defense never did admit that the army jacket was the property of the defendant, we do so now. And in doing so, agree with the prosecution that Dan Morgan, alias Jace Randall, did know Major Sterling and in truth did communicate with him in the settlement of Monument, where the major was shot and killed. We, however, deny emphatically that he, the defendant, is guilty, and we will prove, beyond a shadow of a doubt, his innocence of the charges of murder alleged against him."

"Your honor," the prosecutor rose from his chair. "I must object to this unorthodox procedure insomuch as this is now a part of an inquiry and not a fully constituted court of law, to use your very own words, General."

"Your objection is well taken." The General's face clouded. "Lieutenant," he said pointing to the army jacket, "this is and still remains a matter for the due process of the court when it reconvenes."

But the lieutenant would not yield. "You granted me permission to speak, your honor and at the risk of revealing confidential army matters in court, I insist this board of inquiry hear me out here and now." The defense counsel walked over and put the blue jacket in the general's hand.

"I discovered this quite by accident," he said, probing a small opening in the frayed collar and withdrawing a thick, folded length of paper from between the stiffened layers of fabric. "I am sure when you read it, you will understand why I could not, in good conscience, reveal this new evidence in court."

"I warn you, Lieutenant—" The general cut him off as the lieutenant unfolded the mildewed paper and handed it to the commandant.

"I will withdraw my objection," the prosecutor said over his shoulder at Murdock. "Any new evidence that gets to the truth of this matter is welcomed," he added haltingly.

All eyes were on the general, who was carefully unfolding the sharp creases that threatened to tear as he examined the paper. His eyes swept across the page for a brief second and then he looked up at his audience.

"Everyone is dismissed from this meeting until the court is reconvened. That is, except for my fellow judges and Mr. Morgan. Both counsels will leave also. Lieutenant, you are invoked to silence in this matter until further notice."

Dan Morgan, as astonished as everyone else, looked on in disbelief as the room emptied, leaving him alone in the room with the judges.

"I assume you know what's in this letter, Mr. Morgan," the general said, waving the paper in front of him.

"I am having trouble remembering details, General," confessed Dan. "I can't explain this to you."

"Well! Under the promise of secrecy, I will tell you it is a note supposedly entrusted by Major Sterling to a gunman posing as Jace Randall, the outlaw. It states you agreed to act as a guard to protect the life of our courier, John Walkingstick, who was supposedly carrying dispatches to the commandant here, which carried the name of the army traitor who was working with a gang below the border, supplying guns to the Indians. The note goes on to say that Major Sterling was aware you were not Randall, but he had to trust you." General Warburton, who was still having difficulty believing in Dan's innocence, stopped reading and turned to the defendant.

"This note does not exonerate you completely. There is an eyewitness claiming you are the one who killed Major Sterling." He continued, "The court is adjourned until it has had time to go over your case and consider this new evidence. At that time your verdict will be announced, but don't feel too lucky. You are still responsible for a murder, regardless of whether you remember it or not."

Chapter 18
Closure

The wagon master was having a rough time of it. It was not his best day. "Maybe," he was saying to his side kick, Swamper, who he'd hired to help bring the wagon train safely through the trail to a new settlement in the West, "I've just gotten too dang old for this kind of business." He gnawed at a hunk of chew. Now everyone was able to notice the space between his teeth that had resulted from his nasty tobacco habits.

"Well, boss, dunno what you'r so hung up about. They's a blacksmith at the fort an we can get that wheel fixed while were thar." An afterthought struck him. "That's if them pesky redskins don't pop up in front of our noises before we make it." The wagon lurched as it went over a rock, and the driver braced himself. "Next trip I think I'll just stay in Juarez an' shack up with one o' those senoritas—just take it easy for a spell," said Clyde. The wagon gave another lurch. "Goddamn ruts!" His whip sailed out with a loud snap over the heads of the lead animals even as his foot rode the brake, just in case. His partner rose from beside the driver and shifted from the buckboard of the prairie schooner into the saddle of his palomino as he quickly grabbed the reins to keep himself from falling.

"Goin' to have a look see." Swamper spit copiously. "Can't be far now." He rode away quickly to check out the trail ahead, having lots on his mind, including the eternal grumbling of his friend and escort Clyde, who had relieved him of driving the team. As he rode, he spoke to himself out loud, "Figger we'll make the fort tomorrow lessen we get held up." His brow furrowed as he blinked into the distance before swiveling about in the saddle to wave the lead coach on.

Swamper, answering to a name pinned on him years ago when he'd accidently fallen into a swamp at a logging camp, had a heart as big as all outdoors. He was looking forward to his stopover at the fort. Well into the wrong side of sixty, the years had failed to dampen his bright, effervescent spirit. His life had become an open book to everyone who had come to know him. Most everyone loved his down-to-earth and fun mannerisms. His established friendships were countless. Notwithstanding the rigors and hardship of his calling, he lived his life in the sun and like the mountains about him, endured. A stop at the fort gave him a chance to refurbish his personal supplies from the army store. In addition, there was usually a slew of immigrants waiting to join his wagon train in an effort to keep themselves safe from the outlaws that threatened their freedom this side of the mountain flats. The extra money he made always came in handy when stocking up for his return trip.

He looked back at the wagons some distance behind him. He stepped down to tighten the cinches while taking a moment more to rub the circulation into the seat of his pants before getting back into the saddle.

It was high noon the next day when the wagons hailed at the fort, and a heavy timber gate swung wide open on the twang of a high nasal voice inviting them through.

Once inside, Swamper patiently waited for the wagons to clear the gates before seeking out his friend, the commandant.

Almost immediately, he spotted General Warburton coming down the steps from headquarters and hurried to meet him.

"Well, Swamper, welcome! It's been a long time. Things are good with you, from the looks of the people with you. Come on in an' tell me all about those streets in California paved with gold," he said, his chuckle obvious.

Swamper winced. He never would get used to being ribbed by his longtime friend, but he was always graciously pleased when the two of them met.

"Who you hanging this time, General?" They were on their way to headquarters and both stopped to watch an army of men swarming over a scaffold, their saws and hammers almost drowning out his words.

"An outlaw convicted of murdering an army intelligence officer by the name of Major Sterling back in Monument. Think I have him dead center guilty. A man who saw him do it showed up to testify as an eyewitness. In fact, the man is over there, just riding out now—fellow named Jukes, the one with the black horse." The general purposely left out the information that had recently been presented on behalf of the defendant.

A look of surprise grew on Swamper's face as he stood staring at the commandant, who was standing aside so his guest could pass by. "General." The wagon train boss hadn't moved. "You could be hanging the wrong man!" he said softly, unsure of his right to suggest such a thing, yet forthright enough to blurt out a personal conviction if need be.

The general's jaw dropped as he stammered for words, not sure if he was subject to some joke or errant message. Whether his reaction stemmed from the effrontery of the bland statement or the esteem he had for an old friend seemed of little consequence.

"You're joking of course, Swamper. For a minute I thought you were serious."

"Not by a damn sight, I'm not, General—unless the news I heard when I checked into the last ranger headquarters is a lie. They claim they got a confession from the murderer, and the case is closed."

"You are saying the rangers found the man who confessed to the murder of Major Sterling?" The general's face whitened, the seriousness of the disclosure seemingly affecting his composure.

"You all right, General?" Swamper reached to steady the general, but the commandant, recovering his composure, waved off the overture, taking command. "Tell me what happened, Swamper, and all you know."

"Well, I learned a fellow named Luke Jukes was picked up by the rangers wandering in the desert. He got bit trying to kill a bull rattler with his bare hands after his horse throwed him. He was jest walking around in circles, mumbling something about a black mare he was promised if he killed an outlaw back in Monument, but he had bushwacked the army officer instead by mistake. The man, Red Reagan, who had promised him the black horse had told him he could still have the mare but had to earn it by killing the outlaw. With the help of some other evidence, the ranger was able to piece the story together. He learned that the mountain man had failed to kill the outlaw in a personal grudge fight. That's when he'd decided to find the mare for himself and take it, but he never did get it."

"Did you find out the name of the outlaw he was supposed to kill? Hurry, man, its important."

"Yep! The outlaw's name was Jace Randall, but a funny thing about that, General: the rangers said that wasn't possible. Randall was dead and buried in Texas some time ago. His body had been discovered by two men who were looking for another man by the name of Dan Morgan. Apparently, Jim Clay Elkins, recently sworn in a second time for the army, provided verification of the fact that Dan Morgan, who he had resided with for the past five years, had been assuming the identity of Jace Randall after finding the outlaw fatally shot." Swamper continued to explain the circumstances of Dan Morgan's run-in with the Jukes brothers and Red Reagan.

"My God!" The general shouted for his orderly. "We almost hanged the wrong man." His voice trembled out of control as the orderly saluted. "Get me Murdock, and don't stand there like a damned fool! Scat!"

Dan Morgan was pacing back and forth the length of his cell, tormented by the oppressive heat that riddled the jail house. He sensed something was up when work on the gallows halted. He hardly dared to perceive the glimmer of hope that crept into his soul when he saw Monty whip past his cell window and cut through the open gates as though all hell was at his heels.

Two days later a grinning army scout returned with a memorandum sent and signed by Captain Trent and General Warburton informing the defendant that the murder of the army intelligence officer Major Thomas Sterling had been solved with the confession and subsequent mysterious death of one Luke Jukes from parts unknown. His body had been buried in a field on the outskirts of the village. The notice of his death was on file. No one to date had come forth to inquire about him. A note was also written regarding Dan Morgan— whose name had been mentioned by the scouts—saying that he was not wanted by the law and was advised to return to his family in Texas, who missed him.

Murdock was the first to advise Dan of his freedom and apologized for what he termed as "official blockheadedness red tape" for which no one could be held responsible.

Morning came and before Dan knew it, he was sitting in court one last time, with all the bystanders waiting to hear the verdict.

The general asked the prisoner to stand. Dan eagerly got up from his chair to await his judgement.

The general read to the court the following statement. "We find the defendant Dan Morgan to be *not guilty* for the murder of one Major Sterling of the United States Army. This court is adjourned!"

Relief spread over Dan Morgan's face.

"General," he spoke up, "I am mighty glad to hear that, but one thing puzzles me. How did you make the decision to keep me from hanging?"

"Was it the note from Sterling? Is that what changed your mind?"

The general replied, "Sterling's note did have an effect, but you can thank a man named Swamper, who was able to explain your innocence. His story was backed up by firm evidence that your good friend Monty was able to obtain so that your life could be spared."

"What happened to the shoulder braids, or whoever sewed the letter into the collar so neatly, no one knows. It's one of the things no one can understand," stated the general.

It was during the lull of early evening that Dan went to thank Lieutenant Murdock for his forthrightness and counsel on his behalf. He found the officer and Monty together, having a nip.

"We were lucky," the lieutenant said, smoothing his hair before the cracked mirror in his room. "We probably would not have made it if it hadn't been for this darned excuse of a scout, Monty, here. He got downright rude when he insisted you had searched the army jacket for something you couldn't find back there at the mission, and he threatened to have me court marshaled if I did not search the jacket myself. I will confess I wasn't sold on your innocence until I heard the general's story that he'd heard from his old friend Swamper. You can thank him if you like. He is hanging around for the night so he can get some rest before he ventures out tomorrow with his wagon train. If you look to the west side of the fort, you can't miss him. The old coot is always making food for his buddies before settling for the night."

"Haven't any more time to discuss it now. Maybe Monty can fill you in. I gotta admire that rascal. He got the guts to take a chance. He's a know-it-all around here; ask him." Murdock straightened his collar, taking a last glance at himself in the mirror. "Damned handsome," he said, a twinkle in his eye. "Too bad there aren't any young ladies around to appreciate me. Lock up when you leave, men," he added from the door. "They'll steal a man blind around here."

"Let's go! bottle's jest about empty—an I ain't ate for a long time," Monty said, rising.

As the two men walked across the grounds, Dan turned to the scout, a serious look on his face. "What do you know about Clay Elkins? Everybody seems so fascinated every time his name comes up."

"Yeh, about that; he used to be a special agent working for the army, very well respected for helping get rid of a famous gang. Wouldn't be surprised if he wasn't out looking for you. That's all I know, amigo, and a man can't know less than that." He spit his chew into his hand and flung it aside. "Yu free. Ain't that enough for you?"

"Well, tell me this," Morgan insisted. "How do you suppose that note from Sterling got into the collar of that army jacket?"

The plainsman stopped in his tracks for a side glance at Dan. "Wouldn't be a bit surprised if your lady friend had something to do with it." He turned to walk on. "Yu don't believe me when I tell you about that gal. Wal! Someday, maybe, you jest might recollect," he said, taking the mess hall steps two at a time. "Come on," he shouted, "let's put on the feed bag!"

It was late evening when the general stopped in to see Dan. He explained how small this big country really was and how close-knit and well-formulated the army's plans were to bring peace and security to the wagon trains that were moving West in ever-increasing numbers.

"You see, Morgan," the general said, "I did not completely reveal the contents of Major Sterling's report. However, be that as it may, I called upon you to ask a favor of you."

Relieved by the general's confidential tone, Dan relaxed, awaiting the reason for this visit.

"Morgan, I have decided to take you into my confidence," the general stated, as Dan finished rolling his weed. He leaned forward to take a light. "Truthfully, I have not much choice to do otherwise, but if Tom Sterling trusted you, I am sure I can, too."

Dan's interest peaked; the blue smoke streamed from his nostrils. He brushed the brown flakes of tobacco from his lap and waited. "One question before I divulge an extreme confidence to you. I assume, now that you are starting to gain your memory, you're going home, are you not?"

"Trying to figure out what I know and what I don't know about the things that have happened over the past few months. My hope is that soon I will get things in order, that by the way, General, includes my gun belt, I plan to leave," he replied.

Without hesitation, the general walked to the coat rack near the door where the gun belt hung and handed it to Morgan. He continued, "Sterling's message states—a part I didn't disclose—that he uncovered information about a big gang meeting in Mesilla and believed this a golden opportunity to smash the entire organization, including the higher-ups."

"Where do I fit into your plans, General?" Dan asked.

"Let me finish," the general punched out his cigarette and ground the butt into his ashtray. "Sterling's message states that this meeting will be held at the Double Eagle Bar in Mesilla the twenty-seventh of this month—and what makes it so urgent— is that there are only two weeks left in the month."

"You want me to pass the word to someone up that way, General?"

"Will you?"

"No reason why I shouldn't, General, I do owe Major Sterling something for that note that saved my life," Dan acknowledged.

The general was visibly excited and spoke hurriedly. "You are to convey a dispatch from me to the sheriff in Mesilla—this gang meeting is right under their noses—which must be delivered personally to a Captain Purdy. He will know what to do." He took a breath and looked at Dan. "The army will always appreciate what you are about to do for your country, Morgan. It could mean everything to the settlement of the West—and the end to the long list of men who are giving their lives every day for it. How soon can you leave?"

"At sunup," Dan proposed. "Gotta check out the trail with Monty, General—he'll know the best way."

"That he will—might even go part of the way with you if you'd like. Your orders, Morgan."

The general picked up a sealed envelope. "Remember," he said as he handed Dan the dispatch, "there is a lot riding on this, and it is all up to you." He extended his hand as he opened the front door for Morgan to pass.

The general stood watching Dan walk across the compound, his thoughts pragmatic. He had made his choice—if he was wrong, he'd hear about it soon enough.

Dan made his way to the west of the camp, where he spotted a large wagon train. Everyone was huddled around a fire. The men were having their evening whiskey while the women busied themselves putting their children down for the night.

Dan was able to identify Swamper, who was sitting with the men and talking loudly about his experiences on the trail.

Dan walked up to Swamper, reached out to shake his hand, and thanked him for his courage in revealing what he knew about the murder of Major Sterling and for saving his life. Swamper did not hesitate to include Dan in the evening festivities. He and Dan quickly developed a friendship as they exchanged stories about life on the trail. Swamper confided there were times that his heart would go out to someone lost on the trail with no family. Somewhat a typical story, he described a young woman that had ridden in one storm-filled night.

Swamper continued. "She came across our wagon train, fever-stricken and terrified, collapsing when she got here. Turns out she was a domestic worker. She did not disclose the name of the person she worked for but did say he was murdered. She was fearful for her own life, so she left to pursue a friend of hers who she'd found and then lost. She was chased by a gang of Indians but somehow managed to hide and stay ahead of them. After wandering for some time, she met up with a Texan, who befriended her. After a week, she said the man deserted her when he found she had the fever. She had ridden through the night until she saw our campfire blazing. The women here took care of her for many weeks until she was able to regain her strength. She managed to connect with a family of settlers who had decided to search for land somewhere in the northeast section of New Mexico and build a home for themselves."

Unsettled by the story Dan's mind flashed to a vivid memory. He pictured a woman with a ribbon in her hair, and an angry exchange, but he was unable to recall the full details of the image. Instead, he forced himself to look to the present. He soon left the wagon train, somewhat perplexed, but he knew he had to focus on his trip to Mesilla.

Dan went right to his bunk, his gun-belt slung over his shoulder, a light-hearted whistle on his lips. He packed up his gear, blanket, slicker, and essentials issued by the camp store. The doctor had given him a small can of salve to ease the occasional soreness in his side. The bandage, now removed made him more comfortable.

Monty, watching him pack, sat on his bunk. He took a mouth-full size of chew from a new plug of tobacco as he advised, "Yu ride north of here, holding along the river, and hit the hills just west of the desert peaks. Yu ride into the morning sun and head fur Mesilla, New Mexico. Them Indians might be on your tail ever' minute, so watch your scalp. General says I better ride a piece wif yu to get yu started proper."

"Glad to have you, Monty. Maybe you know a short cut."

"Ain't no such thing, Dan. It's straight north and west—ain't got no chance crossin' over them mountains. I guess I dern better go wif yu to see that yu make it—cause you jest might take a notion—"

"Now, Monty, you know you are just dying to get out of here to stretch your legs—and I sure could use the company."

The scout chewed phlegmatically for a moment.

Dan finished his packing and turned to the scout. "Thanks for the buckskin jacket, Monty," he said. "Sure you won't need it?"

"Nope!" The plainsmen rose from the bunk. "I ain't never

wore it. It's a little tu big for me—won it in a poker game from a buffalo hunter a right smart time go. Been gettin' the smell outen it ever since. Yere welcome to it— smell an' all."

Dan sniffed at his sleeve. "Amigo," he said, his attempt at humor falling somewhat short. "It still stinks like hell."

Monty opened the door. "Yu don't smell it outside," he said, walking out into the sun, "and then you can't tell iffen it's the coat or a stray skunk hereabouts."

Dan laughed.

After a long, challenging, and successful day, both men turned in early.

Sunrise, splashing high color over the sky, found the two friends making their way through the river junction above the fort and after a few days, passing through a large gap in the early morning hours.

The scout, familiar with the mountains towering over them, knew they had made good progress. After crossing the flat marshland, they held their direction between the high-rise escarpments as the day wore on.

Travel was pleasant and invigorating this bright, clear day as the men talked over the creak of saddle leather and the jingle of bridles. "To tell you the truth, Randall, the man yu was— is no longer an issue. What you are doing wipes out all charges against you." The scout gnawed at the corner of his plug, eying the country about them as he tucked what was left of his chew into his pocket.

"See something up ahead?" queried Dan, pinching out his match as he drew in the blue smoke of his cigarette.

"That man Pete coulda come this way, and I don't rightly

figure tu get a bullet from behind them trees," responded Monty.

Heeding the scout's warning, Dan rode slightly behind. He checked his six-gun, feeling somewhat defenseless without a rifle. The day passed uneventfully as they hit the high passes. There was a nip in the air they hadn't felt before, and an apron of light snow covered the bare rock ledges.

At a vantage point, the scout motioned to the level land below them and a silver course angling its way into the distance. Swatting at an insect buzzing around his horse, he said, "This is as far as I go; colonel's orders."

Dan nodded and stepped out of his saddle. Hat in hand, he wiped the sweat from his face.

"Recken you've come further than you should have at that."

Monty swung down to join him.

"Good place an' good time for coffee," he said, stretching his legs.

"Best idea you've had all day, Monty. I'll get the fire going."

"No! I'll start the fire—we don't want no extry smoke—woods air full of them Apache."

Dan got his point and started to unpack the gear.

"Yu'll find beans in my saddlebag thar, Dan."

Shortly a brisk fire crackled, wavered, and steadied into a smokeless flame. The coffee was not far behind.

After this quick break, both men said their goodbyes.

"Jest follow the river upstream. Yu'll strike the Rio Grande jest south o' a settlement of some size. From thar, yu head west as the crows flies to Mesilla, New Mexico. Yu'll cross one high butte, then yu'll be on your way. Keep yor eyes peeled, an' good luck."

The men shook hands. "Thanks, Monty, for all you've done. If it hadn't been for you..." Dan trailed off, unable to find the right words to express his gratitude.

"Wal I ain't never was tu bright, Dan, but like Murdock says, I must be part jackass to be so stubborn." He grinned and stepped into the saddle.

"I won't forget you, my friend. If you ever get to Sweetwater, Texas, look for the Boxed M ranch. You are always welcome," Dan said sincerely and touched his cap in parting. A moment later, there was stillness in the air as the scout faded into the thicket. Dan felt a profound sadness when Monty left, but he put his feelings aside because he knew he had a task to complete and then he would be finally going home.

Many days later Dan Morgan had come across what seemed to be the roof of the world. Once through the tall butte country, he was riding into the dawn, swinging through the rolling buffalo plains—heading west—always west. Light of heart, the nightmare of the past weeks behind him, he breathed deeply. As he rode closer to his destination, he began to think about his life away from home. True, there were things he couldn't remember, but as the doctor had said, it would take some time for his memory to return, and he needed to be patient. He had no regrets—no ax to grind, no lingering remorse. He thought of what the scout had said about the army jacket. Maybe he was resisting old memories. Someday, perhaps, he would go back to the old mission to revisit that part of his life. In the meantime, he had only to feel the scar on his side to recall the gunfight with Red Reagan.

Riding across the open prairie, taking the land swell in

stride, he was grateful for the gray's stamina. He shifted in the saddle to look back. The mountains appeared to be a faint gray against the blue sky, no longer menacing. He felt enveloped in the lazy afternoon when he suddenly spotted a girl atop a beautiful black horse with unusual markings of white on each leg sitting on top of the hill. The rider had long black hair. She was holding her hand over her brow and looking straight down at him. Dan was suddenly paralyzed as he recognized both the horse and rider. Then, all to quickly they disappeared into the horizon. He raced towards them once again searching, but she was gone. After sitting on his horse and lingering for a very long time, he came to the difficult conclusion that he needed to continue ahead on his journey. He just wanted the story to end.

Peering across the sun-drenched prairie lands, he began to tremble. He pulled his hat lower against the sun as a momentary sadness overtook him. He touched the spurs to his animal while trying to control his wondering thoughts. He knew ahead lay Mesilla. Dan hesitated, then patted the envelope in his pocket. Mesilla first, he thought, then the rolling plains of home.

Chapter 19
Mesilla

The day finally came when Dan Morgan rode into the town of Mesilla.

He went straight to the sheriff's office. The door was slightly ajar. He banged on the door and waited.

The sheriff, finishing some last-minute work, looked up after he heard the noise.

"Come in," his voice rumbled. "Don't knock the confounded door down." A moment later he was looking into the face of a stranger whose eyes made him appear much older than his years and noting the heavy six-gun resting at his hip.

"Judas priest," he blurted out. "Whar in tarnation did you come from?"

"Name's Dan Morgan—Boxed M—Sweetwater, Texas."

"I could use a little more information." The lawman shoved his pencil and paper aside. "Sit," he said, pushing up a chair. The chair screeched as Dan sat down. "Yu with the crowd thet rode in this morning?"

"Nope—I am looking for the ranger around here," Dan stated.

"Well! Just so happens he was just here a few minutes ago. Be right back. You wait for him?" The lawman rose to take a tin cup from a wall peg, moving it to the potbelly stove near the window.

"My name's Whalen," he introduced himself. "Dud Whalen. I'm the sheriff here." Dan noticed his hand was none too steady as he poured the coffee and continued, "Thought far shor you was one o' them riders."

"Nope," Dan reached for the coffee. "Anything special about that bunch?"

"Well! Tu tell yu the truth," said the sheriff, "we're expecting trouble in this heah town, and this could be it. Stable boy reported a big, tough-looking hombre on a gray had ridden in. Since we had asked him to report any strangers coming to town, I thought I'd ask you if you had seen the hombre—no offense intended, Mister."

Dan grinned, "I guess I've come to the right place, Sir. I am the man he saw. I suggest you stay to listen to what I have to say. I have a message for Captain Purdy of the Army Rangers, and it might explain the riders you've seen coming into town and confirm the trouble you are expecting."

Just then, Ray Purdy entered. "He was just startin' tu talk when you came in, Ray. Let me introduce you," said Whalen. "This feller is Morgan—Dan Morgan, from a ranch over Sweetwater way. Mr. Morgan, meet Captain Ray Purdy."

"You could be the very man I've come to see," said Dan, as he eagerly handed the envelope to the sheriff, who was standing closest, purposely withholding the note regarding Major Sterling's death.

Dan began slowly at first, telling of his journey from the fort to Mesilla and the reason for it, omitting his trial and acquittal. He did mention that Monty Hayes, an army scout had been assigned to guide him through Indian country. The conversation lasted for what seemed like hours. Purdy stood back quietly without comment as he listened to Dan's story with a questioning look. Callously he forced a smile before curtly dismissing Dan and changing the subject by pointing out a few places of interest in town for him to see that included the Double Eagle Hotel down the street. The sheriff watched the cowboy, puzzled for the moment at the captain's behavior, but just shrugged his shoulders and handed the envelope to him. Dan just stood there in annoyance, and said nothing.

"Dud," said the captain, obviously more excited about a telegram he proceeded to wave under the sheriff's nose continued talking. "I wired El Paso when that gang rode in this morning and got a reply just a few minutes ago. Listen! Assigned Major James Clay Elkins working undercover-special governmental decree-left enroute a week ago-request you give him utmost cooperation-Personal Regards." It was signed Captain Trent, Headquarters, Texas Rangers, Division B, El Paso, Texas."

Dan angrily listened to the captain read the telegram, said nothing, then made his exit. The morning was bright with the subtle tones of fall, and the air was clear and crisp. Several ladies who were engaged in animated conversation in front of the dry goods store stopped talking to stare as he tipped his hat. The smell of spices and freshly ground coffee tickled Dan's olfactory senses as he peered into the store's cool, dim interior.

A storekeeper washing windows from a stepladder shouted good morning as Dan passed by. The merchant watched him until he turned into the stable on the edge of town.

"Humph! Up to no good, I wager," he muttered to himself, the mop sloshing water over the dirty windowpanes that ran rivulets down the wall. "Anybody wearing a gun that low must be looking for trouble."

Dan, oblivious to the commotion his presence had created, stepped into the livery. His eyes rapidly grew accustomed to the poor light.

"Hey, Mister." A high, piping voice came from somewhere above.

Dan looked up to see the tousled head of a youngster, grinning down at him from the hayloft.

"Got somepin for yu," the stable boy squeaked, coming down the ladder. In his hand he held a folded piece of paper.

"Feller rode in last night. He was drunk an bedded down in an empty stall. Was gone afore I got here at sunup—did not pay no money neither. Found this letter in the straw when I went to call him. Fell outa his pocket, I reckon. Don't know what it sez 'cause I can't read, but figure it could be important folded so nice and neat like." The boy handed Dan the note. "Seed yu wif the ranger, so I guess it's all right to give it to you."

Dan stepped to the door where the light was better and unfolded the paper. A dry whistle died on his lips.

It read, "Final meeting, Double Eagle, 10 o'clock, October 27th. Be there."

The note was stained with sweat and printed in heavy lines. There was nothing more, no name, no address, no signature.

Cognizant of the note's importance, Dan flipped a silver dollar to the lad who stood silently by and then in good faith hurried to find the ranger Captain and Dud Whalen.

Excitement grew as they examined the note.

"This is it!" shouted the lawman. "I am sure of it—just the break we needed."

Dan, annoyed with the captain's former disregard, responded blatantly. "You know, Captain, if you open that envelope, I think you will find the message inside confirms what the note says." At that point, the captain picked up the envelope, read the letter, then looked up at Dan somewhat embarrassed and surprised. He held out his hand in a gesture of friendliness. "I am sorry son," he said. "I only half believed your story earlier. Can we begin again?" Dan nodded but did not respond to the handshake. He had promised himself he would no longer be taken for granted. He had seen too much. His friendship would have to be earned.

"What's that date again?" Whalen, changing the subject, leaned forward, looking over the captain's shoulder. "It's my guess that the gang will continue to drift into town in small groups. That must be why all these unknowns are showing up every day. We'll just have to sit tight and wait. Let's get together at my house tonight to work out a plan. Make it after dark so as not to arouse suspicion."

Shortly after dusk, Moore—the ranger from Abilene—rode in...and soon after, Bill Linkletter arrived. During the next few days, Smith of Austin, Daily of San Antonio, and Ross Weir from the El Paso office completed the group. The exception was the arrival of Major James Clay Elkins.

Here at Headquarters was the most efficient group of rangers from Texas and New Mexico ever assembled under one roof. Each an expert in his field and never outfought, these dedicated men carried the beacon star of Texas. Dan remembered his father had always said that the history of the Lone Star state was written by men who had served valiantly and gone above and beyond the call of duty.

Thus, they planned and waited—and watched.

It was at the captain's house that night that Elkins' anticipated arrival was discussed, but Dan again remained quiet. The captain's daily excursions through town failed to turn up any evidence of his presence, and he could only conclude that Elkins was still on the trail. There was nothing to do but wait. Time dragged on. One by one, the lookouts reported the presence of strangers drifting into town.

Disturbed by Elkins' failure to arrive, Captain Purdy went ahead with his plans for a showdown.

During the final meeting, it was decided that the rangers, undercover, would saunter into the saloon one at a time to divert any suspicion of their presence. They would take their places in prearranged positions. The signal for action would come from Captain Purdy stationed on the balcony, overlooking the bar. The only way to the balcony was the main staircase in the center of the room, and it would be in full view.

Captain Purdy continued, "There is one thing we must remember. The leaders of the gang are probably here, but if they haven't come, they'll probably arrive in full force tomorrow morning, sometime before ten o'clock. These men are hardened criminals, and they won't hesitate to kill on sight." He continued, "Don't take any unnecessary chances. Start drifting into the saloon so that you are in your designated positions before ten o'clock. Oh! One thing more...Morgan and I will remain hidden in a room off the balcony and will have scattered guns in case anything goes wrong. Morgan will cover one door, and I will cover the other. When you hear a shotgun blast, you'll know I've blown the door open. Moore and Weir, you cover the downstairs, and Linkletter, you join the deputy outside to watch the rear door and windows. The rest of you stand ready for action."

Early on the morning of the 27th, the men congregated in the sheriff's office, awaiting their final orders. As the sheriff looked out of the window, replacing the coffeepot on the stove, he stated, "There goes another one. Seems they jest keep coming." Dan rose to join the sheriff, craning his neck to see a tall man dismounting in front of the saloon. "Holy smokes!" his voice burst with excitement. "Shore as hell looks like Clay Elkins from here." He turned from the window to sip his coffee.

"Wal!" The lawman walked to the gun rack to take down a double-barreled shotgun. He slid two shells into it and snapped it shut. "Better git him outa that saloon. There's gonna be trouble; I feel it in my bones." Before he could question Dan about his sudden familiarity of Clay Elkins, he was gone. A minute later Dan was in front of the saloon, staring at the big bay with the Boxed M Brand on its flank.

The sheriff pulled the front door wide open to search the street when he noticed Captain Purdy heading toward his office. Once in, the sheriff handed the captain his shot gun while taking another from the rack. Pressing some of shells into Purdy's hand, he helped himself to more from his desk drawer.

"Come on!" he yelled, "That man Elkins is in the saloon, and Dan went to get him!"

"Wait a minute, Dud" the captain interrupted, grabbing the sheriff by the arm. "What is this all about? How'd yu know Major Elkins is here?"

"That feller Morgan came in a few minutes ago. He recognized Elkins when he rode in. Didn't know he knew him, said the captain. "Well," responded the sheriff. "Yu ain't got time tu figure it oot now, be'-cause if I'm right aboot that gang, hell could break lose any minute, an' Elkins is alone in there." The sheriff then turned, raising his voice to a shout, "Yu all coming?"

The captain, still with a questioning look on his face, followed the lawman. "Hold on, Dud. I sent the stable boy for Smith and Daily at headquarters when I first saw that gang ridin' in, and I want to be sure they are in position before we move in." Dud had just about had it with the captain's arrogant attitude and sternly replied. "You and me need to get to the balcony on the second floor. If this is it, we need to be ready. I got a deputy watching the front like we planned. Do you see Bernie yonder across the street acting sorta sleepy like? Lets move it!" he continued angrily.

Shortly thereafter, the sheriff, captain, and the men entered the saloon. They unobtrusively placed themselves on the balcony overlooking the barroom. From their vantage point, they could see three rangers, no badges revealing their identification, two standing along a side wall and one remaining man near the door.

A strange hush had fallen over the place. Cautiously, Whalen raised his head to take in the scene below them. "That's Elkins," he whispered to the ranger."

Captain Purdy, standing beside him, nodded, his finger to his lips, and inched the shotgun forward.

Chapter 20
The Final Showdown

Clay Elkins had counted twenty horses tied up in front of the Double Eagle Saloon that morning. Somewhere, a mission bell had rung at the hour of ten as he'd tied his spent animal to the hitchrail.

An old Mexican dressed in tattered thin cotton pants and with rusty graying hair straggling over his ears, a tobacco-stained drooping mustache, and a frayed sombrero slanted over his eyes stood leaning against the adobe wall, asleep on his feet in the warmth of the Southern sun. An old Mexican woman, her head covered with a flowering red shawl, wearing an exquisite dress that perfectly matched the shawl, stepped quietly along the cracked walls amidst the voices of the young women and the shouts of their children. Pausing only long enough to check his six-gun, Clay eased the gun into his holster as he headed inside the saloon.

He wanted one man and one man only. That man was Gnome. He wondered if, at long last, this was the end of the trail for him. He would take care of things here, find Dan, and finally go home.

Clay Elkins knew that to walk into a room of dangerous outlaws with the intention to take out one man of a possible twenty was next to suicide. It never occurred to him to do otherwise, and if it had, he would not have given it a second thought. The fact that he didn"t know Gnome personally was inconsequential. He was going to arrest him or kill him. What happened after that rested on fate.

Outside the swing doors, Clay paused to cast a last glance up and down the street. Only one man was in view on the far side of the street, and he made a mental note of the deputy's badge pinned to his shirt front. A double-barreled shotgun rested against a porch chair within easy reach of his hand.

Pushing the batwing doors wide apart, Elkins stepped inside the saloon. A quick glance confirmed that the meeting had not yet started. The tables were filled with drinking men. Boisterous talk produced a harmony of sound.

This was no picnic. Elkins knew immediately he had stepped into a den of rattlesnakes. Mentally, he recalled the names of some of the most feared desperados on the border.

At the bar were Sam Trayner, tremendously fast with a gun and a ruthless killer; Jed Bannister, a cold-blooded outlaw, whose gun was for hire to the highest bidder; and the Ames brothers, who plundered and murdered for the sheer love of killing.

Clay scanned the far side of the room. Mendoza Sanchez, a gunfighter from Mexico, was seated at a table and looked right at him, no hint of recognition on his face. He returned to his drinking. Clay's observation continued. The Abilene Kid; the two Marino boys; and Shorty Reeves, a member of a local gang, made up the list of those familiar to him. Another Mexican, his back turned to Clay, stood apart from the others. There was something familiar about him that eluded Clay. He drank alone. The others did not register as Clay's eyes came to rest on the back of the big, baldheaded individual drinking at the center of the bar. If his glass was not raised in a toast, he would have escaped Clay's notice. The man's shrill laugh, suddenly recognizable, sounded a knell in Clay's ear.

Slowly, Elkins walked toward the bar. His spurs chimed musically with each step.

The hubbub and conversation died down as all eyes came to rest on the tall Texan, quickly the center of attention. It was impossible to ignore the easy swing of his right hand as his fingers grasped the butt of his forty-five.

Clay realized that the man and his friends at the bar, were undisturbed by the sudden silence.

He came to a dead pause.

"Gnome!" Elkins' voice exploded across the room like a whiplash.

The big man turned and looked straight at Clay. One look at that evil expression vaulted his memory to a wild night six years ago that included the lacerated body of a dying soldier. Gnome had no left hand. The stump ended in an iron hook. Clay knew this was his man.

"Jim Elkins," hissed Gnome. "God! I thought you were dead." A look of surprise crossed his face as his cronies retreated, leaving him alone.

Clay wasted no time. "I arrest you in the name of the United States government for selling guns to the Indians." The words fell from Elkins' lips like the sound of doom as he continued. "I charge you with the murder of Lieutenant Nelson committed in Texas six years ago."

A murmur ran through the room as Elkins, his feet spread apart in the familiar stance of a gunfighter, raised his left hand. The silver star glistened in his palm.

"I aim to take you, Gnome, dead or alive," said Elkins.

"Make up your mind."

Gnome's eyes flashed with hate as he faced Elkins. For the first time in his life, he had come face-to-face with this big, rangy gunman who had been his nemesis throughout his gun-running career. His face was pasty with sweat, and aware the odds were against him, Gnome stalled for time.

A slight movement at the end of the bar caught his Clay's eye. Trayner had shifted his position to face him.

"You sittin' in on this one, Sam?" Elkins used a mimicking drawl.

"Nope!" answered Sam Trayner, keeping his hands a safe distance from his gun. "I'm standing pat. I pass.

"Then take your hoss and ride," snapped Clay, his eyes never leaving Gnome.

"Wait, Sam. I'll go with you," spoke up Bannister, rising from his chair. "This excuse for a sidewinder ain't got the guts of a jackrabbit." He spat contemptuously at Gnome as he followed Sam Trayner into the street. Two more men rose and left.

Gnome caught the disgust in Trayner's voice...and Bannister's added insult was more than even he could take.

Desperate now, the outlaw pleaded with the man at the end of the bar. "Yu ain't gonna let . ." his words broke off as the Mexican nearby turned. Moving closer and slowly hooking his heel over the foot rail, he faced Clay, his right thumb hooked in his cartridge belt, a cynical look on his face.

Recognition was instant. Clay was facing the Mexican who had invaded his camp that night near Big Spring.

Clay, now in the unenviable position of facing two men,

was aware that he would have to go through this man before he could get to Gnome. He instinctively waited as Gnome edged further away from the bar, now standing in full view.

Suddenly a door opened off the balcony, and all eyes shifted to the figure descending the stairs. Clay desperately tried to keep both the Mexican and Gnome in focus without losing sight of this third person.

Begrudgingly, with uncharacteristic admiration, Clay could almost feel the man's majestic personality. He cut a handsome figure with deep-set eyes; a crop of graying hair shot with white; and a narrow, close-trimmed mustache. Impeccably dressed in a white shirt, gray-striped vest, black tie, and frock coat with a velvet collar, he carried himself in a manner bordering on arrogance—a man who knew his power and meant to use it.

The man stopped on the lower step with an unlit cigarette clenched in his even white teeth. Relentlessly, his right-hand finger embraced a small cameo suspended from the heavy gold chain draped across his vest and threaded through the lower buttonhole pocket.

"So, you are the great Señor Elkins. I could not help but overhear," he said, coming to a halt as he spoke. "Your fame is known to us, even as far south of the border as we are. You are indeed a brave hombre but a foolish one to walk in here alone and arrest one of my lieutenants, especially surrounded by men such as these." A flourish of his hand conveyed an elegance seldom seen by men in these parts of the South.

"Now, your gun will again have to speak for your shining star of Texas, as mine will for the Mexico I serve."

His fingers slid along the chain to reveal the gold medallion for all to see. Clay recognized it as the ancient Aztec symbol of Mexico. The emblem dated back to a time when the Aztecs were coming to the Valley of Mexico and was based on a legend, that they would find a lake and an eagle holding a snake in its beak would be standing on a cactus growing from a rock, designating where they would build their city.

"Your cause against my cause, amigo, my gun against your gun. The stakes are high, much higher than you think."

Thoughts of doubt—disturbing ones—bothered Clay as he stood there with the odds stacked against him, and the question he'd always known would one day have to be answered. Was his gun after all these years still fast enough? He was about to find out.

Clay spoke loudly with conviction. "I'm waiting," he said, the determination in his voice never more serious as he realized that he faced the man who was the ringleader and probably the head of the gunrunning combine.

"Si, Señor," the gang chieftain nodded, his answer low and distinct. Clay tensed as the man stepped down.

Almost too late, out of the corner of his eye, Clay caught the motion from where Gnome stood. Striking fast and hard, emerging from his leather holster, Clay's Colt roared twice. Gnome's body jerked backward as the slugs ripped into him. He collapsed into a shapeless huddle. His gun clattered harmlessly to the floor as he fell. Clay, swinging on his heels, brought his Colt about and in that fleeting instant, knew he couldn't make it. The shuddering impact of lead staggered him, but he persevered. He saw the gang chieftain reach for the support of the stair post on the heels of a shot that came from the rear of the room. Someone was covering Clay, but he couldn't make out who had come to his aide. There was a strained look on the man's face, and his gun wavered when a second shot rang out. Elkins knew the man had been hit and hard. For a short space of time, Clay held his fire.

"You're all under arrest," came a voice of authority, and Elkins looked up to see two men with badges looking down from the balcony. Both held shotguns covering the crowd. For a moment, he thought he saw Dan dodging behind an upstairs door.

"It's a trap!" someone yelled.

Then all hell broke loose. Guns roared, and men went berserk, falling over tables and chairs, scrambling for cover.

Elkins' Colt boomed again and again as orange-and-red flashes of gunfire stabbed the pungent smoke eddies that rose and whirled over the scene of battle. Above the inferno, Clay could hear the heavy blasts of shotguns spreading death and destruction in their wake.

Elkins saw the Mexican at the bar go down, a shotgun waist high blasting him to hell. A wounded man reeled past him drunkenly and fell on his face. The gang chief, his six-gun flaming red, sagged against the banister dying on his feet, refusing to go down until Clay pulled the trigger point blank.

Pandemonium ensued. Men were screaming in a wild scramble to escape. Suddenly, the big window fronting the street caved under the smashing impact of a card table as the outlaws fought to get clear of the rain of death from above.

A sudden pain stabbed through Clay's chest as he slammed

his last shot into the face of Shorty Reeves whose face disappeared in a mist of gun smoke.

Clay reeled as he futilely tried to reload his gun. The growl of a six-gun over him told him that again someone had come to his aid—then suddenly, something seemed to tear his head from his shoulders and the lights went out. His gun dropped from his nerveless finger as he plunged down, down, into bottomless darkness. Red-and-black flashes jettisoned across his brain, and his body exploded with tremendous pain.

Beth's sweet, troubled face rose before him, hauntingly, pleadingly, as he plummeted into the soft darkness of oblivion.

Chapter 21
A New Beginning

The fight was over, and the rangers closed in. Nine members of the gang lay dead or dying on the bar room floor. Outside, the deputy stationed across the street had knocked one more gang member trying to escape from the saddle.

One ranger, Smith, was dead. Moore and Daily were both hard hit but would live. The sheriff, Dud Whalen, would never walk again without a limp, and Elkins lay unconscious in an adjacent hotel room, hovering between life and death. Counted among the outlaws to escape were the two Marino brothers —along with Sam Trayner—and Bannister—who had left earlier —as well as a Mexican official whose body mysteriously disappeared and whose identity was never brought to light.

The rangers posted guards to keep spectators out of the saloon as the dead bodies were removed for burial on Boot Hill.

The saloon was in shambles and would be closed for some time to come.

Captain Purdy shook his head as he and Dan walked back to the sheriff's office.

"I sure hope Clay makes it. Doc only gives him a fighting chance and a poor one at that." Concern showed in the ranger's voice.

Dan nodded and echoed fervently "I hope so. To think I lived under the same roof with Clay for over five years and never knew much about him."

"I haven't words to describe him," stated the ranger captain. "Everything I ever heard about him was great; but today—

today, he was magnificent."

With a look of concern, Dan responded softly, "Yes, he is the best."

Both men walked the rest of the way in silence, each occupied with their own thoughts, until Captain Purdy turned to Dan, and a second time reached out to shake his hand, and said, "Dan, thank you. You didn't tell me you know Major Elkins or that you were so experienced with a forty-four. You Boxed M men musta cut your eyeteeth on barbed wire, taking on odds like that."

Dan grinned and was strangely pleased at the left-handed compliment. "I sure would have felt a lot better if I was more prepared to help Clay." He poked a finger through a hole in the upper part of his jacket sleeve.

"By the way," he said. "I have a letter for you from General Warburton, but wasn't sure you'd read it." Dan fumbled in his shirt pocket with a smirk on his face and handed the ranger the message.

"You know its contents, I assume?"

Dan made no comment.

Purdy immediately opened the message.

"It recommends you as an extremely good ranger and suggests I ask you to join. How about it?" Dan wryly smiling respectfully refused the request.

Back at Ranger Headquarters, an urgent call went out over the new wireless for a surgeon to attend to Elkins. It was early the next morning when Dan received a message from his sister, Elizabeth. She and his dad were catching the first stage West.

It wasn't too long before John Morgan and his daughter, Beth, arrived at the stage depot in Mesilla, where they met the physician that had been providing medical care for Clay. The brief introductions over, Beth was led the way to Clay's bedroom.

"I can't understand how he stays alive," said the doctor sometime later. "I took three bullets out of him—any one of which would have killed an ordinary man—but he continues to hang on." He reached for his hat and picked up his black bag. "If you are Beth, Miss Morgan, then you are the one he keeps calling for. He is running a high fever, and he's had only flashes of consciousness. I must warn you, though; he may slip away any time. If you can get through to him during one of his conscious periods, you may be able to give him something to fight for. He has the constitution of an ox, and he's still alive—that much I can tell you." Beth was unable to reply as she was overcome with emotion.

In the days that followed, Beth maintained a vigil at Clay's bedside, cooling his fevered brow with cold compresses and covering his pain-wracked body when he turned restlessly in his delirium.

It was in the early afternoon of the third day after Beth arrived that Clay looked at her with sanity in his eyes. Beth smiled and put her hand on his. A hint of a smile graced his lips. He sighed and fell into a sound sleep.

The doctor followed Beth into the bedroom and put his hand on Clay's forehead. Carefully and at some length, he examined the patient. Then he straightened up and smiled. "His fever has broken."

Quietly, Beth drew the shades to darken the room. Then she knelt at Clay's bedside. For a moment she watched the rhythmic rise and fall of his chest as he slept on. She laid her head against the bed and with tears streaming down her face, she gave a sigh of relief now knowing that she was finally going to have the life she had always dreamed of with Clay at her side, always and forever.

Clay, having refused all mention of a reward, was pleased, although embarrassed, when Beth proudly showed him a certificate, awarding him an honorary membership in the rangers—signed by the governor of the state. He was told that most of the gang had been annihilated. The ones that had gotten away posed no threat at this point. That evening they learned the rangers had raided the gang's hideout in a deserted canyon. A cache of army rifles and ammunition had been recovered and turned over to the military authorities. They had found Jud Crawley's dead body in the corral. He had been shot twice in the back. The rangers had buried Crawley and burned down the shack.

Remaining days would speed by as autumn's golden brush relinquished the Southwest to the season's change. From the window, Beth would watch the transition, impatient of its magic. Clay was well on his way to complete recovery, except, as the doctor had promised, he would always be able to tell when it was going to rain.

Finally, the day came when they were able to begin their journey home. The early snows had fallen, and the earth was a shimmering carpet of brightness. The invigorating freshness of a whole new world was in the offing. Beth tucked a warm blanket around them both for the stagecoach ride, and at long last they were on their way—together.

Meanwhile John Morgan and Dan had elected to go on ahead. Dan and his father took their own good time on the trail home. In the mountain passes a light snow started to fall, and Dan could feel the wet on his face.

John could not help but notice the change in his son. At first, he almost didn't recognize him. Dan looked much older and very thin. He had grown a beard, and his hair was longer than he had ever seen it.

Dan glanced at his father and was grateful for the softening light that hid his face. He pulled the bay about and moved ahead. He father held his horse back to let his son pass.

John Morgan's eyes followed the manly figure of this lad who seemed to be deep in his own thoughts, buried somewhere on the night trials. His attention dropped to the brass-studded cartridge belt and the long-nosed forty-four as he stopped to turn his collar up against the cold. He pulled his own coat closed and moved up beside him.

Finally, after weeks had passed and many discussions had taken place between father and son, Dan knew he was coming close to the Boxed M. He could feel it in his bones. Emotions began to take over as he rode his mare down the long, dusty trail, to find himself looking at the beauty that encompassed the rolling hills and the fence that had been waiting for him to fix.

As he gazed at the house in the distance, he saw a woman working in the garden. She must have noticed him as he rode into the driveway because she immediately stood up. She had on a beautiful blue dress and her yellow hair was blowing in the wind. Her hands were shading the sun from her eyes as she watched his every movement as he approached.

He pulled up abruptly and slid off his horse. Within minutes, she ran to him and threw her arms around him. Sarah was more beautiful than he had remembered. There was no talking. They both stood motionless as they embraced. Suddenly he felt old. He was aware of the sorrow within him that still lingered, had affected him deeply...would be present for a long time. He held on tightly to Sarah as he extended his free arm to reach out for his dad.

The End

Acknowledgments

The picture on the book cover was designed by Denise Sepot. Denise has created other items of art that have been beautiful and thought provoking throughout the years for family and friends. Denise resides with her family in Oxford, Connecticut. She is the sister-in-law to Susan DeLeon.

Many thanks to Aimee Zaleski for her design ad layout of this book. Aimee is a freelance designer and actor who resides with her husband and two children in Connecticut. She is the granddaughter of Hank Scott.

I would like to thank Sandy Koorejian, a very special friend who had a hand in editing this story. Her keen attention to detail has allowed me to continue with the manuscript and bring it to completion. I am very grateful for her guidance as well as her friendship over many years, which began through a close working relationship while advocating for the rights of domestic violence survivors. Sandy was the executive director for thirty-five years of a domestic violence organization and for the last ten years has been preparing and managing grants for a city police department with a strong community policing philosophy.

A special thanks to Adrienne Makowski, a book editor, writer, and actor who lives in Stamford, Connecticut. I had the pleasure of being introduced to Adrienne through my daughter Aimee who has maintained a close working relationship with her for many years.

Thankyou to Juliann Lutinski for her keen input into the manuscript. Juliann is an editor residing in Connecticut.

About the Authors

Hank Scott, the pen name chosen by Henry (Harry) A. Prescott, was born in Philadelphia, Pennsylvania, on July 11, 1906. His father was a machinist. His mother, a homemaker who was hearing impaired for most of her life, gave birth to eight children, four of whom survived. Hank was the third in line.

Hank spent his early life in Pennsylvania. He attended Temple University, where he studied industrial engineering somewhere between the years 1928 and 1930. He entered the workforce during the first years of the Great Depression. He met the love of his life in the late 1930s at the then Philco Corporation in Philadelphia, where they were both employed. They married in 1940.

Hank's ambitious nature and can-do attitude prompted him to purchase a quarter-acre plot of undeveloped land in Fairfield, Connecticut, in the 1940s where he built his home.

Hank loved playing golf with friends and business colleagues; fishing for trout in a local river; and dabbling in home improvement, landscaping, and construction. Too old to serve in the military in the Second World War, he focused on his career in the defense industry, where he worked for most of his life.

He loved the popular 1950s Western-movie genre, especially color films with his favorite Western actors. The novel *The Man from Sweetwater* was inspired both by his interest in the history of the Old West and the popular romantic notions of the roles that cowboys and Indians played in molding the

Southwest at the time of its writing.

The book was unpublished at the time of Hank's death in 1973.

Susan Elizabeth DeLeon, Hank's daughter assisted her dad by typing up the drafts of this book as they were hand-written by her father when she was in high school. It was much later in 1973 when Susan had the benefit of spending some special time with him that he turned to her, and with a somber look, requested that she take over the responsibility of getting *The Man from Sweetwater* published after he was gone. He passed away three days later.

Recently, she created the final version of this novel by combining four similar manuscripts, all originally written around 1959.

Susan graduated from Fairfield University in Connecticut, with a Master of Arts Degree in Marriage and Family Therapy. She was employed as the director of a nonprofit program, where she advocated for the rights of domestic violence survivors for over twenty-five years. Susan recently moved to Tucson, Arizona where she has enjoyed reliving the adventures of Dan Morgan, the young man at the center of this entertaining story.